The girls are taking Manhattan, but how will Manhattan take to the girls?

Joan has met a new man in New York—but there's always a "but" in her relationships. Not to mention she already has a man back home.

Toni needs an escape from Los Angeles, and her business could profit from some East Coast clients. Her drive to succeed has been known to take her far. Sometimes too far.

Lynn never has a problem finding a man. This time she might have a problem letting one go.

Maya is single again, but how soon is too soon to get involved with someone new?

William has run into an old high school flame in the big city, but it may prove better that she was one who got away.

New York is a 24-hour town where anything can happen—and does!

Coming September 2003

GIRLFRIENDS: GUILTY PLEASURES

THE FIRST ORIGINAL NOVEL BASED ON THE HIT SERIES

GIRLFRIENDS

TAKING
MANHATTAN

JAZZ NOLAN

ibooks

new york
www.ibooks.net

An ibooks, inc. Book

Copyright © 2003 Paramount Pictures Corp.
All rights reserved.

An Original Publication of ibooks, inc.

Distributed by Simon & Schuster, Inc.
1230 Avenue of the Americas, New York, NY 10020

ibooks, inc.
24 West 25th Street
New York, NY 10010

The ibooks World Wide Web Site Address is:
http://www.ibooks.net

ISBN 0-7434-5826-5
First ibooks, inc. printing April 2003
10 9 8 7 6 5 4 3 2

Edited by Jan Miles

Cover design by Jason Vita and Joe Bailey

Printed in the U.S.A.

GIRLFRIENDS

TAKING MANHATTAN

CHAPTER
ONE

JOAN

I'm a California girl, but I'm fast becoming a New York woman. For instance, I have mastered the three rules of a New York pedestrian. First: never make eye contact. Second: don't wait for a green light to cross a busy street. Just plunge in. It's all about the goal. Third: the taxi belongs to the person who opens the door and gets inside first. I was about to demonstrate this third rule one rainy spring morning outside the Plaza Hotel when I found myself in a standoff with a tall, black prince in a Burberry trench coat. Prince or not, wherever he was going, it could not possibly be as important as my meeting downtown.

I had the taxi. I got myself inside and was busy placing my umbrella on the floor when I realized he was holding on to the open door. Until that door closed, the taxi would not move. This did not seem to bother the turbaned taxi driver, who was deep in a discussion on his cell phone, but it did bother me since I hate to be late.

"I saw it first," I said. I tried to soften things by smiling at him, but he wasn't having it. "And I'm really late for an important meeting," I added, giving him my I'm-sure-you-understand look.

I could tell he was not impressed, but at least he let go of the taxi door and stepped back, leaving it to me. "You must be from out of town," he said with a sneer. I sneered back, noticing that his leather briefcase was expensive and monogrammed in gold with the initials BEH.

"Yes, and thanks for confirming everything I've heard about rude New Yorkers," I retorted. I turned my attention to the driver and told him to take me downtown, to the City Hall area. In the morning traffic, the drive would take a minimum of twenty minutes. It would give me a chance to go over my notes one more time.

My colleague William Dent and I had been stuck in New York for a week, working on the Emerson case. I had just learned this morning that I was going to be there for at least another seven days, which didn't thrill me.

Please don't misunderstand. Every junior associate at Goldberg, Swedelson, McDonald and Lee wanted this assignment, and William and I work well together. We are friends as well as colleagues, except when we are competitors. William has gotten a lot more competitive since he got involved with his new girlfriend, Monica. William is the reason I was running late. We were both staying at the Plaza and he was supposed to call me in the morning. I had expected that we would head downtown together, but at 7:45 A.M. I called his room and learned that he had already left. This is not the William I know. I am sure Monica is behind it.

I decided to try to relax during the ride, and I

settled back, concentrating on my notes from yester-day's settlement meeting. The talks had gotten nowhere, much like my hard-won taxi, and now the opposing counsel was bringing in a big gun from Chicago. As the cab rolled forward another inch, I could see that Mr. BEH had moved farther out on the corner and was standing under his big black umbrella with no other cab in sight.

I tapped on the glass that separated me from the cab driver.

"Could you pull over for that man?" I said.

"Make up your mind, lady," he muttered, but he did pull over to the corner, another one-inch man-euver, to where Mr. BEH was standing. I rolled down the window. Mr. BEH just glared at me. In spite of his umbrella and his Burberry, those fine Italian shoes were going to be soaked pretty good if he stood there much longer.

"Look, I'm heading downtown," I said in my most professional manner, "If you are too, we can share the cab."

For just a second he looked surprised, but he was not going to pass up a ride. Not in this rain. He moved to the door and closed his umbrella. I scootched over so he could get in beside me in the back seat.

The taxi was warm and I had already opened my coat. As he got in, his eyes immediately locked onto my legs, where my skirt had ridden up. Embarrassed, I tugged at it. For the first time, his face softened and smiled. I was almost having a moment when suddenly the calm of the cab was pierced by the shrill voice of Joan Rivers, who was apparently locked in the car's trunk.

"Don't forget your seatbelt!" she screamed. It was the latest innovation in New York City cabs: recorded messages from celebrities reminding you to buckle up.

"If that woman wants to tell me what to do, she should pay for my ride," Mr. BEH said.

"Amen to that," I replied.

His eyes flashed something. Recognition? Curiosity? I was wearing my lucky earrings and my new purple Chanel suit. I wanted to feel strong and prepared for this meeting. I wasn't especially aiming for sexy, but it's funny how often sexy and powerful go together.

"Do I know you?" he asked.

"I'm Joan Clayton, from L.A. How about you?"

"Bradley Houston, from…Chicago. How far are you headed?"

"All the way downtown. City Hall," I said.

"Same here."

We exchanged some inane chit chat about the weather—L.A. vs. Chicago vs. New York. And how the Plaza compared to other hotels in New York.

There was a time, not too long ago—okay, a few months ago—when I would have gone all fluttery about the idea of sharing a cab with a man who could easily be mistaken for Michael Jordan and was clearly on the success track. But at this particular moment, I am in a relationship with Ellis Carter, who just might be The One. So, although I can enjoy the view, I don't need to jump into the pool. On the other hand, I have two very single girlfriends, so there's no point in letting this fine specimen get away.

I'll tell you what I didn't tell him: I'm Joan Clayton and I grew up in Fresno, California. I'm single but

I'm currently in the most satisfying relationship of my 32 years of life.

The only reason that Ellis and I are not together this very minute is because Ellis is an actor and is making a movie on location in Vancouver, and I am a lawyer and am working on this case in New York. Thank God for phone sex.

Let's see. What else about me? I love the law although I'll admit that I do not always like my clients.

My parents are divorced and I'm not close to either one of them. My father lives and works in Washington, D.C. He only comes to Los Angeles once a year, and he always calls me when he does. Well, almost always.

So, I've created what a psychiatrist would call a family of choice, which is kind of fitting for a sometime control freak like myself. My girlfriends have always been there for me. It's important for me to know that I can always count on them. And they can always count on me.

My closest friend is Toni Childs. We have been friends since we were eight years old. Toni is a little self-absorbed, a little high maintenance, but she has a heart of gold. She has created a niche for Toni Childs Real Estate as the realtor to young Hollywood. And, after years of searching for a millionaire with a big penis, Toni has finally found her Mr. Right, a Beverly Hills plastic surgeon. He's short, white, and shares her love of Willy Wonka and the sharp comeback.

Then there's Lynn. We met as freshmen at UCLA and we were together at college for four years. I went on to law school and the partnership track at Goldberg, Swedelson. Lynn has been kind of stuck: she's managed to collect four graduate degrees without ever establishing herself in a career. This year, with a little help—and a lot of positive reinforcement—from her friends, she's finally managed to get and hold a real job. I spent about an hour on the phone with her last night, giving her a pep talk about sticking with her job, at least until she can line up another one.

Maya is a few years younger than the rest of us, but in some ways she is more mature. As my father would put it, she has not had "our advantages." She is also my assistant and yes, if you must know, my personal project. She comes out of Compton, married at seventeen, had a son, and is now being divorced from Darnell, who was a good guy but just did not share her ambition. I'd like to help Maya make the most of her potential.

Finally, there's William, my fellow junior partner at Goldberg, Swedelson, and an honorary girlfriend. The girls really have very little in common with each other, besides our friendship, but we do share one other thing: we all hate William's latest girlfriend, Monica. She's beautiful and intelligent and classy and just all wrong for our William. Not because of those good qualities I just mentioned but because she's also a conniving and manipulative and ruthless. Not that there's anything wrong with that, I suppose. She has the makings of the kind of attorney no one wants to be up against. But she has no intention of being an attorney—just of being married to one. I anticipate and dread the day when they announce their engagement.

I've already seen the changes in William—like him ditching me at the hotel this morning. He used to be so kind and thoughtful and considerate. Now that I think about it, those aren't necessarily good qualities for an attorney, but that's not the point. The point is, those are good qualities for a friend. And if Monica keeps changing William, some other things may wind up changing too.

I see Maya and William every day. In fact, I see Maya almost twenty-four hours a day since she has been staying at my house since her husband threw her out six months ago.

We try to get together with the others after work at the Blue Bar a few days a week. And we always meet for lunch and shopping on Larchmont, or 3rd Street or the Beverly Center on Saturdays.

I found myself missing them. Today was Friday and I had been in New York for a week. I could have gone back to Los Angeles. I thought about flying home just for the weekend, but I decided to stick around the Big Apple. I think I love Ellis, and I know I like him a lot. He really could be The One. But he's an actor, with all an actor's insecurities and ambitions. I'm still sore about the way he treated me at his movie premiere. He's at the point now where he has to trust advisors like his publicist Darla. And also noteworthy is that Ellis has not invited me to join him in Vancouver.

"We're here," Mr. BEH—I mean Bradley—said, nudging my arm. Seems I had gone into a bit of a daze thinking about Ellis. I wondered how long the silence had been and if I had made Bradley uncomfortable.

We got out of the cab in front of City Hall. He insisted on paying for the taxi, and we traded cards. I was sure I would never see him again, but I kept the card. I turned to walk away, then turned back to get another look. To my surprise and pleasure, he was watching me. I waved this time and went on my way. I did not look back again.

TONI

Last night Todd and I played our new favorite game: "Hide the Honey." Todd taught me how to play, and we take turns. Last night it was Todd's turn to find the honey. All you need is a blindfold and a teaspoon of honey. What you don't need is clothes. Get naked, blindfold your partner, and then hide the honey somewhere on your body. Without using his hands, or his eyes, Todd had to find that drop of honey with his tongue.

Tonight we were just enjoying William's hot tub. I've always believed that a hot tub is a terrible thing to waste. Just because William was out of town did not mean that his lovely hot tub should lay empty on a Friday night. It just didn't seem right. Since I found him his ranch house in the Valley, I feel it is almost my duty to check up on the hot tub while he was away. William would want me to.

I am the brains—and the beauty—behind Toni Childs Realty. I specialize in results. It's my corporate slogan and it's my watchword in life.

My boyfriend, Dr. Todd Garrett, the prominent Beverly Hills cosmetic surgeon, has more than enough compassion for us both. This Friday night, Todd was with me. Usually he does volunteer work at a soup kitchen on Friday nights, but tonight they did not need him. He's asked me to join him there, but that kind of thing is not for me. I have my own mission: I work among the homeless of Beverly Hills.

This month alone I have found million dollar homes for a rap star, a newspaper heir and one of the last dot com millionaires still standing. They are the kind of people who winter on St. Bart's and summer in St. Tropez. But there's always a big fish, a Moby Dick, the one that got away. For me that was Derek Johnson, the New York Yankees pitching sensation. Everyone knew his next step would be a movie career. That boy was definitely headed for Hollywood, and when he got here he was going to need a house. And I was the one who was going to sell him that house.

Those were my thoughts as Todd and I soaked in William's hot tub.

It was as if I had been driving in the Hollywood hills and taken a wrong turn and ended up in some strange little town called Happiness. When Todd and I made love the first time, it was more powerful than I ever expected. Now, six months later, our sex is even better.

All my previous romances had been so full of drama that I never imagined the sheer joy that could come from knowing that the man beside me wants nothing but to make me happy. It's a calm, secure feeling.

He genuinely enjoys my company. We laugh. We both consider *Charlie and the Chocolate Factory* a book that profoundly influenced our lives. I call him my little oompa loompa and he calls me Veruca, after the Chocolate Factory's spoiled brat.

He is thoughtful. He always calls at the end of the day to find out how I am doing and how my day has been going. And I, Toni Childs, am actually interested in hearing about his.

We speak the same language. The farm girl from Fresno and the Beverly Hills prince had come together, and were still coming together.

I see it in the reaction of my girls. There was instant acceptance, from the first night I impulsively invited him to a dinner party Joan was having. He bonded with William and Ellis immediately. It was as if I'd been dating him forever. And when he took me to one of his client's parties I saw the flash of surprise in their eyes, and then he squeezed my hand and introduced me as his girlfriend.

He takes me seriously. He respects my opinions. He doesn't always agree with them, but he respects them. He has a problem with my work among the homeless of Beverly Hills, but I can see that he is proud of my achievements.

He always has a compliment for me. For a man who works with professional beauties all day, he is never jaded. He treats me like the most important person in his life.

He remembers that I do not eat anchovies and that I love pistachio ice cream.

Now he wants to take this relationship to the next level. He is talking about living together. He throws out little hooks, like "At some point it's foolish to be shuffling back and forth between two places."

I have known more than a few men, but I have never lived with one. I am not even sure that I ever wanted to.

But I know that if I say no, and Todd asks me why, I will have to tell him the awful truth.

"Because, Todd," I will have to say, "I want to marry you."

LYNN

I've never been in a hurry to sell out to the corporate world. I loved college. I love study. I love the structure of it. My girlfriends have never understood that. My adoptive parents have never understood it.

Don't get me wrong. I am very grateful to Bess and Ed. The only thing they did wrong was to be too good to me. If they had not fronted the loan for my fourth master's degree, I could not have completed the program. How was I to know that they expected me to pay it back. How was I to know that it damaged their precious credit rating? Now I'm in this cubicle, toiling away, five days a week, hoping I can pay it off before this bourgeois grind crushes all the soul out of me for good.

I'm counting the days. Thank God that William lets me and Vosco stay in his house rent-free. But if he gets engaged to the dreaded Monica, my beautiful arrangement could come crashing down.

Sometimes I wonder if William and I had kept our fuck buddy arrangement would he still have fallen for Monica. Granted, I'm sure that a lot of men would regard Monica as perfection. William certainly does.

Aside from William, Joan, Toni and Maya are my best friends. Funny thing how we are so different in so many ways.

For example, I am proud that I can take my sex like a man. Hell, I'm way more of a man than William in that regard. I am not a prisoner of the old rules. I can have sex with a total stranger. In fact, I prefer it. No strings, no baggage. No complications. Most women are uncomfortable with that idea. They need emotional intimacy before there can be physical intimacy.

I am not like most women. I say emotional intimacy is a crutch.

For me, it's just sex. Except with Vosco. That's Vosco Wilde, the man, not Vosco the dog. Well, come to think of it, they were both dogs.

I want to explore my sexuality wherever it takes me. I want to push the boundaries. Some people label alternative forms of sexual expression as kinky, freaky or abnormal. People like Maya, for example, label any sex outside the "norm" as strange, perverted, disgusting or just plain nasty. Not me. I want to try it all.

One guy I dated, Howell, liked me to tie his wrists and ankles with my pantyhose. The worst thing about it was that I don't normally wear pantyhose. Heck, I don't even wear underwear. But I wore pantyhose just for him, so I could take it off and tie him. Then he wanted me to whip him on the ass. That was the only part of his body I was allowed to touch. I went along with it until I got bored. Which was by our third date.

I take sex where I can. Sex makes this dreary job bearable. This afternoon, I worked through the lunch hour. Everyone else in the office went off to T.G.I.F.'s to celebrate someone's engagement. Someone in this office is always getting engaged—or having a baby or a birthday or buying a house—and it is all celebrated. If I were back in grad school, studying anthropology, it might make a fascinating study.

I stayed behind in the office. I knew that the plant man always comes in on Friday. I don't know his name. He's a good looking young Taye Diggs type who's probably only watering our office philodendrons until he gets his big break in the movies, or at least a running part on a daytime drama. He was edging his way towards my cubicle with his enormous watering can, singing that song from *Rent*. From the way his voice was soaring over the desktops, I'm not sure he even knew I was there.

I soon fixed that. I stood up from my desk and caught his eye. I smiled. He smiled. I approached then, moved closer to him, so close I could feel the heat through his t-shirt. I sensed he was nervous, so it was up to me to make the first move. I decided to turn up the heat. I put my hand on his belt. He brushed it away. I was startled, but only for a second.

He put one arm around me. Until then, I did not realize how much bigger than me he was. And stronger. With one move, he pulled me to him and began to kiss me. His breath smelled warm and herby, like pumpkin pie.

We ended up making love on my desk, then we moved to the floor. Over his shoulder I could see the digital clock on my shelf marking off the minutes until my colleagues were due back. He was a good finisher, and by the time the gang came back from their margarita party at T.G.I.F.'s I was on my feet, freshened up in the ladies' room.

"Lynn, you missed a great party," was the same greeting I seemed to get from every one of my colleagues from the Xerox machine to the coffee station all afternoon. I didn't bother to tell them that I'd made my own party.

MAYA

I'm just a girl from the 'hood. Straight out of

Compton and come up in the world. I've done alright for myself, what with a steady job at a big law firm and a little more education under my belt than before. And talk about coming up—I've been living in my boss Joan's house, which is like something out of Martha Stewart Living. Except none of it is from Kmart, believe you me.

I've been driving Joan's car while she's out of town. After dropping my son Jabari off at school this morning, I headed to the office. There were probably already a good five messages from Joan, who was three hours ahead of me on New York time and anal enough to leave five messages.

As I drove, I thought about last night. I had dreamed about Darnell again. It's always the same dream: we're still together. In my dream I am rushing home from the office, racing to cook smothered pork chops, his favorite. And I always feel…I don't know…safe. I brushed the dream and the feeling off as just my mind reminiscing. Again.

See, unlike my girls, Joan and Toni and Lynn, I don't need a man. I know that sometimes it's not enough. For ten years I had a fine black man who treated me with love and respect. But it didn't keep me from straying, and I've had to pay the consequences. Now, until I figure out what I want, I have removed Miss Twyla from the social round, if you get my meaning. A man will have to be very special to get Miss Twyla out of retirement.

Mistakes are not necessarily bad. They just prepare you for what you are going to do next. I don't regret my fling, or whatever it was, with Stan. I don't regret my marriage to Darnell, either, and in the big picture, I don't regret the end of it. Maybe someday we'll even be friends. It's just that when someone has been a part of your existence since you were fifteen years old, and then he tells you it's over, it leaves a big hole in your life. An emptiness that no job, no girlfriend can fill. I know, I know…I said i don't need a man, and I don't. At least I don't think so. I have all sorts of other things, like Jabari, to keep my mind occupied. It's just those nights, when I'm asleep—and my mind is occupying itself—that make me wonder. Maybe, deep down, I really do need somebody?

The horns from the cars behind me startled me out of my thoughts. The light was green. Time to get moving again.

WILLIAM

This morning I was not proud of leaving Joan behind at the hotel while I headed for our meeting down-town. Now she was going to dog me out about it for the rest of the trip.

"I tried your room, Joan, but the line was busy," I explained. It was no excuse, and she called me on it.

"I just don't understand, William. I thought we worked together as a team."

Someday I'll explain to her that even on a team, there's a line between offense and defense, but I'm not sure she'd ever understand. I love the ladies in general, and I love Joan and the rest of the girls, but there's always that gap between them and those of my gender.

This has become especially clear since I met my current lady. She is gifted in so many ways, and they refuse to accept her. Monica knows they don't like her and she doesn't care, which, of course, drives the girls even crazier.

But I consider Monica my secret weapon. The tiger in my tank. Together she and I are going to conquer new heights. Heck, anyone can have great sex, but to have a great career takes planning and the support of the perfect partner. And I think that I've found her in Monica.

CHAPTER
TWO

JOAN

We were in Monroe Foley's conference room. It was designed to impress: lots of mahogany paneling and a fabulous view of the New York harbor and the Statue of Liberty.

We had split up into several smaller groups and taken a quick break so some of my colleagues could dash down to the street for a restorative cigarette. I decided to take a chance on calling Ellis in Vancouver. I guess it was too early for him to answer his cell, but I liked hearing the sound of his voice on the message anyway. Then it was back to the conference room.

It's amazing but when I gave up looking for a relationship, I found a wonderful man. Ellis has it all: looks, style, a sexy voice and a genuine good heart. I was thinking about how lucky I was while I tried to concentrate on hammering out the details of the settlement. There were still a few points on which neither side wanted to budge. Monroe and I were alone in the room, huddled at one end of the long conference table, Monroe on one side and myself on the other. William was in another room with Monroe's junior partner, Marva Troy. The idea was that we were preparing for our next round of settlement talks with the Emerson team. But Monroe was resisting all my suggestions.

All of a sudden, Monroe surprised me by standing up and coming around to my side of the table. He sat next to me and said, "This would go so much better if we were talking in a less formal environment."

I balked for a moment but recovered quickly. "Okay," I said. "How about breakfast tomorrow?" New Yorkers are big on power breakfast meetings, so I assumed that was what he had in mind.

"I was thinking more along the lines of dinner," he responded, "and drinks."

Now I could see where this was going. This was not the first time I'd been hit on while trying to conduct business, and I think I know how to handle it.

At times like this I have to ask myself: How much of myself am I willing to sacrifice to get what I want professionally?

I want to become a partner. It's the Holy Grail of every young law school graduate lucky enough to be hired by Goldberg, Swedelson. I've survived the toughest years, turning out all the grunt work that allowed me to move forward from associate to junior partner. There are few feelings more empowering than reaching a career goal under your own steam. Well, you feel empowered for a few minutes at least, then it's on to the next goal.

I decided a long time ago that although I am very ambitious, I will not surrender my personal code of ethics. I want to go to sleep at night with the knowledge that my friends and colleagues have respect for me. Heck, I just want to be able to go to sleep at night period. I believe that a woman in business should not have to sacrifice her principles to be successful. In situations like the one Monroe was putting me in now, I have learned to accede to a point—just far enough to keep everyone happy and my principles intact. And my knees together. He wants to talk business and flirt at the same time? I can handle that.

So I went to dinner with Monroe Foley at Lotus, which is a hot new restaurant in what was formerly the meatpacking district. It was full of beautiful people, and I was glad I had worn my new coral dress that I bought to celebrate finishing the L.A. Marathon. Toni had even talked me into buying the big jangly coral earrings that matched it. I toyed slightly with one of them while Monroe polished off yet another in a series of single malt scotches. I took a sip of my first and only kir royale, and outlined for Monroe a few of my ideas for a compromise settlement. But Monroe wasn't interested in the settlement.

Monroe wanted to dance. So I reluctantly let him pull me downstairs to the dance area. That's when things started to go awry. How can I put this delicately? Well, I can't. Monroe was intent on acquainting me with his 12-play, so to speak. It was like he had taken lessons in pelvic thrust dancing from the original king of R&B himself. And I was his Whitney, or whoever had consented to him for the moment. I started to get a funny feeling—call me naïve, you won't be the first—but it finally hit me that tonight was never about business at all. The question now was how to get away without alienating my firm's biggest client. This was not a man who was going to accept a polite lie about a headache.

I finally got Monroe to leave the dance floor. We

went back to our table to get another round of drinks. That was probably more than he needed, but it gave me time to think. I excused myself to freshen up in the ladies' room, and I was on my way there when I saw him: My black knight. My answer.

"Bradley!" I said as if we were old friends. He was talking to a tall blonde model type, and for about three awful seconds he looked at me blankly. "It's me, Joan, from the cab," I added. Then blessed recognition dawned.

"Oh, right," he laughed a little and shook his head like he was just coming to. "Hey, thanks again for the lift today. I just made it to my meeting in time. I owe you."

My eyes went huge with relief. "I'm so glad you said that—because I need a favor." The blonde excused herself and Bradley looked wary, but I sensed that this was a man with home training and he would never ignore a lady in distress.

"I saw you dancing out there with Monroe Foley, Joan. I don't think you need any help at all," he said, smiling.

"You know him?" I puzzled out loud for a second, then went on. "Well, he's not a friend. He's one of my firm's biggest clients, and I need to get away from him without any hard feelings. Can you help?"

Now he chuckled. I think he was enjoying my discomfort. Men love to have the upper hand, and he had it now. But before I could rethink this, he had taken my hand in his and was heading over to the table where Monroe was sitting. His grip was gentle but firm, and I knew that this was a man who could handle the situation.

"Monroe Foley! Long time no see," he said warmly. "How long have you known my girl?"

"Your girl?" Monroe looked confused. And drunk. All those single malts he'd been downing were starting to take their toll.

"Joanie didn't mention me, did she? That's 'cause I wanted to surprise her. And here I am!"

"And here you are," grumbled Monroe.

"So I hope you won't mind if I take my little lady off your hands," Bradley said. "Maybe we can give you a ride home?"

Monroe was starting to look a little green, and he actually seemed grateful to concede the field to Bradley. He stumbled to his feet, and we managed to get him out of Lotus before he collapsed. Lotus is at the far west end of 14th Street, and the sidewalk outside was dark and deserted except for a few limousines idling across the street. Suddenly Monroe pulled away and began to heave into the gutter. Bradley watched him and shook his head with disgust.

"I don't understand people who lose control," he said. He made some subtle signal that I didn't catch, or maybe he had some kind of beeper, because suddenly a long, sleek, black limousine cut away from the pack across the street, made a U-turn and pulled up to the curb beside us.

"This is my car," Bradley said smoothly. "If it hadn't been in the shop this morning, we'd never have met. Now, do you know where your friend lives?"

"He's not a friend; he's a client," I reiterated, then gave him Monroe's address at Park Avenue and 65th Street. Bradley repeated the address to his driver then helped Monroe into the back of the limo, where he promptly passed out. As he started snoring loudly, Bradley turned his attention back to me.

"What's a nice woman like you doing with a slug like Monroe Foley?"

"I told you: he's just a client."

"Maybe you should be more selective about your clients," he said.

"He's a client of my firm," I said. "I'm just a humble junior partner."

He grinned at that. He was a good looking man, but when he smiled a light seemed to go on inside him and he moved up several notches.

"I don't think there's anything humble about you, Joan Clayton," he said.

"Talk to me Monday, when I have to face Monroe again. Do you think he'll remember any of this?"

"Don't worry about it," he said. "He'll either have a total blackout and remember nothing after his first few drinks, or he'll remember everything in which case he'll rely on your lawyerly discretion to cover his sorry ass. Either way, you hold all the cards. Just remember that."

I wasn't expecting a pep talk, but I suddenly felt better. Especially since we had reached Monroe's address and we could turn him over to Reynaldo, the very large uniformed doorman guarding the front entrance to his building.

"Thanks so much for helping me," I said as we watched Monroe disappear inside the building lobby in the arms of Reynaldo. From the way the genial giant handled Monroe, he was probably used to helping him make it up to his apartment. Monroe would have until Monday to sober up.

Bradley and I were left alone on the sidewalk. I

thought we'd get back in the limo, but he had a different idea.

"You know, Joan, I was about to tell Khalil, my driver, to take you back to the Plaza, but this night is too beautiful to waste. How about walking back?

I was wearing 3-inch high Jimmy Choo sandals, but do you think that stopped me?

It really was a gorgeous night since the rain from earlier had cleared out. We walked across 65th Street, then down Madison to 61st. We looked in the Barney's windows then walked west to Fifth Avenue and Central Park, past the huge gold statue of General Sherman. From there I could see the Plaza, all lit up like a birthday cake. Well, if it was for someone my age.

I felt a twinge and realized I didn't want the night to end. "Can I buy you a drink? I'm sure the Oak Room is still open," I asked when we reached the front steps of the hotel. "I want to thank you for helping me out."

Although it was now almost one in the morning, the steps were crowded with people, men in black tie, beautifully dressed women dripping jewelry, and uniformed hotel staff moving among them.

He shook his head. "Another time. I've got to get going. Business."

Khalil must have been following us at a discreet distance because he suddenly pulled up.

I did not feel I knew him well enough to ask exactly what kind of business happens at one in the morning, or maybe I just didn't want to know. But I did know that I wanted to see Bradley Houston again.

Standing there, a funny thing happened. The chattering crowd, the bright lights, the doormen and porters all seemed to fade away. There we were, like Barbra Streisand and Robert Redford in *The Way We Were*, only those two had a history, and Bradley and I had so far shared less than one fractured day.

He must have felt the same way, though, because he lingered there, his hand on the limo door. He seemed to be reconsidering, but just for a moment. Then he leaned forward and pulled me to him with those big strong arms. He kissed me on the forehead, then the lips. They were chaste little non-committal kisses, but kisses nonetheless.

"I'll call you," he said and sank into the back of his limo.

Yeah, right, I thought, as I walked up the shallow steps into the hotel. When I reached my room I was not surprised to find a message each from Toni, Lynn and William and several from Maya and one from Ellis. I realized with just a pinch of guilt that this was the first time I had thought of Ellis all night.

TONI

"Joan, I'm afraid that I'm losing my edge." There. I blurted it out on the telephone. It was the kind of conversation I would have preferred to have face-to-face, but my best friend in the world was on the other side of the country, and this could not wait until she came home. I have built my business on edge. Toni Childs is all about edge. I could not afford to lose my edge.

Joan is almost as compulsive as me about returning calls, so of course she called me back as soon as she returned to her hotel room. It was after eleven in Los

Angeles, and I was just curling up in bed—alone—and planning to watch my new DVD of *Brown Sugar* and ponder where my edge had gone.

"You've always had a lot of edge," Joan told me. "You can afford to lose a little."

"You don't understand," I said, "this is serious." And I proceeded to tell her about my blackout in Beverly Hills.

I had spent most of Friday showing mansions to Vonda Regal, a founding member of the Beverly Hills Fourth Wives' Club. I had managed to convince her that she was destined to live in a French Provincial fantasy just off Rodeo Drive. The next step was to show it to her husband, Arnie Regal, who was currently getting some kind of youth-restoring treatments in Switzerland and would not be back for two more weeks.

Everything on my life seemed on track, and I decided to reward myself with a little shopping tour of Rodeo. I was moving along briskly, picking up a new bag at Vuitton, a new pair of red lizard sandals at Charles Jourdan, trying a suit at Escada, and then it happened at Neiman's.

"What happened?" said Joan, like the good friend she is.

"I don't know," I admitted. That was the truly most terrible part. "All I know," I explained, "Is that I got home with my usual collection of shopping bags from all my favorite stores: Ralph Lauren, Neiman's, you know. And I started to empty them out on my bed, and that's when I realized what I'd done."

"Toni, don't tell me you pulled a Winona Ryder!"

"Worse! I bought presents for everyone I know!

Joan, I spent the whole night shopping for other people! And it's not even Christmas!"

"Oh, Toni." Joan sounded genuinely concerned, which only made me worry more. "Have you been cutting down on caffeine?"

"No! I think love is making me soft! I'm losing my edge. Joan—when I start thinking about other people it could be the end of me as a real estate broker!"

"Don't say that, Toni. Your business is all about people. You help people find their dream homes and they love you for it."

"Sure, but I don't do it to make them happy. I do it for the money and plenty of it. I can't start thinking about other people now," I wailed.

"Have you talked to Todd about it?"

"Joan, I'm not so sure I want to tell the man I love that I'm afraid his love is making me a nicer person. I don't think he'd understand. You're my only hope."

Joan sighed. Then I realized I hadn't even asked her how her work in New York was going, so I did. She told me the settlement talks were dragging, and that one of the principles behaved like a pig at Lotus, but she had met an interesting man who helped her get the pig home.

"Are you going to see him again?" I asked.

"Maybe. I do have a boyfriend, you know."

"Yes, but Ellis Carter is an actor. You need a man with a *real* job."

"Toni, it took me this long to find Ellis."

Joan is the queen of bad dating experiences. She is the nicest person in the world, but she always accepts the "buts" in her relationships. She thought Sean was the one, *but* he had a sexual addiction. She moved on to Chris, *but* he let her take Ecstasy. And then there was Marcus—he just had a big butt. Ellis is an actor and he has made it clear to her that his career comes first. She needs something better. She deserves something better. But there I go again—thinking about somebody else. It worries me, and it should have worried Joan.

"You know, Toni, you would love it here in New York," she said. "It's full of people with edge. It's the edge capital of the world."

I thought about it. I was not so sure I wanted to leave town before I close the Vonda Regal sale. While I thought this over, my eyes scanned my bedroom where I had piled the day's purchases on top of my dressing table. Inside one of the boxes was a nice pair of earrings from Fred Leighton for Joan, and another had a vial of patchouli for Lynn. And—

"Oh, my God!" I said, a little too loudly.

"What's wrong?" Joan asked.

"I'm just looking over at the presents I bought. Joan, I even got a sweater for Carmella!"

"Oh, Toni, no."

"Oh, Joan, yes! I'm buying presents for my cleaning woman! And you know I don't believe in spoiling my employees. Joan—I'm turning into you!"

She tried to soothe me. "I think it will take a little more than a shopping spree to change your personality. But maybe you need a change of scene. Come on…why don't you come to New York next weekend? There's so much edge here—I'm sure you can find some to replace what you think you've lost."

I thought about it for a minute. I had only been to New York once, on a college trip, and that was years ago. Maybe it was time to go back. Besides, there were a lot of potential clients there. It could be good for my business.

"Yes, I think that's the solution," I decided. "I could take the redeye this coming Thursday night and hit Manhattan Friday morning."

"Sounds like a plan!" said Joan.

"And then I can meet this Bradley Houston," I added. "And give you my assessment."

"Careful, Toni. You're thinking about someone else again."

LYNN

The best thing about the past year has been reuniting with my birth mother, Sandy. Don't get me wrong, my adoptive parents were wonderful. They gave me everything, the whole suburban Seattle 1970s package—soccer, ballet and a pony. I'm sure I've been a disappointment to them.

That's why it has been so great to meet Sandy, who is as much of a free spirit as I am. I thank the Goddess that Sandy didn't raise me, but now I know where I get my own personality. I don't need material things. I don't need a car or a house or a hot tub.

Well, scratch that. Monday morning I needed a car, and I needed one bad.

How bad, you might ask.

So bad that I called Maya and groveled, begging her to bring my dog Vosco and me to the vet. The poor thing was just lying there.

"He's *always* just lying there," said Maya. "Sometimes I mistake him for a rug." Maya is not an animal lover. "Anyway, I have to get to the office," she added.

"Joan will be calling me at noon and she'll have a ton of stuff for me to take care of."

"But you know that Joan loves Vosco as much as I do, and she'd want you to help me."

Maya is from a different world, where they don't treat their pets like surrogate children. In fact, they don't use the word surrogate unless they're in family court. My childhood pony Starlight probably had more advantages than many of the kids Maya grew up with in Compton. But I didn't need a lecture about how spoiled I am, especially when poor Vosco was lying there, staring at me with those soulful brown eyes that remind me so much of the man I named him for.

"He hasn't been the same since I fed him the peach pie Monica bought for William," I told her. "Do you think Monica could have poisoned him?" William's girlfriend has never been happy with me as his semi-permanent houseguest, but hey, I was there first. "Maybe she thought she could get rid of us both? "Suppose Vosco ate poisoned pie that was meant for me?"

"Serves you right for taking something that wasn't yours," said Maya.

"That's just it. You know how diabolically clever that woman is. Suppose Monica planned to poison me and Vosco, but she knew that I'd be suspicious if she brought us a pie. So, she only *pretended* it was for William and left it on the kitchen counter with her cute little note, knowing I would take the bait. It was all a trap. I fell for it and now poor Vosco is paying the price."

"I think you should stop watching *Law & Order* and go back to your porn."

"I can't go anywhere until I find out what's wrong with my dog. Please, please, please Maya. I'll make it up to you."

"How?" That's our Maya. So literal.

"You decide. Just remember that I'll owe you a favor."

Maya sighed. But twenty minutes later, she was there and I carried poor, half-comatose Vosco out to Joan's car.

While we were still on the road to the vet's, Maya's cell phone rang. It was Joan. Really, Joan has been my best friend since college, but I'm not so sure I could stand working for her the way Maya does. She seems to expect Maya to be available 24-7. She also seemed surprised when I answered Maya's phone.

"Lynn?" she said.

"Yes, Joan. I'm in your car with Maya. She's driving Vosco and me to the vet. He's having a medical emergency. I told Maya that you'd understand."

What could Joan say? That she didn't understand? She's a little more flexible on animal rights than Maya, but still far from a PETA member, if you get my meaning. I put her on the speaker, so Maya could get her marching orders while driving. From the back seat, my poor Vosco whimpered like he was having a sad, sad dream. I reached back and stroked him.

"How's New York?" I asked her while I ran my hand down Vosco's back.

"It's good, but I miss you guys. Why don't you two come here next weekend? I'll treat you both. Toni's coming Thursday night. You could stay here at the hotel with me. I'll get us upgraded to a suite."

"I don't know, Joan," I said.

Maya laughed immediately. "I've never heard you turn down something free before, Lynn!"

"I'm worried about Vosco." My friends think I only care about sex. They never take my other feelings seriously. They didn't take Vosco the man seriously. Why should I expect them to care about my dog?

We had reached the vet. I left Maya to confer with Joan while I carried my baby inside where the vet and her assistant were waiting. The vet, Amber Phyllis Giddings, could be an *Essence* cover girl; she's that gorgeous. All her assistants are young men and sometimes I picture her in the middle of a harem after hours. But right now all I cared about was my poor Vosco.

We went inside to a consulting room and I placed him on the table. Dr. Giddings began to check out his paws and neck as I held him. He was too frightened or sick not to behave himself.

Every once in a while she'd say "hmmm," then go back to another body part. She had the assistant draw some blood.

"It will take a few days for the results but what I think we have here is a simple case of indigestion."

"Indigestion?"

"What are you feeding this dog, Lynn?"

"I believe that dogs should eat at least as well as people," I told her. "I give him whatever we have in the house. In other words, whatever *William* has in the house. Which could be pizza, pate or steak. If he has a steak dinner, he always brings home a doggie bag for Vosco. Yesterday he had peach pie, didn't you Vosco?" I rubbed his head. He was unresponsive.

"Is there an avocado tree in your neighborhood?" she pressed.

"I think there are a few. Vosco loves avocados."

"Lynn, I'm going to be frank. This dog has over-dosed on rich food. The pie pastry, the avocados…"

"But I only give him the best."

"Dogs are carnivores, Lynn, not gourmets. He'd be much better off with some canned food from the su-permarket."

"With all those chemicals?"

"Trust me, Lynn. I'm a doctor."

At her instructions, I left Vosco behind with Dr. Giddings. Maya still in the car, just wrapping up her phone call with Joan. She didn't ask about Vosco, but I told her anyway.

"Vosco has to go into detox."

"What?" Joan said from the speaker.

"Too much rich food. Dr. Giddings wants him to stay with her to de-tox for a week."

"That's great!" said Joan, then she must have real-ized how that sounded. "I mean, with Vosco in good hands, there's nothing you can do. Come to New York. How about it?"

MAYA

Every working mother has mastered tricks to arriving late at the office. Mine is to slip in as quietly as pos-sible and act like I've been there all the time, only folks just didn't notice. As the mother of a nine-year-old boy subject to everything from missing homework to a medical emergency, I have mastered this art to the limit.

By the time I dropped Lynn off at her so-called job, picked up a mocha latte and made my own way to the Goldberg, Swedelson offices in downtown L.A., it was already past noon. That meant that most of the lawyers and support staff would be out to lunch, which was a break for me. It was a beautiful spring day and the plaza outside the Goldberg, Swedelson high rise was filled with office workers taking their lunch breaks in the sun.

I was making my way across the plaza when I heard my name being called by male voices.

"Maaa-ya!" called one of them, then *"Maaa-ya!"* echoed the other.

I'd recognize that vocal arrangement anywhere, as well as the accompaniment.

"Damn, how can that girl move so fast in those Charles Jourdans?" projected voice one.

Only two men in my life would know a Charles Jourdan from a Michael Jordan. It was my cousin Ronnie and his sidekick Peaches, two style queens who fancy themselves the Dolce & Gabanna of the ghetto.

I stopped in my tracks, busted.

"Girl, what kind of office hours are you keeping? How do you expect to hold on to this job, which you need, since your husband threw you out and all," said Peaches. He was wearing gold Seven jeans, a pink Moschino t-shirt and turquoise flip-flops. Ronnie was all Armani casual from his black t-shirt to his black cargo pants to his black slip-on loafers.

"I'd tell you what kind of office hours I'm keeping if I thought it was any of your business," I said. I did have to watch myself, though, because Ronnie has a good heart and he's a great back-up sitter for Jabari. He can also do a fierce press-and-curl for those in-between but in a hurry times. It's just that he and

Peaches are way too interested in my life. Not wanting to be spotted by any of my co-workers, I decided the best move was to get these two up to Joan's office to find out what they wanted.

As I had hoped, the workstations were all deserted, and we had the office to ourselves. I herded Ronnie and Peaches inside Joan's private office and Peaches was soon absorbed in voguing in front of the full length mirror she keeps behind the door.

"We don't want anything from you, Maaaya," said Ronnie, who I had settled into the chair across from me, in front of Joan's desk. He sounded hurt. "I want to *give* you something."

I perked up. "What is it?"

Have you ever noticed that hair stylists always have connections to those people standing around to catch things when they fall off a truck? Ronnie has friends like that. A few months ago, he came by with a Roberto Cavalli jacket for me. It fit like a glove. And when I wore it to the movies with the girls, Toni turned up in the same jacket. You can be sure hers didn't fall off no truck, either. Somehow it doubled the pleasure.

"Well, you know, cousin Maya, I keep in touch with all our far-flung cousins. Did you know that Cyrinda's boy is with the Marines in Iraq? And that cousin Marcus Dorrance is a big banker in Singapore?"

"No, I didn't, Ronnie."

"Well, you would know if you read the newsletter I send out to you periodically."

I sighed. "Ronnie, I've got a busy day. What's your point?"

"My point, cousin Maaaya, is that you would know that our cousin Jacqueline Dawkins is celebrating the

fifth anniversary of her business and you never responded to your invitation to her party. She's hurt."

Oh, no. I confess, I do let some mail pile up, and
Ronnie's newsletter definitely makes the pile. But I'm
in the middle of a divorce I didn't want and I don't
even have a home or a car at this point. It won't lift
my spirit to read about how well all my cousins are
doing. On the other hand, Jacquie is special. We had
a bond once. She spent a few summers with my family
in Compton when we were little. We haven't laid eyes
on each other since! I think about her and we ex-
change Christmas cards with photos, but it's not the
same as a face-to-face. Now Jacquie is a teacher and
she and her husband are running a bed and breakfast
in Fort Greene, Brooklyn.

"I don't suppose you will be able to go, but don't
you think you owe her the courtesy of an answer. The
poor girl thinks you don't want to see her."

"Oh, alright. Give me her phone number, Ronnie,
and I'll call her and make my excuses. When is the
party?"

"Next weekend. Next Saturday. I believe Peaches
and I will be Jet Bluing it for the day."

"True," Peaches chimed in from by the mirror.

You know, they say that when God closes one
door, He opens another. Just this morning, Joan had
invited me to come for a weekend in New York. I had
real doubts about it because Jabari and I are already
living in her house and using her car. I want to pay
my own way, and I can't be going off to New York
just for fun. But now I had a real reason for going: a
reunion with my cousin Jacquie.

"Next weekend? Saturday?" I asked.

"Yes, ma'am."

"If Jacquie's party is next weekend, I can go, Ronnie. I was going to go to New York anyway." I acted nonchalant, like I can just pick up and fly all over the world any time I like. Sitting behind Joan's desk made me get beside myself like that sometimes.

"And what about Jabari?" He looked me up and down in the utterly disapproving way that only a black woman or a gay man can. Honestly, first he's up in my face about my work hours, then it's my correspondence, and now it's my parenting.

"It's none of your business, Ronnie, but my son is with his father for spring vacation. So I believe I will be joining you and cousin Jacquie next weekend."

Peaches turned around and stared at me. He looked as surprised as Ronnie. For once Peaches and Ronnie were at a loss for words.

WILLIAM

Joan thinks I was avoiding her this weekend, and she's right. But sometimes a man wants to hang with other men. Saturday morning I caught the A train down to the Village and found the basketball court. There I played in a pickup game and indulged my fantasy that if I hadn't gone to law school I might have played for the Kansas City Kings, what with my manly stature and athletic ability. These guys at the courts on West 3rd Street played hard and they played to win. It's another example of how men are different from women: here we were, all kinds of guys, all colors, all ethnic groups, playing for sport. Some of the guys might not even speak English but I couldn't tell you because we didn't engage in much chitter chatter. I couldn't even begin to imagine the girls playing cards or some such with a pack of strangers and not quizzing them about their marital status and career goals.

Another funny thing about New York and a big reason why I love it: it's the biggest small town in the world. I recognized one of the players on the court that afternoon as Rhamses Day, a guy I went to college with. He's with Goldman Sachs now, and it never hurts to network. Together we hit Bleecker Bob's where I got a classic vinyl recording of the great Roosevelt Sykes. Then we went for some pizza in Little Italy and caught up on our respective career paths since college. Remembering my legendary status as a poker player, he tipped me to a game later that night and I said I'd try to join them. But I had to head back to the hotel. My firm's client had arranged a dinner party for all their lawyers who were in town to save their sorry corporate ass.

Back at the Plaza I rang Joan's room, just to touch base, and suggested that she and I grab a drink before the dinner party. We agreed to meet in the Oak Room.

I got there first and was already downing my first apple martini of the evening when Joan turned up. I have to admit that she looked radiant. It made me wonder if she was seeing someone in New York, although she's not the type to balance two men at one time. An arrangement like that requires a gift for deception, and Joan has a weakness for the truth. In fact, with her literal interpretation of truth, it's a wonder that she was ever attracted to a legal career.

I kissed her on the cheek, New York style, and ordered a kir royale for her. "You look great," I told her. "New dress?"

She shook her head. "New earrings," she said. "H. Stern on Fifth Avenue."

The earrings were big dangling things, like miniature glass chandeliers. "I like them," I said truthfully. "Maybe I'll stop by and pick up a present for Monica."

Joan's face clouded at the mention of Monica, so I quickly backtracked and started telling her about the basketball game and my theory about why men can play in a pickup game and women can't, and about running into Rhamses Day.

"Is he single?" she asked.

See what I mean? I had to tell her that I wasn't sure. Rham didn't mention a wife, but that didn't necessarily mean anything.

"Does it matter?" I asked.

"Oh, it might. We're going to have some company next weekend. Toni is definitely coming, and I invited Lynn and Maya too."

"That's great!" I said. "Let's hope this settlement is wrapped by then."

"Amen to that," said Joan.

"Joan, I want you to know I'm sorry about Friday. I should have waited for you and I didn't."

"No problem," she said evenly, which worried me more. Was she cooking up something? In my experience, women are at their most dangerous when they are at their calmest.

I'll confess that I barely got through the elegant dinner they laid down for the visiting lawyers. My mind was on the game downtown.

I took Joan back to the Plaza in a cab then told her I had other business to tend to. I could see that she was dying to know what it was, but she would never give me the satisfaction of asking where I was going.

I had the taxi driver head downtown and drop me at a drab storefront on Carmine Street, just a few blocks south of where I played basketball earlier that day.

I wandered into a smoke filled room. How many of those do you see these days? Especially back home. In L.A., smoking has dang near been banned anywhere within the city limits.

The smoke was so thick that I was afraid I'd have a coughing fit and my childhood asthma would kick in. I searched the room for any sign of Rhamses, but if he was there he was lost in the clouds of smoke. The crowd was mainly old timers, serious players who rarely spoke.

All this room needed was the theme from *The Godfather* playing in the background. Instead they had Sinatra and Al Martino on the jukebox, which was close enough.

At one table a cluster of older men who looked like genuine members of the Corleone family concentrated on their cards. At another table, a handful of Chinese looking men were just starting a game.

At that moment, Rham turned up. "Who are these guys?" I asked him.

"You never heard of any of them," he said, "and if their lawyers earn their money, you never will."

I nodded subtly, like a good consigliere.

"The night is young," he added. He reminded me that New York is a twenty-four hour town. While most of L.A. has gone to bed, New York's late night is only beginning its second shift.

Rhamses had a better place in mind. We headed out to the street and walked past a few more storefronts. Soon we were standing in front of a one-way mirror on the second floor of a warehouse. Rham pushed a buzzer. In a few seconds, someone opened the door, and I found myself in a vast converted loft that looked more suitable to a post office than a poker palace.

We each shelled out a C-note (a platinum card is no good there) and took our places. I'm a different man at the table. I have been accused of yammering, but when I pick up my cards I am quiet. I concentrate. After folding my first few hands I found myself on a winning streak.

With four queens I won a $1,200 pot. I was ready to leave with some folding money in my pocket, so I bowed out, said goodnight to Rham and his pals, and left.

You've got to know when to walk away.

CHAPTER
THREE

JOAN

I was walking down Fifth Avenue, on my way to meet my boss for lunch, and simultaneously talking to Toni on my cell phone. She was three hours behind in L.A. and just opening her office for the day. I was giving her the update on what I had seen with my new friend Bradley Houston.

Being in New York on business, I never had time to really get to know the city until now. Bradley has helped. It has only been a week, but he and I have become great friends. Bradley is a free spirit and a native New Yorker who knows the city intimately. He even knows his way around the outer boroughs, the neighborhoods in Brooklyn and the Bronx that are reached by bridges and tunnels. The night before he'd taken me up to the Bronx to a nightclub called Jimmy's. We danced there until 3:30 A.M.

Now the big mysteries of relationships began to intrude. Just exactly what kind of relationship was I was having with Bradley?

"There is no relationship," Toni said firmly. "There

can be no relationship when there's an entire continent between you."

"That's ridiculous," I told her. "Lots of relationships today are bi-coastal."

"Sure they are, Joan. And they always end in bi-coastal divorces."

"Puh-lease, we just met. Let me at least have an affair with Bradley before we start talking marriage and divorce."

"Let's at least be honest, Joan. Have you told him about Ellis?"

"I will when it's appropriate."

"Oh, Joan—"

"Oh, Toni. Just wait until you meet him."

Toni didn't understand about Bradley and me, but I was sure that would change once she got a look at him. I was looking forward to her arriving in New York the next day so she could get face time with him. Toni has been a great success in the real estate business because she's a terrific appraiser. She can size up value in seconds.

While we were talking, I was also giving Toni a description of the store windows I was passing. I described the Badgley Mishka gowns at Bergdorf-Goodman and a pair of ruby earrings at Van Cleef & Arpel. This went on until I reached 52nd Street.

"What are you wearing to your lunch?" she asked me.

"My green Tracy Reese dress and faux emerald earrings from Fred Leighton."

"Good choice," she said. That's high praise from Toni who thinks she has the market cornered on style.

"End of the line now, Toni." I turned off Fifth Avenue for my lunch with Mr. Swedelson.

"Oh alright. Go easy, tiger," she laughed as I ended the call on my cell phone. Toni remembers how two years ago, I exploded at a meeting at Goldberg, Swedelson. It was a turning point for me. I was a struggling associate and I had taken all I could stand. I was just fed up and I said so.

I remember sitting in that conference room with all the founding partners, senior partners and junior partners sitting there and staring back at me. It was one of those moments when you wish that real life had a rewind feature, but of course it doesn't.

It was the kind of event that could destroy a career, send you right off the partner track and into a ditch. But lucky for me, my outburst actually helped my relationship with the law firm.

Since then, I've made it a point to have lunch with Mr. Swedelson every few months. It's a way to keep him informed about what I'm doing and to get a sense of what more I have to do to become a full partner. I mention all this to explain why I was meeting Swedelson at the 21 Club that Thursday afternoon.

William and I had been the foot soldiers in working out the Emerson settlement, but we passed the torch to Swedelson when it came time to sign off on the agreement. He had swept into town for the big event and insisted on taking me to lunch at his favorite New York restaurant for the occasion.

A longtime favorite of old school sports stars and media celebrities like Bryant Gumbel and David Letterman, 21 is a former speakeasy on West 52nd Street. It's just a few doors off Fifth Avenue and you can recognize it by the parade of small cast iron statues of famous jockeys lined up outside.

I passed through an iron gate, walked down two

steps and through two more glass doors before I got to the narrow foyer where a doorman was waiting. I told him that I was meeting Charles Swedelson. Of course he knew Swedelson. He led me to a maitre d' who led me inside the dining room, which reeked of power, money and testosterone.

Swedelson was waiting at a leather banquette, behind the table, which meant he only half-stood when he saw me. It's one of those sweet preppie mannerisms that make him so endearing. Another is the smooth way he ordered me a vodka martini, and another for himself. He was already halfway through the one in front of him.

"You look lovely, Joan," he said as I sat down. Dressing for the big business lunch is always a challenge. In this case, my green dress seemed to be the answer, and I thanked him. Like I said, Swedelson is old school, and harmless.

"Congratulations. You did an excellent job on the Emerson agreement. I know it hasn't been easy," he said.

I decided to take the high road and give William his props. "It was a team effort, Mr. Swedelson," I said. "William was a big part of it."

Swedelson grinned. "Ah, yes, but you were the one who had to deal with Monroe Foley."

For one very long minute I saw my entire career at Goldberg, Swedelson flash before my eyes. I was sorry that I ever accepted the dinner invitation from that lecher.

"Funny thing, Joan. Two other junior partners have tangled with Monroe and complained to me about him in the past. Tough ladies, too, but they were in tears when they came to me."

"I guess they didn't give him enough line," I said. 'To hang himself' was the end of that sentence in my mind, but what I actually said was, "The big fish always need a little more slack." Our drinks had arrived and Swedelson insisted on clicking glasses with me.

"To bigger and better clients, Joan," he said.

And bigger and better bonuses, I thought, but I kept that thought to myself.

"And to the day we can afford to take on only clients we respect," he added. It was his way of acknowledging that he appreciated what I had endured, but business was business. We would not be cutting Monroe loose as long as his company paid ours a big fat retainer.

It was time to order. Swedelson insisted that we share a chauteaubriand and he ordered a Merlot. I gathered that 21 is famous for its wine cellar.

Swedelson tried to get more details about my evening with Monroe Foley. I decided not tell him that Bradley had helped me with Monroe.

Halfway through lunch, I brought up my plans for the weekend. I expected that there would be no problem with me using the company suite at the Plaza, now that Swedelson was so pleased with my performance.

Swedelson suddenly looked stricken. "Oh, dear, I'm so sorry," he said. "Any weekend but this. Didn't anyone tell you?"

I could feel the old paranoia kick in. He'd spent the last hour telling me how great I was, but he wouldn't let me use the suite?

He explained quickly, saying, "Lavinia Lee always takes it in April. She's coming in tomorrow night."

"So are my girlfriends," I said grimly. We had just

been bumped from the Plaza by the widow of a founding partner. I wasn't looking forward to trying to find hotel rooms for us all, not to mention suddenly picking up the tab.

"Don't change your plans," Swedelson said. "I insist you've earned this weekend. I'll arrange for a suite at the Soho Grand, downtown. That's more suitable for four young women anyway. Consider it an early preview of what I expect will be a substantial performance bonus this year."

I was touched by his gesture and couldn't wait to share the new switch with Toni. I excused myself, went to the ladies room and called her on my cell.

TONI

I was thrilled when Joan called me from her lunch at 21 to give me the news that we were moving to the Soho Grand for the weekend. I can't say I was as delighted with the rest of her news.

"What do you mean Lynn is coming?" I asked. "Why?"

"Because I invited her," said Joan.

"Well I hope she's paying her own way," I snapped.

I should point out that much of the huge success of Toni Childs Realty is due to my ability to multi-task. At the moment I was conversing with my best friend while she was in New York and I was in my Los Angeles office, I was also getting a pedicure from the fabulous Olga, and rifling through my rolodex. I was making a list of New York based clients who ought to own homes in L.A. but just didn't know it yet. There was Derek Johnson, of course. And Lenny

Kravitz. And Mariah Carey. If that girl still hoped to have a movie career, she should be here. See how hard I work for the money?

"It's my treat," Joan said. "I'm so proud that Lynn has kept her job for four months."

I rolled my eyes. "Listen, Joan—when you climb the ladder of success, you sometimes have to cut loose the dead wood."

"Toni, you can't call Lynn dead wood. Lynn is your friend too."

"Yes and no, Joan. I only know Lynn because of you. But we both know she's lazy, unfocused and irresponsible."

"Gee, Toni, how do you really feel?"

"I really feel like Lynn is dead weight, dragging you down. Let's face it, Joan. Now that I'm going to be the wife of a Beverly Hills doctor, I have to be more selective about my friends."

"Toni, if you have a problem with Lynn coming for the weekend, you're not going to like my other news," said Joan.

"Oh man," I whined. I knew what was coming. When you've known someone as long as I've known Joan, you can practically read her thoughts. "Maya too?"

"Yes, Toni. Maya is coming too. She helped me a lot during these negotiations. She's a terrific assistant and she deserves a getaway weekend as much as any of us."

"That's just it," I said. Joan still didn't get it, so I tried to explain. "When it's just you and me, we're equals." At least in the professional sense. Anyone in his right mind would tell you that I am gorgeous, far more beautiful than Joan. Just ask Todd, my boy-friend. I do. All the time.

"Joan, you've turned our getaway weekend into some kind of charity outing. If I wanted to baby-sit society's children I could stay in L.A. and go work at a shelter with Todd. Besides," I added, "do you really think it's wise to bring Maya everywhere with you?"

"What do you mean?"

"First of all, it's one thing to slip up and buy a present for the help; it's quite another to let them move into your house and then, on top of that, to go taking them on vacation with you. Second, Maya is from a different world, Joan. She's not comfortable in ours. At least not the one I was looking forward to experiencing in New York. We'll just expose her to things she can never have."

"Toni, do you ever listen to yourself? Is this the farm girl from Fresno I grew up with?"

"I've moved on, Joan. Some of us have the ability to do that, and some of us don't."

"Did you tell me you were worried about losing your edge?" Joan asked, suddenly flipping the script.

"Yes, I admit my fear that love is taking away my edge."

"Yeah? Well, don't worry. You've still got more edge than Ginsu."

Joan hung up on me, leaving me alone with my thoughts, my rolodex and my pedicure. Olga is brilliant with feet, but I'm not sure how much English she understands.

"You see why these two women shouldn't come on my weekend, don't you Olga?" I said as she rubbed cream into my feet. "It would be like me inviting you.

We respect each other as fellow professionals, but you go your way and I go mine."

"Yah," said Olga. Then the bitch stabbed me with her cuticle scissors. It was an accident, I'm sure.

I missed Todd, but he was off doing good works. I needed to talk to someone about what Joan had said. But I don't have any other close friends but Joan. Very few women can bear to be in my shadow.

Much to my chagrin, I was so desperate to discuss this that I actually called Lynn. I decided not to say anything about my real feelings about her coming to New York. After all, I was not the one stuck with paying her bill.

"Hey, girl. Are you excited about our weekend?" I asked her.

"Who is this?" Lynn asked, pretending not to recognize my voice.

"It's me. Toni. I wanted to talk to you about our plans. Isn't that what friends do?

"Toni? Is this the first time you've ever called me?"

"I'm sure it's not, but why quibble? Have you heard the latest? Joan is moving us to the Soho Grand downtown. We'll be near all the hot clubs and new stores."

"Oh, that's great."

We talked a bit about what we planned to pack, and I gave Lynn the benefit of my outstanding fashion sense. But of course, the problem with people like Lynn is that you can't talk to them for long before they're hitting you up for something.

"Toni, since I've got you on the phone, how about a ride with you to the airport tonight?" Lynn asked.

Yes, in spite of all those degrees and a lot of attitude, Lynn does not have a car. Why should she bother with the hassle when she can freeload from her friends?

"Oh, I don't think so," I told her. "I don't think I'll have room."

"Toni! You won't have room in a Range Rover? How many bags are you bringing for three days?"

"I believe in being prepared."

"Well I believe in traveling light. I'll have one little backpack. Please, please, give me a ride already."

I knew her pleading would give me a headache. I decided that she might be able to help me with my luggage, so I graciously agreed to give her a lift to the airport.

Joan is so wrong about me. I *am* losing my edge.

LYNN

I don't know what gets up Toni's butt sometimes. I mean, what's the big deal about giving me a ride to the airport tonight? We're going on the same plane. We'll be staying at the same hotel when we get there.

I was explaining this to Sandy when we were having lunch that afternoon at The Sweet Life. Sandy was in L.A. for a few days, still working on raising money for her next documentary. We believe it will do for sex what Ken Burns did for baseball. Sandy was as excited as I was that I was going to New York for the weekend.

"How did you manage to get the time off from your job?" She knows that my boss, the hearing-impaired but bitch-enabled Roberta would never cut me any slack.

"Look at me, Sandy. Don't I look a little pale?"

"No, honey. You have beautiful coloring. You'll always be blessed with a beautiful complexion."

"Well, I'm feeling poorly. By the time the red-eye leaves for New York tonight, I'll be sick as a dog. At least, that's what I'll be saying when I leave my message for my boss to explain why I won't be in on Friday."

My adoptive mother would go nuts at the idea of a little white lie like that. She would not understand my desperate need for a little rest and recuperation after working non-stop five whole days a week and six whole hours a day for the last six months. This relentless pressure has almost broken my back on the wheel of corporate America. I don't know how women like Joan and Toni and Maya do it. Maybe I'm just more sensitive. I'm an Aquarius, and we're more artistic. That must be it. Quite frankly, if it wasn't for my lunchtime quickies with the plant man and such, I don't think I could stand cubicle hell another day.

Unlike my adoptive mother, Sandy is a free spirit who understands completely why I couldn't possibly pass up a free trip to New York just because I've already used up all of my pathetic five vacation days. Oh, how I miss the days when I was terminally unemployed and every day was a vacation day.

Sandy loves New York and was stoked to give me tips on places to go and things to see. "You have to check out the Museum of Sex," she said. "We're going to want to include it in the movie. And I'll get you a list of fetish clubs—"

"Sandy…?"

"What, honey?"

"I'm going to check out some film schools while

I'm there. I'm thinking I'd like to work behind the camera more."

"But I thought that we agreed you'd be starting as my assistant. I can teach you what you need to learn."

"I know that, and I really want to work with you. But now I feel I've found my spirit. I want to make movies, and I can't wait around for you to raise the money for yours. I want to get started."

Sandy looked puzzled. "Going back to school, Lynn? Won't this be your third degree?"

"Third, fourth, fifth...who's counting?" I shrugged. "But this is different. Now that I've finally found my spirit—"

She shook her head and changed the subject abruptly. "Tell me about Vosco," she ordered.

I was startled. I stammered, "What...what about him?"

"You tell me. When did you last see him?"

I was touched. None of my girlfriends ever ask me about Vosco. They have never understood what my relationship with Vosco Wilde did to me. That man truly broke my heart, but every time I bring it up they brush me off. They just don't take me seriously. But here was Sandy, showing some genuine feeling for my situation.

"That's so sweet of you, Sandy. Nobody ever asks me about Vosco Wilde."

"Your dog has a last name?"

That's when I realized she wasn't talking about my former lover.

"Oh," I looked away. "Vosco will be fine. He's lost a little weight already, and he has a lot more energy. He even gets along with the other dogs. Maybe I'll start bringing him to a play group after he's released."

Sandy's eyes narrowed. For a blowsy ex-hippie chick she can sometimes be pretty perceptive.

"Lynn, who is Vosco Wilde?"

I sighed hard. "Only the great love of my life, Sandy. And nobody cares." With that I started to sob like a baby. It was embarrassing, but fortunately it takes a lot to embarrass Sandy. She just let me pour it all out. How Vosco and I fell in love in Jamaica and tried to make a business there, and how it didn't work out and we came back to L.A. and struggled for a time living in Maya's mom's garage until Vosco took off, leaving me with nothing but his dog to remember him by. And how I discovered later that he was still in L.A. and never even tried to call me. I mean, talk about hurt.

Sandy took my hands and looked into my eyes. "Oh, honey, I'm so sorry. I had no idea you were hurting so. You go on your weekend. You go look at your film schools. And you have a good time. You deserve it."

By this time, Sandy was no longer looking into my eyes. Her attention had strayed to something beyond my left shoulder. I turned around to see what she was staring at. A tall, brown skinned man who could double for Morris Chestnut had walked in and taken the table behind me.

She smiled at him shamelessly.

"Sandy!" I said. Sometimes I wish she would act like a mother, but that's not going to happen.

"What? This is how you meet people, Lynn. Didn't you learn anything in anthropology?"

Sandy turned her attention to the newcomer. "Are you lunching alone? Why don't you join us?" she said.

To my shock and surprise, he actually seemed amused and got up and moved to our table.

"I'll bet you're East Coast," said Sandy. She is amazingly flirtatious for a 50-something broad. This man was a lot closer to my age than hers.

"You're correct," he said. "I'm Malcolm," he added, extending his arm for a handshake with each of us. "Malcolm Diggs."

We soon learned that he was a venture capitalist. He was in Los Angeles to look at a small radio station that he was considering acquiring. And he was going back to New York that night.

"On the red eye?" Sandy could hardly contain herself. "So is my daughter." She put a hand on my arm, indicating that she was referring to me.

He looked a bit surprised for just a second while he digested the information that blonde, full-figured Sandy is the mother of lean, black—okay, beige—Lynn, then his expression changed to pleasure. He was definitely interested. I guess Sandy does have an eye for men. Let's hope that she has an eye for good men. Or at least men who are good at it.

"Long story," I said.

"I'll bet. Maybe you'll share it with me later? I have a car taking me to the airport tonight. May I offer you a lift?"

"You may. I'd be delighted."

"Excellent," he said crisply. "I'm sorry we won't have time to pick you up, but if you can get to the Mondrian Hotel, I'll see that we have some champagne in the car."

"Vive le Mondrian," said Sandy, grinning a devious little grin.

MAYA

Lynn called me at the Goldberg, Swedelson office to offer me a ride to the airport with her new acquaintance, some guy named Malcolm Diggs. I'm sorry, but I'm not in the habit of trusting something that important to a man I've just picked up in a coffee shop.

"Thanks anyway," I told her, "but I have my cousin Ronnie bringing me. I'll see you at the airport later."

I was about to go to lunch. Goldberg, Swedelson is so big that they have their own cafeteria. They make a fish fry that's as good as Red Lobster, and I was on my way to partake when Joan called from New York. She sounded a little buzzed from her lunch with Swedelson. Joan is one of those women who should probably drink more. She is a lot more fun when she loosens up.

"We're changing hotels," she said. "I'm packing up now. The next time we talk, I'll be at the Soho Grand downtown."

I made the appropriate notes in all the office systems so all the very-important-people around the firm would be able to reach Joan with their very-important-thoughts.

Then I brought her up on the daily activities in the office. Besides the Emerson case that had kept her in New York for two weeks, she also worked with four other major Goldberg, Swedelson clients. Each of them had to believe that he or she was the most important fish in our little swamp. That's a large part of my job, and I like to think I do it very well.

When I had finished the office updates, we moved on to our plans for the weekend.

"It was so nice of you to include me," I said. "You know, I've never been to New York."

"I couldn't have gotten through this last year without you, Maya," Joan said. "It's just my way of saying thank you."

Frankly, I like a cash thank you, but I knew that a cash bonus would have to come from the great man, Charles Swedelson, himself.

I'd like to say that Joan is a nudge, a control freak and a woman obsessed with appearances...well, I guess I just did say it...but she is also generous and kind and patient, and she's been a rock during the painful collapse of my marriage to Darnell.

"Now it's time to rebuild," Joan was saying, as if she could read my mind across the country. "Maybe you'll meet someone."

"Let's not rush things," I said. "My divorce isn't even final."

"Alright, alright, but I want you to pack some really sexy clothes. We're going to some clubs and the women really dress here. Or *don't* dress, if you know what I'm sayin'." I could hear the wink-wink-nudge-nudge in her voice. "So bring your *un*-clothes," she said, laughing at her little joke.

"By the way, my cousin in New York is having a party on Saturday," I told her. "We're all invited."

"Oh, that's great. Where does your cousin live?"

I could hear Joan's mental brakes squealing when I told her that Jacquie lives in Brooklyn. I don't know much about New York, but I guess Joan was not thrilled about going outside of Manhattan.

"I don't know about Brooklyn," she said slowly. "Why don't we see how things work out when we're all together tomorrow?"

"Sure, Joan," I said. I hate it when she gets in that patronizing mode, as if she's the teacher and I'm the schoolgirl. In Joan speak she'd just told me to forget it, nobody wants to go to Brooklyn and chill with my homies. Okay. Whatever. That wouldn't keep me from seeing my cousin. In fact, it convinced me more that I had to go.

Darnell and Cousin Ronnie had often accused me of forgetting my roots. For me, this was going back to my roots, to my oldest friendship. Jacquie and I go back almost as long as Toni and Joan, although Jacquie and I haven't stayed in touch the way they have.

I was wrapping up my packing when my mother called. I was surprised that she wasn't more excited about my trip.

"I worry about you, honey," she said. "That's all."

"There's more, isn't there?" I pressed her.

"Yes, Maya. I just know how hard you work at your job. I just wonder if maybe you put as much time and attention into your relationship with Darnell you might not still be married."

"Mama, you of all people should know better than that. Darnell and I just outgrew each other."

"Don't rush into anything, Maya. That's all I'm saying. Give yourself some breathing space. Enjoy being a single gal for a while." Mama's just seem to know when you're chewing on something in your mind, don't they? Just seem to know when you got a mental Jolly Rancher stuck in your back teeth, so to speak.

But I didn't want to talk about it. "Since when are you the Ebony Adviser?" I asked her. I frowned up my face in that way she hates and said, "Uh-oh...I think Ronnie's here! Gotta go, mama. Love ya," and hung up the phone.

Seconds later I heard the roaring voice of my cousin Ronnie from outside. It was time to leave for the airport and Maya's excellent New York adventure.

WILLIAM

I was naked in my room at the Plaza, packing my bags, when Joan called with the news that the girls were all coming to New York for the weekend.

"That's great," I said. Although Joan and I had had our small competitive tensions during the last two weeks, I missed the girls. I missed Toni's colossal ego and Lynn's flower child spaciness and Maya's street-wise skepticism. But I also missed my beautiful four-bedroom house in the Valley, and I definitely missed my hot tub and my wine cellar.

Oddly enough, though, I hardly missed my girl-friend Monica, but that might be because the woman calls me every hour just to check up on me. People who pine for relationships sometimes don't think about the down side. If I don't respond to one of Monica's calls, she leaves more and more messages wanting to know where I am. I know that my girl-friends consider Monica cold and calculating, but when it comes to the telephone, she's just like every other woman I've ever known. She goes crazy when you don't call.

Am I yammering here? I've been accused of yam-mering and Monica had me working on it. In fact, Monica has me working on so many things to turn me into her idea of the perfect mate that I thought I needed to take a little vacation in New York before I returned to Los Angeles and all the many plans Monica had for me.

My work in New York was done. Like one of the Seven Samurai, like one of Ocean's 11, it was time for Big Will to move on to new battles. My brilliant legal mind was through representing for a while.

I did not consider it necessary to circulate my schedule to Joan or to Monica. But I did tell Joan that I'd be staying in town.

"I'm moving down to the Mercer Hotel," I told her.

"That's great. We'll be nearby." Joan is like Miss Congeniality. The one you knew in high school, not the Sandra Bullock character.

"We'll have to get together," I said, and left it hanging.

How do you say "fuck you" in L.A.? The answer: "Let's have lunch." How do you say "don't bother me?" Answer: "We'll have to get together."

But Joan is a perfectionist. She wants all her relationships to be perfect and she wants her friends to be too. She was not letting me off the hook so early.

"Speaking of getting together, I had lunch with Swedelson today," she said.

Was she trying to make me nervous? Was she scoring points with him ahead of me? This was something I actually would have to discuss with Monica. My lover is a master strategist. Or is that mistress strategist? Whoops, this might be considered yammering.

But anyway, Joan is not a strategist. She's a Good Girl. "William, I told him about everything you did to work out this settlement. He is really so grateful to both of us."

There she goes again. When will she understand that we are more powerful if we separate? If it were up to me, we'd create a mystique inside Goldberg, Swedelson that would have everyone convinced that we hate each other. We'd meet secretly and trade information. I'd have information from her rivals, and she'd have information from my competition. There would be no stopping us. The power of two!

Even Big Willie was alert and erect at that thought. But was it the idea of seizing power at Goldberg, Swedelson? Or was it talking to Joan while I was standing completely naked? Sometimes a man just shouldn't ask questions.

CHAPTER
FOUR

JOAN

I am all about control. I am not the kind of woman who has tearful conversations with her boyfriend on the telephone. No, I am the kind of woman who calls her boyfriend and when a woman answers, I hang up.

The day started out so well. After lunch with Mr. Swedelson, I was free. I had the rest of Thursday to play in New York. I would not have to think about Goldberg, Swedelson again until Monday morning when I would have to be back at work in L.A.

The first thing I did that afternoon was to check out of the Plaza and move downtown to the Soho Grand. The hotel is on West Broadway between Grand and Canal Street, at the edge of Soho, and Swedelson had arranged for me to have one of the four penthouses for myself and my friends. Our penthouse even had its own private terrace. As I un-packed, I noticed that the bar was stocked with goodies from Dean & DeLuca and the bathroom had all the latest Kiehl's beauty products. After hanging up my things, the next step was to call Ellis in Vancouver. I wanted to let him know that I had moved. I dialed and sat on the edge of my bed gazing out at the view of lower Manhattan's skyline until someone picked up. That someone was definitely not Ellis.

"Hello?" she said. She sounded groggy as if the call had just awakened her. I hung up, mentally cursing the hotel operator for giving me the wrong room.

I tried again and got the same woman. This time when she picked up she sounded groggy and angry.

"Who is this?" she snapped. "Do you realize what time it is?" I cringed. I'd forgotten about the three-hour time difference between New York and Vancouver, but what the heck? A quick calculation on my part discerned that it was already noon where Ellis was. And who was he with? Who was this woman answering his phone?

"I'm sorry," I said. "I'm trying to reach Ellis Carter, and they gave me your room."

"This is Mr. Carter's room," she said crisply. "What do you want?"

I was speechless for what felt like a very long time, during which I heard someone else enter the room on the other end of the line. The woman greeted the new person, then added that she thought she had "some Ellis groupie" on the phone.

"I'm so sorry, sugar, let me handle that," I heard the new person, another woman, say. And then she was on the phone with me. "Hello? How can I help you?"

"I…was calling to speak to Ellis," I stammered.

"Joan? Is that you?" she asked.

Now I recognized her voice. "Yes, Darla, it's me. How are you?" I wanted to add, 'and who the hell is that woman in my boyfriend's hotel room?' but that would be undignified, and Joan Carol Clayton is all about self-control and dignity. I wanted to express my consternation, but I was at a disadvantage. When you deal with Darla it helps to know what current medication she's on. Is it Metabolife? Prozac? Ritalin? They all contribute to the magic that is Darla. So I ventured a tamer version of my question: "What's going on?" I asked.

"Oh. Didn't Ellis tell you?"

"Tell me *what?*"

"Well, it's a great story," she started gleefully. "It involves his ex-girlfriend. She lives in Canada now, you know."

I tried to play it cool. "Ex-girlfriend? Is that her that answered the phone?"

"Why, yes it is," Darla gloated. "Last night...."

I decided to cut her off. "Can you just put Ellis on the phone?"

"Oh...sure," she said. "No problem. But I better warn you, Joan. The phone service here sucks. Don't be surprised if we're cut off. Why just the other day—"

The line went dead. Did she expect me to believe that we were cut off? That wench hung up on me!

I was in a fury now, and I tried to Blackberry Ellis, but he wasn't answering his two-way either.

So I started my fun weekend in New York with the knowledge that my man was sharing a hotel room with some woman, a woman who apparently was in the favor of his publicist Darla, who would rather take a bullet than let me near him in the first place.

There are three things a girl can do in a situation like this: (1) get drunk, (2) call her best friend or (3) go shopping. But drinking alone is a little too *Waiting to Exhale* for me, so two out of three ain't bad. I grabbed my cell phone and punched up Toni on speed dial as I headed for the elevator.

By the time I was outside on the street, I had Toni on the line. We would shop together while I told her the latest.

"What's up," Toni said when she picked up. "Where are you?"

"I'm having a crisis," I said. "And I'm on Canal Street."

"If you're changing hotels again, Joan, I'm not coming," she said.

"No, honey. The hotel is great and you'll love the penthouse. I can't wait for you to see it."

"Then what's wrong?"

I suddenly felt ridiculous, like a child. Why was I so upset? There was probably a perfectly good explanation for why this woman was in Ellis's hotel room, answering his phone. I told Toni that.

"Umm...okay, Joan. If that helps you sleep at night. But from the sound of the it, she sure wasn't doing any sleeping last night. Where are you now?" She had wrapped up her commentary and changed the subject.

I signed and went along. "I'm walking up West Broadway, heading for Spring Street," I said. "I'm going to Ferragamo. There's a pair of red lizard slingbacks there with my name on them. I want to wear them tonight."

"Relax, Joan. Our plane doesn't get in until Friday morning. And you don't have to get all dressed up for us. We like you despite your clothes."

"They're not for you, Toni. I told you about Bradley. I'm having dinner with him tonight. He's taking me to Mr. Chow."

It's hard to impress Toni, but this did. It's pricey, it's stylish and it caters to the in-crowd, from the music industry and beyond.

"You should have told me sooner," Toni said. "I would have called one of my cool friends, like Beyoncé, and made sure you get a good table."

"You haven't met Bradley," I said. "Somehow I don't think he'll need Beyoncé's help. He really knows his way around this town."

"What else do you know about him?" Toni asked. For some reason she's skeptical about all my boyfriends. Not that Bradley is my boyfriend. I can't believe I just lumped him into that category. I wondered to myself if this mental slip had anything to do with my still-simmering anger at Ellis. Who, by the way, still hadn't called.

"I know all I need to know: He isn't sharing a hotel room on the other side of the country with his ex-girlfriend. Who is sleeping in his bed."

Toni's tone turned serious. "Now, Joan. That's not enough. Don't get carried away. Wait until I get there and inspect him."

"Toni, he's not a piece of property. He's a nice guy who's been showing me a great time. And now that my eyes have been opened, it seems to me that maybe the rules don't apply anymore when you're out of town. I think there's some travel exception that makes your behavior not admissible in court if you leave the state or the country. And Ellis seems to be taking full advantage of said loophole."

"Girl, don't get all lawyer on me. All I'm asking is that you wait a day. Don't do anything foolish. Wait 'til I check him out. *Then* you can do something foolish. Okay? I'll see you in the morning."

"You'll see us both then," I spat out, still upset. "He's coming with me to meet you at the airport."

"Ah, a man who meets me at the airport," she said. "Watch out, now. He's getting points already."

TONI

After Joan's semi-frantic phone call about her nonexistent love life, I got back to packing my wardrobe for the weekend. Actually, Shelby technically was doing the packing while I received a massage. I say technically because all Shelby was doing right now was staring at the luggage that was spread out all over my bedroom. I myself was laid out on a massage table. Ilsa the masseuse was laboring over me as I directed Shelby.

"Are you really going to take all this for three days?" Shelby asked. One of Ilsa's virtues is that she hardly says a word. She just kept silently kneading oil into my tender muscles.

I understand that even my lowly Shelby wants to learn, to soak up some of the genius of me, so I was willing to be patient. "If you own 15 pieces of Vuitton luggage, you ought to use them. That's the whole point of having good luggage," I explained.

Shelby eyed the open luggage scattered around my bedroom. "Your hair care products have their own suitcase?"

"Hair care and make-up," I corrected her. "And those will be two of my carry-ons," I said. "I'm not letting them one out of my sight." Shelby has frizzy over-bleached blonde hair. She clearly could not begin to understand the maintenance requirements of hair as exquisite as mine.

I relaxed as my body responded to Ilsa's skillful ministrations. The woman is to massages what I, Toni Childs, am to real estate.

"Are you sure you're not going over the weight limit?" she asked. "I hear the airlines are really cracking down."

Her negativity was amazing. "The airlines cannot stand in the way of my life," I explained to her. "Besides, all of this is part of the magic that is Toni Childs. The weather in New York can change in a minute, especially in the spring. It's been known to snow there in April, in which case I'll need my lynx coat. But it could suddenly turn warm, in which case I'd want to wear shorts and a t-shirt."

"But don't you want to do some shopping when you're there?"

"Of course I'll be shopping. But I can't take a chance on not being prepared. This is also a business trip, you know."

"Is that why you had me research that list of Manhattan properties for you?"

"Yes, Shelby," I sighed. I had instructed her to prepare a list of home addresses for entertainment people like Spike Lee and Damon Dash and business types like Robert Johnson and Malcolm Diggs. I don't understand why folks with all their money are living in New York when they could be buying gorgeous luxury homes from me in Los Angeles. "I intend to visit their homes so I can get a sense of their housing needs," I explained. "When I do approach them, it will be with a portfolio of houses that are just right for them."

"Aren't you worried about being mistaken for a stalker?" she asked.

"You have to think outside the box, Shelby," I said. It was clear that this concept was beyond her. "You can't get bogged down in what is. You have to look beyond that, to what might be."

"And that requires 15 pieces of luggage?"

"Well, I have to pack my Cavalli suits for business. We're going to do all the clubs. Lotus. Spa. Bungalow 8. Suede. And then there's Derek."

"Derek?" Shelby asked.

"Derek Johnson. The Yankee."

"Do you know him?"

"Know him, honey? The man was crazy about me. He'd be furious if he knew I was in New York and didn't call him."

"Does Todd know?" Shelby asked.

"Todd's not the jealous type," I said. But the truth was I had not mentioned Derek to Todd. What's the point of mentioning an old boyfriend to your new one?

"Besides, Shelby, this isn't a romance. I want to sell that dude a house. A player like him ought to be living in Los Angeles."

We put together a few outfits. Or rather, I put them together. Shelby does not have my awesome fashion sense.

"We better move, girl," I said. "We still have to pick up Lynn before we head for the airport."

"Oh, she called to say don't bother," said Shelby. "She got herself a ride. She'll meet you at LAX."

"Now who would give her a ride?" I wondered out loud. "Must be that plant man she's doing it with in her office."

Shelby seemed to perk up at this.

"Don't get any ideas, Shelby," I warned her. "I do not tolerate that kind of behavior at Toni Childs Realty."

"Nooo, that's not it. It's that Lynn told me about her movie," said Shelby, brightening even more. "She said she might want to interview me."

"I just have one warning for you, Shelby: Don't give up your day job. Or you'll end up like Lynn, begging for rides from men who water plants for a living."

"Actually, I think she said that she was getting a ride from…Malcolm Diggs," said Shelby.

"Malcolm Diggs? The businessman?" I pushed myself up from the table, knocking aside Ilsa's hands and exposing my perfect, nakedly chocolate form. I have a stack of the latest magazines on the table beside my bed. I reached for it and pulled my latest copy of *Black Enterprise* from the pile. I waved it at her.

"This man on the cover is Malcolm Diggs, Shelby," I said. "Remember that. He is one of the most successful men in the country, and I can assure you that he would not go anywhere near Lynn Searcy."

"Vill you return to this table or must I leave?" said Ilsa. I could see that she was angry that I had interrupted her work. To tell the truth, one of the reasons I like Ilsa is that she's the only woman I know who's tougher than I am. Of course I returned to the table at once. But all the time Ilsa worked on me, I couldn't stop wondering who was actually bringing Lynn to the airport.

LYNN

No one would ever believe that Lynn Searcy, rebel, professional student and free spirit, would turn up at the Los Angeles airport on the arm of Malcolm Diggs, but that's the way it happened Thursday night.

Malcolm had told me to meet him at his hotel, the Mondrian. I soon learned that when you travel with Malcolm Diggs, it's first class all the way. From the minute his driver picked us up at the Mondrian, we were representing like mad. Malcolm's only luggage was one large, sleek black garment bag. If he was embarrassed by my well-worn, old-hippie duffel bag, which has been with me since college, he didn't show it. I sat beside him in the back of the limo. It was my first chance to talk with him since Sandy picked him up for me in The Sweet Life.

Malcolm was very open, and I found myself telling him all about the weekend my girlfriends and I were going to have in New York.

"You'll have to come to my birthday party on Saturday," he said.

"Oh, a birthday party? I'd love to, but I have a feeling that Joan has the entire three days scheduled for us."

"Bring her. I want the four of you there."

The way he said it, I understood that Malcolm Diggs was the kind of man for whom "I want" meant "I will have." By the time we got to the airport, I felt that we were old friends. We even checked in our luggage together at curbside: his expensive garment bag, my ragged duffel bag.

"How about a drink in the VIP lounge?" he asked.

"I'm not a member," I told him. As if he couldn't

guess. Frankly, I find things like VIP lounges elitist and obnoxious. Where's the brotherhood? On the other hand, I never turn down a free drink. And a drink with a man like Malcolm doesn't come along every day. I wasn't even sure they'd let me into the VIP lounge, dressed as I was in a wife-beater, long skirt, platform boots and floppy hat. Everyone else going inside looked very corporate. Even Malcolm, in his expensive Diesel casual and Gucci loafers could never be mistaken for just another brother from the 'hood.

"Don't worry about it, Lynn," he said smoothly. "They know me here. And you're my guest."

But as we approached the VIP lounge, we could hear shouting. And the voice doing the shouting was very familiar to me. It was the unmistakable sound of Toni Childs at war. That's a sound once heard, you never forget.

"What do you mean I can't carry these bags on?" she was positively shrill.

"Oh, no," I mumbled. We turned a corner and I could see Toni surrounded by four—count them, four—Vuitton bags. She was at the check-in counter, behind which were two harried-looking clerks in airline uniforms, one male and one female.

Frizzy-haired Shelby was standing next to Toni, her face red with embarrassment. "Code red." I said. I thought I said it under my breath, but I guess it was a little louder than I intended.

Malcolm heard me. "Do you know her?" he asked.

"Unfortunately yes. Remember I told you about my girlfriends? That's one of them."

"I'll bet I can tell which one." He smiled. "It has to be Toni."

"None other," I admitted.

"It looks as if she's having some trouble."

"Some trouble is right. She's going to get herself bounced from this flight if she keeps it up."

I waved at Toni and Shelby to get their attention, but Toni was too wrapped up in her argument with the people at the counter to notice me. Shelby looked relieved when she saw me. As they say, misery loves company. She walked quickly towards us. A look of recognition flashed in her face as she registered who Malcolm was. She gave a smug little smile.

"Aren't you Malcolm Diggs?" she asked.

"None other," he said graciously.

"I was just reading about you in *Black Enterprise*," she said. "My boss will be so glad to meet you."

I grabbed Malcolm's arm. "You know, if she's going to be bounced from this flight, I'm not so sure we want to get attached to her," I warned him. I guess that establishes what kind of a friend I am. But you have to know that Toni has never been my best friend. She's never approved of my lifestyle.

To my surprise, Malcolm was not concerned about getting barred from the flight. On the contrary, he waded into the fray, or rather, strode up to the counter. I was too surprised to remove my hand on his arm, so he carried me along with him.

That's when the drama that Toni loves so much suddenly stopped. While I approached Toni, Malcolm took the two clerks aside and spoke to them very softly. They nodded, but I really couldn't tell which way the conversation was going until I heard the man get on the phone and then tell Malcolm that the person wanted to speak to him. Malcolm spoke briefly, then the call was ended. That was it. In my periphery,

I saw the man's face break into a smile. The woman beamed broadly. The sun broke out. The planets had aligned. Everybody was happy.

"You're back on the flight, Ms. Childs," said the female clerk as she came over to us.

"Thank you," Toni said, scooping up her bags.

"Don't thank us," said the clerk. "Thank Mr. Diggs. He's agreed to be responsible for your luggage on this flight."

Toni then looked past me and took in the full splendor that is Malcolm Diggs. Of course she recognized him. Unlike me, she reads the business press and knew all about his income (huge), marital status (single) and residences (Manhattan and Sag Harbor). And I had the pleasure of introducing them.

"Toni, I want you to meet my new friend, and your benefactor, Malcolm Diggs."

"You have my eternal gratitude, Mr. Diggs," said Toni who can be extremely gracious when it suits her.

"Please, call me Malcolm. And I'm looking forward to being part of your weekend in New York."

"What did you tell those people at the counter?" she asked. I was wondering about that too.

"I just got them to listen to reason," he said coolly.

All this time Shelby had looked like she was about to explode. At that point she could contain herself no longer.

"He owns the airline!" she crowed. "It was all in *Black Enterprise*."

He looked slightly embarrassed. "That story did go on a bit," he said. "Actually, I just own a piece of the airline. Not a terrific investment these days, but at times it pays off. Like now."

Malcolm was not through with rescuing my girlfriends, however. For at that moment the last remaining traveler appeared. Maya was breathless as if she had been running, or possibly because she was carrying with both arms an enormous box, the kind a winter coat might come in.

"Will one of you please help me," she wheezed. "I can't carry this cake another minute!"

MAYA

The waiting area after the last checkpoint was strangely quiet when I arrived. It had that strange stillness that makes you suspect you just missed some big dramatic moment, like a car crash or some Toni Childs production.

If I seemed a bit ragged when I got to the waiting area, you can't blame me. Cousin Ronnie had convinced me to take the trip to New York so that I could go to Cousin Jacquie's family reunion in Fort Greene on Saturday. He and his pal Peaches were supposed to be coming too, but at the very last minute, a crisis at the latest branch of Ronnie's hair salon empire, Situations, meant that he and Peaches had to stay behind. They did drive me to the airport, but Ronnie actually expected me to carry that 20-pound ambrosia cake all the way to the waiting area all by myself. Ronnie is over six feet tall and twice my weight, and I insisted that he carry that thing through LAX.

"I should have left this home," I told him and Peaches as we weaved our way through the crowds. "I don't believe for a minute that I'm getting this box on the plane. Who carries a homemade cake on the red-eye?"

"Maya, you should be ashamed for even considering leaving this delicious cake behind," said Ronnie. "This cake is part of your family history. This is a treasured family recipe." Ronnie likes to act as the family griot, whether you ask him or not. "This was handed down from your ancestors in the African Diaspora. They passed this recipe on through drumbeats and dance."

"Don't even try it, Ronnie. I don't think our ancestors knew about tiny marshmallows and fruit cocktail."

Ronnie shrugged. "Then consider it a symbol of what they were deprived of. It's still a tradition."

"I don't see why I just couldn't e-mail Cousin Jacquie the recipe so she could make the cake herself."

Ronnie shook his head with disgust. "The point of the ambrosia cake is fellowship. It's about love and sharing, not about some old printed recipe. Besides," he reminded me, "she had enough details to handle without adding this to the list. And you promised you would bring it."

"A promise is a promise," echoed Peaches. "You don't want to be breaking a promise before a flight. It's bad luck."

"Thanks, Peaches. If I wasn't nervous before, I sure am now." I haven't done much flying in my life.

At the last checkpoint, Ronnie turned the cake over to me. He and Peaches were not on a flight so they couldn't go any further. There was a lot of kissing and hugging as if I was leaving for forever instead of just three days. Made me even more nervous, to be honest.

Nerves were quickly losing the battle to exhaustion, though. I had been up half the night baking the ambrosia cake. Mama had even given me her recipe and helped me through baking it by coaching me by phone

from San Bernadino. There was no way I was gon'
to tell my mama that I didn't bring the cake because
it was inconvenient. But I was sure that once I got to
the gate the security people were going to confiscate
it and eat every damn crumb themselves.

But no.

As I came to the waiting area, I was struggling to
balance the cake box and wishing that I had rented
a luggage cart for the damn thing. Then I realized that
I had just walked in on the end of a Toni episode. All
of them: Toni, Lynn, some over-permed white girl
and a tall good-looking black man turned to look at
me. My facial expression must have given me away,
or maybe Lynn read my mind.

"Don't worry, Maya," she said. "We're still on the
flight. No thanks to Toni."

The man didn't wait to be introduced. He reached
for the box I was carrying and took it off my hands.
He flinched a second when he realized how heavy it
is—for a cake. "You must be Maya," he said. "I'm
Malcolm Diggs. Let me find you a place for this." He
turned away to whisper something to the female clerk
behind the counter. She smiled and took the box from
him.

He turned back to me and smiled. "Don't worry,
Maya. Your cake is in safe hands."

"I don't like letting it out of my sight," I admitted,
squinting over his shoulder at the suspiciously hungry-
looking counter clerk.

"I asked her to keep it in the first class galley. You
can come up and take a peek at it any time you want."

Who was this man, I wondered? And who was he
with? Again Lynn managed to answer a question before I asked.

"Malcolm has invited us to his party Saturday night," she said, putting her hands on his arm possessively.

"Does Joan know this?" I had the feeling that Joan had a full schedule for us and God forbid anyone should tamper with Joan's plans. You move one half-hour in one of her schedules and she can go to pieces. I swear, I've seen that girl freak out when I printed a memo on canary yellow instead of colonial yellow.

"Joan doesn't know yet," said Malcolm Diggs. "I'm looking forward to meeting her and inviting her myself."

"In that case, I'm there," I said. Jacquie's party was an afternoon thing, so I would be free for night-time activities on Saturday.

"I knew I should have booked myself in first class," muttered Toni to no one, and everyone, in particular. As usual, she was unengaged by anything that didn't center around her or cause drama. "If I had called Russell Simmons I could have chartered us a plane. Still, I'm going to ask about first class. Maybe it's not too late to get a seat."

"Oops…you dropped something Toni," I said. She looked around the ground quickly, reaching for her ears to make sure those diamonds—not diamondelles, diamonds—were still there. "Where?" she said, irritated.

I rolled my eyes. "That name. You dropped a name, baby." I patted her on the shoulder and she sneered at me. She wasn't fooling me one bit. I could see that Toni wanted that seat in first class to be next to Malcolm Diggs. But if she was trying to impress Malcolm with who she knew, it didn't work.

Then Malcolm spoke up again. He really was a

smooth operator. "I'm not making any promises, ladies, but if we ever do get on this flight, and there are vacancies in first class, I can probably get you upgraded. If I'm able to do that, would you like to join me?"

Toni gave an arrogant little glance each to me and Lynn and then, in disgust, folded her arms across her chest (no small feat for her, I might add). For Toni, half the attraction of first class is that it keeps out folks like myself. It's not enough to soar; one's lowly little friends must also crash and burn.

WILLIAM

Swedelson offered to set me up at the Soho Grand, but I opted for the Mercer Hotel instead. It's not far from the Grand, in the heart of Soho at Prince Street and Mercer, but it's smaller and it won't have the girls monitoring my every move. Women are treacherous. I think the word some of them use is "catty." That's one of those words that women are allowed to use but we guys can't. And don't get me started on what the hell the difference is between "catty," which is okay if a woman says it, and "pussy," which is never okay. But I'm yammering.

The point is that at any given moment any one of them, Joan, Lynn, Toni or Maya, might suddenly decide that Monica is her new best friend and go filling her head with all the dirt she knows about me. I have no doubt that Toni would throw our friendship out the window in a minute if she thought it would help her sell Monica a million dollar house.

But I had other, bigger fish to fry that Thursday

evening. At the hotel bar, I ordered myself an apple martini and savored it. I was free to indulge and happy that I didn't have to pretend away my preference for fruity drinks for the sake of pleasing Monica. I waited, watching the parade of chic downtown types move through the lobby. I was soon joined by my buddy Rham. They teach those young investment bankers to be prompt. No CP time for those working on the Goldman, Sachs plantation. We were planning a guy's night out: drinking, steaks, and then a card game.

Yes, more poker. Having tasted that game in Little Italy, I couldn't wait to get back.

"My nose is opened. My senses are sharpened. I'm ready," I announced.

Rham laughed. "Careful man. You can't lose your cool. Poker is all about keeping your cool."

But my blood was pumping. "Have you ever hunted? " I asked him.

"Sure, man. Everyone in Minnesota hunts before the winter," he said. "You too?"

"Not in Kansas City," I told him. "And I was one of those kids who never got over the death of Bambi's mother. I could never go into the woods tracking some defenseless, gentle creature."

"So why are you asking?"

"Because that's the feeling I get when I play poker, Rham," I explained. "I think it's the same kind of excitement. The same kind of using your wits, even your whole body, because in a moment of weakness you can scratch your ear and, if you're playing with people who've studied you, you give yourself away. You blink and a smart player knows you're holding a busted flush."

Rham laughed. "Careful man. You have all the symptoms of a gambling jones. I heard a commodities trader talk like that once, just before he bet the farm."

"Was it a good bet?" I asked. I ordered another round for us: apple martini for me, single malt scotch for Rham. Monica would like him.

"It was, actually. Maybe you know him? Malcolm Diggs? But he's out of commodities now. He's representing the community these days."

"Oh, yeah. I've been reading all about him. Does he need a lawyer?"

Maybe the martinis were kicking in. I found myself telling Rham about my life at Goldberg, Swedelson. About the competition with Joan. About how she makes it so hard because she takes it so personally. Instead of focusing on winning, I had to think about hurting her feelings. Damn feelings. They have no place in business. Especially not in a law office.

Rham was a good listener. When I finished my rant, he nodded.

"All of us have been through some version of this," he said. "I take my advice from John Gotti."

"Put a hit on Joan? I don't want to go that far." But I was thinking, maybe I could hire someone to scratch her car? God forgive me.

"No. When Gotti went to jail, he said, 'Do the time, don't let the time do you.'"

"So you're saying that while I'm at Goldberg, Swedelson, I should treat it like a prison sentence?"

"All I'm saying is that at Goldman, Sachs, I do the time, I don't let the time do me." With that he pulled out an onyx American Express card and insisted on paying for our drinks. Who was I to argue?

Then we were on to dinner at The Kitchen, right

in the hotel. No, not the actual kitchen. The Kitchen. It was Asian-American-Provençal cuisine of the highest order, but I'll admit that in spite of the dinner and the wine and the career advice from Rham, at least ten percent of my brain never stopped thinking about the poker game.

I was the happiest man in town when we finally made our way to a smoke-filled room in the warehouse district and I could finally sit down at a table and pick up the cards. It was a seedy neighborhood, but inside, in spite of the smoke, you could tell this was a first class operation. Two beautiful girls moved around offering drinks and cigars like we were in Vegas. There were even a couple of women at the card tables, which wasn't that unusual. I barely noticed them. They were all older, well dressed in mafia matriarch fashion, and they were totally focused on their cards.

Rham was about to take the other empty seat across the table from me. Suddenly he paused and stared past my shoulder as if he had seen a ghost.

This was New York. My first reaction was that it was a raid. Then I thought maybe a celebrity. Maybe Mick Jagger. I turned around.

I'm not going to yammer on about all those people in history who were warned not to turn around. They turned around anyway and created all kinds of disasters.

But nobody told me not to turn around.

So I did. And before I could say anything, there she was. Honey Hayes. And although it had been about sixteen years since I had seen her, she was even more beautiful than I remembered.

I got to my feet. "Honey," I said. My heart was pounding.

The rest of the table was not so romantic. "Do you mind?" one of the mafia matriarchs growled, clutching her cards to her chest, "We're playing cards here."

Honey smiled at me. A million dollar smile that could light up the Empire State Building and still have enough watts left for Times Square.

"William Jerome Dent," she said and gave an eye gesture in the direction of the bar before retreating into the smoky darkness as quickly as she had appeared.

FIVE

JOAN

Bradley was picking me up at the Soho Grand at nine o'clock that night. That was late for L.A. standards but not for New York. I knew in advance that we'd be pulling an all-nighter, so I decided to pamper myself then get some beauty rest. I had a spa all picked out for the pampering part.

The hotel doorman hailed a taxi for me, and I gave him the address of the Just Calm Down Spa on West 22nd Street. Their Malt Shop Wrap turned out to be everything I'd heard it was.

As I lay naked on a table, a masseuse named Shannon scrubbed me down with sugar and coffee grains and a detoxifying paste made of coffee and cocoa powder.

"Vanilla or chocolate?" she asked me at the end.

I looked at her, unsure what she was talking about. Truthfully, I like my chocolate over six feet tall and built like Bradley Houston. She seemed to read the confusion in my face.

"I mean moisturizer," she said. "We have it in vanilla or chocolate."

"Chocolate," I answered, without hesitation. It was the right choice.

After that, I felt so fabulous I walked down Fifth Avenue the half-mile back to my hotel. I wanted to call Toni or Lynn because they'd really appreciate details about the spa, but I figured they were probably busy taking care of last minute things for the trip. Instead, I got a little beauty rest, bathed and played with some new M.A.C. cosmetics I had picked up. I think I looked pretty darn fabulous when Bradley called from the lobby downstairs.

As I headed for the elevator, I checked myself once more in the mirror. My hair was fluffed, my earrings were the new chandeliers from Paul Morelli, and I was wearing the new red Ferragamo slingback sandals and a magenta slip dress and jacket from Versace. I thought I looked pretty good. Bradley confirmed that when I stepped out of the elevator.

The response was mutual. Now that I was accepting the out-of-town loophole that Ellis—who still hadn't called—had already slipped through, I was free to look at Bradley Everett Houston as more than my new New York friend and guide. This was one sexy guy. A thrill went through me as we exchanged New York-style air kisses. The thrill intensified as he took my arm and led me outside. His chauffeur Khalil was standing at the curb, and he opened the door of Bradley's limo so we could step inside.

As I leaned back on the leather seat, I remembered what Toni had said on the phone earlier that day. She really touched a nerve when she reminded me that I didn't know very much about Bradley. I intended to change that tonight.

Mr. Chow was on the east side, not far from

Jimmy's downtown, which Bradley had mentioned to me on our foray to Jimmy's in the Bronx. By now it didn't surprise me that the hostess recognized Bradley or that the maitre d' led us to our table immediately while another couple, who had arrived before us, was sent to the bar to wait. Hanging with Bradley I was getting very spoiled.

There were no menus, and when our server asked what we'd like to order, I was flummoxed. But Bradley did the ordering, and the food—course after course of it—was to die for. Over lettuce wraps, our second appetizer, Bradley said he wanted to hear all about my shopping and my experience at the spa. That got me started.

"Bradley," I began. "I had a funny thought tonight."

"Uh oh," he said, with a smile. "That doesn't sound good."

"Oh, no, nothing serious," I assured him. "It's just that I realized that we women always say that we want a man who listens."

"I seem to have heard that a few times," he agreed.

"But you know what? You've been such a good listener this week that I've done most of the talking. I really don't know much of anything about you."

He stiffened just a bit, sitting up a little straighter across from me.

"I mean, sometimes you have a chauffeur and a limo; sometimes you don't. You've only given me your cell phone number. And sometimes you answer; sometimes you don't."

"I always call back," he said quickly.

I patted his knee, which was as far as I wanted to go. I'm not like Lynn. I'm not into the bad boys.

"When we met, you said you were from Chicago,

but you seem to know your way around New York like a native."

He relaxed.

"I guess it's time to come clean. I have commitments in Chicago, and I've been spending most of the year there. But New York is my home and always will be."

That wasn't quite satisfactory, so I decided to ask the Big One. "Bradley, are you married?"

Much to my relief, he laughed. It was a big, hearty, authentic laugh, like a young Eddie Murphy. It was at least a minute before he could speak.

"No, Joan," he said. "I am not now, nor have I ever been, married." He paused and added, "Not that I have anything against it."

Lynn would say that I hold on to things and that it was time to let the subject go, but I couldn't. Part of my control issue is my need to have a mental file on everyone I know. Besides, I'm a lawyer, and I know how to keep pressing for information.

"Bradley, I don't even know where you live."

"I told you. I'm a native New Yorker."

"But Bradley, you've taken me all over town, from Tribeca to the Bronx. The city's a big place. Where exactly do you live? I'm sure it's not in your limo."

He smiled. "No, Khalil would never allow that. He loves that car too much."

He reached for my hand. "Okay, Joan. Here's the truth. Have you ever heard of Sugar Hill?"

I hadn't.

"Well, it's an old neighborhood in the heart of Harlem. That's where I live. In a very nice brownstone that I'd like you to see. In fact, I could take you there tonight."

His eyes, his smile, his honesty, and possibly the

second round of ginger Cosmopolitans had an effect. For a short time that night I found myself wondering whether I had made a mistake by inviting my girlfriends for our New York weekend. If I was on my own, who knows what could have happened? But I'm a responsible person who was going to see that we met my friends when their plane came in at dawn.

TONI

When the red-eye finally took off from LAX that night at 10 P.M. I was not even sure that I still wanted to go to New York. I had been disgraced more than once and we hadn't even arrived in New York yet. Now I was sitting in the tourist class section in my effort to be a team player, and the team wasn't even together. I was seated with Miss Girlz N the Hood, bless her heart, and being serenaded by a screaming set of triplets across the aisle.

At least I was not alone in my misery. Maya and I exchanged grimaces every time one of the noisy crumbsnatchers erupted.

"I had to pass many tests to get my license to sell real estate," I said loudly enough so that the parents could hear. "Why are these people allowed to take fertility drugs and multiply without any qualifications at all?" The happy parents just smirked at me. Some people have no shame.

"Please don't get us thrown off the plane," Maya said quietly. "Lynn's new friend Malcolm can only do so much. After that incident at the ticket counter, I think the flight attendants have been warned to keep an eye on you."

"Ridiculous. This would never have even happened if I had been flying on Russell's plane. After this trip, I'm never flying on a commercial airline again."

Maya looked unimpressed. "At least we're not on Southwest," she said. "Those people don't even feed you. Won't even toss you a cracker. Talk about cheap. It's not like the fares are that low. This airline charges about the same but you get more for your money."

"What's it to you?" I snapped. "It's not like you paid for your ticket."

Maya glared at me. "Hey, if Joan wants to treat me to a trip, that's her business." She turned away from me and concentrated on her paperback. It was the latest John Grisham legal thriller. That's all she reads, as if she doesn't get enough law working for Joan in a law office. Soon she dozed off, so there was no company coming from her. I was too antsy to sleep.

I decided to amuse myself with the in-flight magazine. That turned out to be a good thing because I read an interesting article about a book called *Personal Magnetism: Discover Your Own Charisma and Learn to Charm, Inspire and Influence Others*. I was completely caught up in the article. If I had only had this information, I would not have suffered that humiliation at the ticket counter. I would not have had my luggage snatched away from me. I would be the one sitting in front of this plane in first class next to Malcolm Diggs, not Lynn.

The theme of the book *Personal Magnetism* was that the way to get people to go your way is with compliments. I was amazed at the simplicity, the genius of this idea. The article suggested that you start a notebook of compliments that you've paid individuals in your life so that you don't repeat yourself.

I wasn't sure if this was Palm-worthy, and I didn't have a notepad, so I flipped through my old Filofax looking for a page I wouldn't need. Success: I found one headed Birthdays/Anniversaries. I started the list with my boyfriend. I always compliment him after we make love. But was I going to have to think of something new to say every time? I mean we make love twice a day sometimes, and most of the time all I can think of after is "Wow." And that works for him.

So I moved on to a list of people in my life. I started with Joan. Then added Lynn. And I had to include Maya because Joan insists on including her in everything. Besides, Maya might see the list when she woke up. I added our friend William and wondered if he was going to be joining us during this weekend. Things had been so strained since he took up with his girlfriend Monica. That woman wasn't getting any compliments from me. I added William to the list alone. I also added Shelby and Carmella.

And then I sat there while Maya snored softly and the triplets screeched, until the flight attendants came through with the rickety drink cart. That woke Maya up.

"You're a really good sleeper," I said to Maya. I wrote that compliment down on my list.

"What are you writing?" she asked.

I explained to her about the compliment list.

"Toni, it's not a compliment to tell someone she's a good sleeper," Maya said.

She's so short-sighted. It's that Compton mentality. She doesn't understand my drive for self-improvement.

"Of course it is," I said. "And now I won't say it to you again."

She gave me a smug, superior look, like she knows

more about the world than I do. "Toni, that just means you'll have to think about a new compliment next time." She took my Filofax from my tray and looked at the rest of my list. She started to laugh.

"Oh, Toni. How long have you been trying to think of compliments? Face facts, honey. You have to start by thinking good things about people, then the compliments will come naturally."

"It's not that easy," I said.

"It's just a habit. Like now. Watch me." She leaned across the aisle to the mother of the terrible triplets. "They're such good babies," she said. "You're so lucky."

I couldn't believe it. When Maya turned back to me, I gave it to her. "Since when is a compliment an outright lie?" I demanded. "You're just giving her delusions that those babies are not the horrifying monsters that everyone else knows they are."

"It's my own idea, Toni. Compliment people in advance. Try it some time." She downed the little plastic cup of ginger ale she had requested from the sky-waitress. I didn't have a drink. I had frowned about the cup and asked for a white wine instead, which I also declined after being told that it, too, would come in a little plastic cup. Maya went back to sleeping. I went back to my list, which was easier now because the triplets had quieted down and, wonder of wonders, were all asleep at the same time.

I made a new section for my compliments list and headed it "Compliments to Give." The first name that came to mind was Malcolm Diggs. When we arrived at JFK I intended to lather that man with compliments. He was exactly the kind of customer Toni Childs Realty was created for. He might think he had everything, but he was about to learn that until he had acquired a home from me, he had not really made it at all.

LYNN

I could only imagine what was going through Toni's mind in the back of the plane. I knew that Maya couldn't care less as long as her ambrosia cake was safe. But Toni thought she belonged in first class and, more than that, she believed that I didn't.

I'll admit that I've been vocal about my political issues with first class. I don't believe in this kind of elitism and separatism. On the other hand, when a man like Malcolm Diggs upgrades your ticket and invites you to join him in the first class section, you know that it would be rude to turn him down.

I don't usually go for businessmen like Malcolm either. I always believed that the more successful they were, the more arrogant and self-centered. But Malcolm had proved he was neither arrogant nor self-centered when he defused Toni's angry scene at the airport. And he was down-to-earth enough to take care of Maya's precious cake.

All the seats in the first class section were full which was why Maya and Toni had to stay in the back with the ordinary folks. Most of the other passengers in first class were either dressed for business or in expensive Armani-type casual like Malcolm. Let's face it, my personal style is unique even in L.A. They probably don't see much of it in first class.

I posed a question for Malcolm that had been on my mind since we boarded. "Is it my imagination,

Malcolm, or are the flight attendants better looking in first class?"

"It's possible, Lynn. Or it could be the free booze just makes them look that way."

Whatever. The man who took our orders looked like Ricky Martin. I asked for champagne. Why not go all the way? Malcolm ordered Chivas.

"We have to make a toast," I said.

"Sure, Lynn," Malcolm raised his glass. "Here's to your trip. Let's hope you and your girlfriends have a weekend to remember."

That was so sweet. I found myself so drawn to him. The fact that he gave me absolutely no encouragement only warmed up my feelings. Was he the big time businessman that *Black Enterprise* described? Or was he the genuine nice guy every woman dreams of meeting?

"What's the first thing you plan to do when you get to New York?" he asked me.

"Don't laugh, Malcolm, but I want to send Sandy a postcard and thank her for introducing us."

"You call your mother Sandy?" he asked.

"Actually, she's my birth mother," I said. I explained how we'd only recently reunited and that she'd turned me on to the idea of making documentary films.

"Maybe I should send her a postcard myself. I have a feeling that this is the beginning of a beautiful friendship."

Suddenly and surprisingly I found myself hoping it could be more than that. I shivered slightly.

"Are you cold?" he asked.

"A little," I said. The cabin had grown quite chilly and my wifebeater exposed a lot of skin.

Malcolm signaled to Ricky Martin, Jr. to bring us

some blankets. When they arrived, he very gently wrapped me. His strong hands brushed my shoulders as if he was tucking me in to bed. But suddenly the last thing I wanted was to sleep. Feeling his touch aroused different feelings entirely.

The cabin lights had dimmed and the movie was coming on. It was Robin Williams in *Death to Smoochy*, a movie I hated the first time around.

"Now let me take care of you," I said in the darkness. I don't think he understood what I had in mind. In fact I know he didn't. He just leaned back and let me wrap the other blanket around him. But unlike him, I wrapped him loosely. Then I moved my hand underneath.

I might not know much about the business world, but I know how to please a man.

He frowned slightly. "Please, Lynn. You don't have to do that."

"But I want to. Besides, I've seen this picture. I know how it ends."

I had a strawberry-flavored condom opened and on his dick before he could say, 'hold up.' In the darkness of the cabin, I ducked under the little airline blanket and my mouth sought his penis. His lips might be saying "no," but sister, his dick was sending an entirely different message. I began to give him my personal version of the Bel Air hello. Once I got started, he didn't put up much of a fight. I thought I had him almost to an orgasm when he surprised me.

Don't ask me for a diagram, but the man managed to lift me out of my seat and onto him, all the time keeping me discreetly covered by his blanket. I guess we owe something to the darkness, the width of the seats and the discretion of the other first class passengers. Who knows what they were doing? Who cares?

All I know is that I was straddling him. In a matter of seconds Malcolm had turned the tables on me and instead of me servicing him, he was suddenly servicing me and I was very glad that I had worn only a little thong under my long skirt.

I started to lose it. I moaned. He lifted one of those strong hands and put it over my mouth to quiet me. I stopped thinking about him. I stopped thinking about anything.

The sound of laughter brought me back to reality. But people were only laughing at the movie. I kissed Malcolm and slipped back into my seat. He leaned over and kissed me again.

"That was very nice," I said. "I think you've done this before."

He smiled. "Never as well, Lynn. Never as well."

MAYA

Sometimes to relax I hum my new theme song to myself. It's Mary J. Blige's "No More Drama." I don't want any more pain or any more drama in my life. Yet here I was on a plane bound for New York sitting next to Toni Childs, the biggest drama queen I know. She had already clashed with the folks at the check-in, and now I could only pray that we make it to New York before she caused any more trouble. Every time one of those three babies across the aisle made a sound, I grabbed Toni's hand to silently remind her to control herself.

Fortunately, she was busy with her list of compliments. The idea of a few kind words for no immediate reward was a concept that was totally new to her.

"How are you doing with your compliments list?" I asked her.

"I'd give you a compliment now," she said. "But then I'll only have to give you one later. At the beginning I'm going to limit myself to one a day."

"I think that's wise, Toni. You don't want to wear yourself out."

"No. I'll need my energy when I start checking out properties tomorrow."

"I'm not really interested in looking at real estate, Toni," I said. "I'd much prefer shopping."

"Don't worry about it, Maya. I intend to go off on my own. I have to conduct some business."

I have to admit this was news to me. I did think that Joan expected us to stick together for the entire weekend, just like Girl Scouts. Not that I ever thought the idea would work.

"Does Joan know you're going off on your own?" I asked.

"I'll explain it to her. If I'm going to deduct this trip as a business expense I have to conduct some business. I'm not about to get in trouble with the IRS."

"Why not?" I mumbled, "You're in trouble with everyone else."

I swear I didn't realize I had said that out loud until Toni glared at me. "What?" she snapped.

"Nothing," I said quickly. "It's just that I thought we all had to stick together 24-7. I think that's what Joan has in mind."

"Joan is a control freak. That's exactly why we will all need some personal time."

"Well, you're all invited out to Fort Greene to meet my cousins."

Toni sneered. "And have ambrosia cake and chittlins? I don't think so."

"No problem. I don't mind going out to Brooklyn by myself." I'm from Compton, I thought. Brooklyn ain't got nothing on us.

My new friend Triplet Mother across the aisle heard our conversation.

"Are you going to Brooklyn?" she asked.

"I hope to," I admitted.

"What part?"

"I have family in Fort Greene," I said.

"Do you know how to get there?" I didn't know it yet, but New Yorkers have no shyness. They'll ask you anything. You don't have to answer, but I did.

"I have no idea," I admitted. "Is it far from the Soho Grand Hotel?"

"Not really," she said. I think she was happy to have something to think about besides the triplets. Her husband was sound asleep. Once I gave her the Jacquie's address, she took out a pad, wrote down the directions and gave them to me.

"Easy as pie," she said. "You'll just be taking the N or R train to DeKalb. It's like ten, fifteen minutes away."

"But it's across the river," observed Toni, who seemed to have forgotten about giving compliments, or even a thank you. "I'm not crossing any water. Nuh-uh. I don't do bridges—or tunnels. Especially not tunnels."

"Suit yourself," said Triplet Mom as she turned back to her babies.

I looked at Toni. "I don't get you. I really don't.

What happened to discovering your own charisma? What happened to your plan to charm, inspire and influence others?"

Toni shrugged. "I can't waste my charisma on people I'm never going to see again."

"Toni, you could use the practice."

"Didn't you ever hear the expression 'leaving it in the gym?'"

"No, I don't believe I've ever heard that."

"Well for your information, sometimes athletes can practice so hard that they wear themselves out. They push themselves to the limit and they do their best work and nobody sees it because it was during practice. By the time they get in the game they're worn out. The coach tells them they 'left it in the gym.'"

"And what does that have to do with you?"

"Maya, I can't wear myself out giving compliments to everyone I meet. I'll be exhausted! I need to strategize, to conserve, to measure. I need to plan my compliments. I need to place them where they will do the most for my charisma."

"I see, Toni," I said. And unfortunately I did. And then I realized who she was reminding me of.

"You know, I think someone else we know has read this book."

"Who?"

"Think. We know somebody who's always handing out hollow compliments, who pretends to be impressed with what you do, then calls your Lynn because she doesn't really remember who you are."

"Monica!"

Yes, our friend William's girlfriend Monica. She was a master manipulator. Was it possible that this was the key to her power over him?

WILLIAM

I was deep into a high-stakes poker game and was completely focused, but not as focused as I would have been had I not known that Honey Hayes was in the house. All week long I'd been looking forward to sitting down at this table, and now I was losing interest fast. The room was large but dimly lit and thick with cigarette smoke. Honey had disappeared into the darkness and it took all my self-control to focus on the game and not get up and follow her.

Fortunately for me, she came back a few minutes later. She leaned over and whispered in my ear. "When you're ready to take a break, meet me in the bar."

I was ready right then, but it took a few minutes for the hand to end. Rham winked at me as I got up. I guess he knew that I wouldn't be back that night.

I made my way through the tables and finally reached the bar area. It was also dim but decorated like a Renaissance palace with big ornate gold trimmed mirrors and old-fashioned red plush upholstered couches. Honey was standing at the bar, which gave me the opportunity to take in every delicious curve.

Have I described Honey Hayes? Well, I'm not a poet, and only the great Luther Vandross is equipped to sing her praises, though not equipped to do much else for her, if you get my drift. Oops...yammering. Now, while I would not throw Halle Berry out of bed, I have to admit I like my women with a bit more flava, and Honey had flava to spare. She looked like a combination of Eve and Aaliyah. She's tall, and most of it is leg. I'm over six feet tall and she comes up to my shoulder, which is just about right.

I don't know a lot about women's clothes, but she was wearing a short gold dress made out of some kind of stretchy material that hugged every luscious curve. Her hair was long and black.

"Of all the bars in all the world, you had to come here," I said, trying to sound like Humphrey Bogart in *Casablanca*. Maybe you've already guessed. Honey and I had a history and not all of it was good.

Honey smiled. "It's good to see you, William. It's been a long time."

We ordered drinks. An apple martini for me, a club soda for her.

"Nothing stronger?" I asked. Back in the day, Honey belonged to a hard drinking, hard partying sorority. I hoped she wasn't going to start lecturing me about the 12 Steps.

"Oh, I think I should keep my wits about me. I'm a little shaken to run into you like this, William. Maybe later you'll come back and have a drink at my place?"

Bake me and call me butter, I was thinking to myself. Because I was on a roll.

We moved to one of the cozy couches.

"How long has it been, Honey?" I asked. "Can it really be sixteen years?"

"Actually fifteen years and eight months," she said. "Kansas City seems very far away, doesn't it?"

We had been in high school together, Honey and me. But we were never actually friends. She moved with a crowd of rich kids. My friends all had jobs after school. She dated college boys with sports cars. I think that she was even engaged to a guy who played for the Royals at one point, but her parents soon put a stop to that.

"What are you doing in New York?" I asked her. I don't know much about women's fashions, but I knew that outfit she was wearing didn't come cheap. And the jewelry was all real.

"Oh, this and that. Since my divorce I've been kind of finding myself."

"Is New York a good place for that?" I thought I sounded totally suave, but it may have been the martinis kicking in.

"After you've lived in Paris, the rest of the world is Kansas City, William," she said. God, she was still so cool. I wanted to knock her to the floor and introduce her to Big Willie. He'd done well in Paris too.

"How about you, William? What have you been doing since you ruined my life?"

"Excuse me?" I wasn't sure I'd heard her correctly.

She laughed. "Oh, just my crazy sense of humor. But remember how you defeated me when we ran for president of the senior class?"

Winning that election was one of my happiest high school memories. I credit my election victory to the diligence and hard work of my fellow Young Republicans.

"I do remember that you took it hard," I said.

"I had to drop out of school for two months, William. Mother took me to the south of France to recover. Everyone thought I was having a baby."

Oh, yes. I remembered all the rumors.

"I was exhausted. That campaign took a lot out of me. I would never get into politics. In fact that's one of the reasons I left my first husband."

"How many husbands have there been?" I asked.

"More than one," she said. "But I don't dwell on the past. My first husband wanted to run for governor of Kansas and I realized that after my experience running against you, I could never survive another campaign."

"I'm sorry you still feel that way, Honey." Suddenly I was beginning to think Big Willie was not going to get to meet Honey after all. Certainly not tonight. Possibly not any night.

But at that moment her lovely hand, glittering with a fat pink diamond ring, touched mine. "Come home with me, William. Come home with me now."

CHAPTER
SIX

JOAN

It was nearly midnight when Bradley and I left Mr. Chow, and we were both high on Cristal champagne and very chi-chi, very expensive Chinese food. The next stop was Lot 61, back on the other side of town in the twenties. Bradley had Khalil drive us there, explaining to me in the car what else he had planned for the night.

"I like to move around," Bradley added as he took my hand. "We'll check out the club, but unless it's really jumping off we won't stay."

Lot 61 was located in a huge warehouse near the Hudson River. It's one of those neighborhoods that's busy during the daytime and almost deserted after dark, except for the crowd outside the entrance to the club. As usual Bradley had no trouble getting us past the line of folks, the velvet rope, and the doorman, and into the inside. Everyone knew him. I felt like the wife in *Goodfellas*. Or like Ashanti in the video for "Foolish," if you prefer. That dress in the restaurant scene was impressive...but I digress.

If you're starting to get the idea that there were

things about Bradley that I didn't know, you're correct. If you suspect that there were things that I should have recognized, I'll give you that too. I'll admit that at home in L.A. my radar would have been sensitive to certain signals. But why spoil the suspense? I will warn you that he was absolutely not a drug dealer. And he was most definitely not gay. Although I had not officially confirmed that fact, every time we danced close, I had ample evidence, emphasis on ample, to suggest that Bradley Houston was all boy.

And we had such a great time. We were surrounded by folks who were as fabulous as we were, if I do presume to include myself—and I do! The men were smooth as silk. Half of them looked like models. And, well, the other half looked like actors. There were even some famous faces in the mix. I recognized Craig David and Tyra Banks. Talk about being in the mix!

Bradley and I moved together like synchronized swimmers. There's no other way to describe it. We just moved alike. Where had he been all my life?

"We've gotta get my girlfriends back here," I shouted to Bradley over the roar of the Lot 61 sound system. The DJ was amazing. He played mostly hip-hop beats, everything from Amerie to Jay-Z, but managed to mix it with merengue and reggae and even some world-music sounding stuff and techno. I swear I heard a techno version of "The Girl from Ipanema" mixed with something by Nas. I was blown away.

"Are the rest of your crew like you, Joan?" Bradley asked. "If so, I can't wait to meet them."

How about that, I thought. My crew. I liked the sound of that.

"I hope you'll still have time for me," he added. I

was hoping I'd have time too. In fact, I was definitely going to make time. I was not going to let Bradley go.

From Lot 61 Khalil drove us downtown to make the rounds of the hottest clubs in Soho and the Village. Well after last call, we were still living it up V.I.P. style at Chaos. We were in no mood to stop, but by 4:30 A.M. Chaos was turning up the house lights. The DJ had stopped playing and had started asking people to leave.

Bradley knew about an after hours club, Free Fall, in the meat packing district, so we moved on to there. We arrived outside a building with a scary looking steel door. Bradley used a key card and it opened automatically. I could hear music as he took my hand and led me down a dimly lit staircase. At the foot of it we were suddenly in the middle of another completely awake, pulsing-with-energy club.

"You'd never know it's after four o'clock in the morning," I exclaimed.

Bradley laughed. "That's the idea," he said.

I could have stayed there at Free Fall all night, but after about an hour, Bradley had another idea. He took my hand and led me back to the limo. I reminded him that we had to meet my girlfriends at JFK at 6:30.

"Don't worry about it," he said calmly. "I just want us to make one stop first." He said something to Khalil and leaned back.

Soon we pulled up to another park, but it was one I didn't recognize.

"I have no idea where we are," I said.

"We're on the upper east side of Manhattan," Bradley answered. " I want you to see something."

He opened the car door and took my hand to help me out. We walked into the darkened, deserted park. He seemed to know his way, and I trusted him. Soon we were on a walkway with park benches on one side and water on the other. Across the water I could see more skyline and in the distance a bridge.

"That's the East River," he said, "and over there is Queens."

It was very beautiful if you like skylines. "Is that what you wanted to show me?" I asked.

"Not yet," he answered and led me further down the walkway along the river.

Then he stopped and looked at his Rolex. "Just wait a minute," he said. "Keep watching." I was a bit puzzled as we stood in silence.

But then it happened. The sun began to rise over the East River. I hadn't greeted the dawn since my college days. I have to tell you that to watch the sun come up over the water and flood the skyline of Manhattan with light is one of the most beautiful sights I've ever seen.

"Like it?" he asked.

I don't know which impressed me more: the view of the sun rising over the East River or the fact that I was with a man sensitive enough to share it with me.

"Yes," I said, one hand to my heart like I was pledging allegiance. "Thank you so much." I moved my hand from my chest to his upper arm.

"That's all I get?" he said. He pulled me towards him. I could feel the heat of his body in the early morning chill. His warm mouth was on mine. He held me in his arms. In the silence of the dawn the only sound was the water, gently lapping against the retaining wall.

I swear, I was ready to give it up right there, but to my surprise it was Bradley who pulled away.

"Come on, Joan. We've got to meet those girlfriends of yours."

TONI

We were waiting at the baggage carousel at JFK when Joan turned up with two of the finest looking black men I have ever seen. There were introductions all around. Lynn introduced Malcolm Diggs. It turned out that Joan had met him before at some legal thing. How typical of Joan that she had let him slip through her fingers. But maybe she was learning something in New York because the young hunk of brown sugar with her this morning was just all kinds of fine. She introduced him as her new friend Bradley Houston. The other man was his chauffeur Khalil.

"Bradley's been taking me all over New York," she said. "I've got lots of places to show you this weekend."

"Sorry I can't shake your hand," said Malcolm to the two men. He had his arms full of the box containing Maya's ambrosia cake.

Immediately implementing my new strategy, I complimented Malcolm on his generous gesture. Of course Maya had to join in. That girl has to imitate everything I do. I suppose I'm a role model for her.

"Yes, thank you so much, Malcolm. You saved my life," she said.

"I just hope I'll get a taste of this famous cake," he said with a smile.

"Only if you can come to cousin Jacquie's party Saturday afternoon," she said.

"I'd like that, Maya, but I'm afraid I'll be tied up with the last minute planning for my own party that night. I hope you'll all becoming to that," he said.

I started lifting the first of my 15 pieces of Louis Vuitton luggage off the carousel. "If it wasn't for Malcolm, we might still be in L.A.," I explained to Joan who was staring at my luggage with a frown.

She turned to Bradley.

"Do you think all this luggage is going to fit into your limo?" she asked him.

Bradley shook his head. "I'm sorry, ladies. If I'd known you had all this, I'd have rented a van."

Lynn stepped in. Or stepped in as far as she could without letting go of Malcolm's arm. She had been clinging to that man since our plane landed. I recognized the sex glow on her and I was convinced that those two had engaged in something while we were mile-high.

"No problem," she said. "Malcolm's offered me a ride into the city. I'll meet you at the hotel." She pointed to the area where the car service drivers were waiting. They were all foreign looking men in cheap, badly fitted dark suits. Each of them held a hand-lettered sign with someone's last name scrawled on it. One of them read "Diggs."

"Lynn, you hardly know Malcolm," I said, like the caring person I am. "Maybe I'll send my luggage with Joan and ride with you, just to be on the safe side."

I could see that Lynn wasn't going to go for that, but Malcolm stepped in.

"No problem, Toni. If it makes you feel better. I wouldn't want you worrying about your friend."

107

That's how I ended up arriving at the Soho Grand Hotel in a Lincoln Town Car driven by a Russian immigrant named Serge. A pair of Asian men in black came outside and began taking my luggage out of the town car and loading it onto a shining brass carrier on wheels.

"I'll hold on to these," I told them as I took possession of two of the bags.

Joan had already checked us in, so we just headed for the elevator up to the penthouse.

"I still don't know what the fuss was all about," Lynn said. "I still don't understand why you couldn't just check these bags with everything else."

"One of them has all my hair care products and tools," I explained.

"Tools?" Lynn sneered. "We should be looking to women like Lauryn Hill and india.arie as our hair models. They know who they are. No apologies. Why kill your hair with heat and chemicals just to appeal to some European aesthetic?"

"That might carry more weight if it weren't for the fact that you *are* the European aesthetic," I retorted. Frankly, Lynn has been unbearable since she learned to cornrow.

My mood improved the minute I saw the suite Joan had secured for us. I had to compliment Joan on her great choice. The rooms met all my standards. Maya started singing the theme song from *The Jeffersons* and Joan, Lynn—and even I—joined in. We all agreed: We were definitely moving on up.

"I've ordered us breakfast," Joan said. "It should be here by the time we all finish freshening up. Then I've got the whole day planned."

I showered and dressed, changing into my new

Manolo Blahnik stiletto timbs, the same ones my new friend Beyoncé wears. I was ready to hit the stores. But Joan had other plans.

Fifteen minutes later, the four of us were on a Circle Line tour bus that was going to take us around the city and point out all the places of interest like the Empire State Building and Rockefeller Center. Excuse me if I yawn.

Our tour guide was a Will Smith wannabe who kept up a steady patter as he pointed out places of interest—to him. I was getting more and more restless. When he pointed out Rockefeller Center and I noticed that Saks Fifth Avenue was across the street, I freaked.

"Stop the bus! Let me off!" I yelled.

"Can't do that, lady."

"Toni, we can come back," Joan whispered. She gets nervous at the slightest hint of a scene.

I forgot about my new compliment strategy and started to tell that guide what I really thought of him and his tour. His reaction was just to stop the bus but to refuse to open the doors. "Listen, lady. I can't operate this vehicle with you standing in front of that line. And I can't let you off the bus because it's against policy. So if you don't move, we don't move."

"I can see you're a brother who's not used to strong-willed women," I said.

I got up in that boy's face and gave him a piece of my mind. He shrank from me like the little coward he was while he called someone on his cell phone. Soon two cops appeared. The male was large and black. The female was small and latina. They both wanted to know what was the problem. I explained that I was being held on the bus against my will.

Joan and Lynn and Maya were huddling together,

acting like they didn't know me. Finally, Joan stepped forward. Or rather, was shoved by the other two.

"Please excuse my girlfriend, officer," she said. "She's kind of overwhelmed by the city."

The male officer smirked. "What do you want to do, lady? Do you want to get off the bus?"

Now it didn't seem like such a good idea. I could see that my girlfriends were not planning to come with me.

I faltered then tried a new approach.

"I just want the bus to move to Madison Avenue so I can see the stores there," I explained. "I paid for a tour, and I want to see what I want to see."

"Lady, this is not a private tour," the guide said.

Not one to back down, I took a deep breath and dove back into my attack.

LYNN

I couldn't believe it. Toni was tearing into our tour guide and now the cops were here.

What happened to her compliment strategy?

Joan was just standing there, looking horrified and embarrassed, as she watched Toni melt down in front of the cops. Maya stood between us, and she just looked disgusted.

I guess I had the least involved reaction of all. I just missed my new friend and sex buddy Malcolm and wanted to talk to him. I wanted to share this wacky moment with him.

"Maya, can I borrow your cell?" I asked.

"Who you gonna call?" she demanded. That's a question that Joan would never ask, but Maya was closer which is why I asked her for her damn phone. Fortunately, Maya didn't wait for my answer; she just handed over her cell with a skeptical look.

I fumbled through my purse for Malcolm's card and punched up the digits. He answered on the first ring.

"Hello." What a deep smooth voice he had. "This better be important."

"You sound just like Barry White," I said.

Quieter now but in the same bassy register, he said, "Lynn? Is that you? I didn't recognize the number."

My heart leaped and almost did a dance down Fifth Avenue. Malcolm knew my voice. Mr. Suave recognized my voice. And he didn't even play games about it.

"Sure is me," I said. "I borrowed Maya's cell."

"Where are you?" he asked.

"I'm on a tour bus with my girlfriends, stalled in front of Rockefeller Center while Toni argues with our tour guide. Am I anyplace near you? I could come and visit your office." His card said his office was at Federal Plaza, but who knew where the hell that was.

"I'm all the way downtown, Lynn," he said. "I look out my window and I can see the Statue of Liberty. But at this very moment I'm in a conference room with no windows, only some very important people who think I'm talking to the President."

"Of the United States," I gasped.

"No, the president of their company," he laughed. "But still very important."

There was a growing buzz from the back of the bus. The other tourists were losing patience. They wanted to get moving and Toni was holding them up.

"Come on, lady," one man shouted. "We're going to miss the Empire State Building."

"I want to see the Intrepid," a little boy whined.

Soon other voices joined in, all of them demanding that Toni put a lid on it so that the bus could get moving. Some of them had turned on their video cameras out of boredom and were filming the crowds on the street.

"What's going on there?" Malcolm asked. "What's all the noise in the background?"

"I think we've got a rebellion here," I said. "It looks as if the passengers want to vote Toni off the island."

He laughed.

"It's not so funny when you're stuck with a bunch of angry tourists. Oh, Malcolm, I wish you were here."

"Sorry, Lynn. I actually have a business to run. I'm in a meeting right now. But I do have some advice for you."

"What's that?"

"Next time you go out with your girlfriend Toni, bring a videocam. I think you've got the makings of a great film. Ton-zilla in New York."

"Very funny," I said. "Will I see you tonight?"

"Try and stop me, babe."

I purred inside—and on the phone—then I let him go back to his meeting.

MAYA

Lynn handed me back my cell. She looked like a cat that had swallowed a whole canary. The noise at the front of the bus was getting worse, and the grumbling of our angry fellow passengers was getting louder. Those folks were restless.

"I've had enough of this," I said. "Maybe Joan wants to stand around and watch Toni drama, but that's not what I came to New York for."

"What are you going to do?" Lynn asked.

I rolled up my copy of *Honey* magazine and started to thwack it into my palm.

"Just watch me," I said as I walked down the aisle until I got to where Toni was still yelling at the driver.

"Antoinette Marie Childs," I said. There is a tone that every child with a black parent will recognize and that was my tone. There is a face that goes along with that tone, and that was my face. Toni turned around, stopped talking and looked surprised. I continued to thwack the rolled up magazine in a meaningful manner. Under the circumstances, it was as close as I could come to a switch, but Toni got the message.

To drive it home, I leaned close and whispered into her ear, "I am counting to five and when I finish your ass better be in a seat."

She snapped to attention. Talk about pressing buttons. Toni was raised right and sometimes all she needs is a few stern words to remind her how to behave in public. The others forget that because they expect her to act like a grown-up. But sometimes she's nothing but a spoiled little girl in need of a whuppin'.

Joan just stared at us; the two cops stared at us. And Toni went back to her seat, as meek as a kitten. The folks in the back who had been ready to kick her off burst into applause.

"I guess our work here is done," said the older cop. "Maybe you should consider joining the force," he said to me, tipping his cap. They looked very happy to be leaving us. I wished I were going with them.

"What did you say to Toni?" Joan asked.

"I just told her to behave," I explained. "No biggie."

"No biggie? You got her to stop! How?"

"Joan, honey. You're not a mother. Anyone with a two-year-old knows how to handle a tantrum like that. I wouldn't tolerate it from Jabari when he was small and I won't tolerate it from Toni."

"That's it?" Joan can never accept the obvious.

"You're worse than William," I said. "Can't you just accept the results? Why ask for details?"

While we talked, we moved together to our seats. Lynn was looking out at the street but she turned around when she heard me mention William.

"Speaking of William, where is he?" she asked. "Wasn't he going to be part of our weekend. Doesn't he get the tour?"

Joan shrugged. "I called him this morning, but he said he's tied up and he'll catch up with us tonight."

WILLIAM

That Friday morning I was more than tied up. While my girlfriends were getting a taste of New York, I was waking up in four-point restraints with the gorgeous Honey Hayes looming over me. You could say that I had one foot in heaven and one in hell and you wouldn't be far wrong.

How did I get there? I would love to tell you that I was drugged and date raped, but if I told you that I would be lying.

No, Honey led me to her loft on Franklin Street

and I followed her willingly. I thought I had my wits about me when we got there.

I remember looking around and telling her that it was a fabulous place. She had wraparound views of New York: the Empire State building on one side and the Worth building in the other. Looking up, I saw a starry sky and below I could see the Hudson River. It was the perfect setting for the glamorous Honey. I forget if she said that her second or her third husband paid for it. I should have wondered about that. What made a man so anxious to dump a beauty like Honey that he would give her millions and a crib like this?

The answer, which I soon learned, is that Honey Hayes is crazy. But I didn't know that yet.

Oh, no, not yet. For the moment I let her mix me up a pitcher of apple martinis. She was drinking Cristal.

I'll admit that my mind started to cloud after the second martini. Could it be the apples were sprayed with Alar? Could I have drunk too much vodka? Maybe it was the wrong vodka. But I had soon drunk enough to start making my moves, and she had drunk enough to respond.

I kissed her on those full, luscious lips that I lusted after in high school. I grabbed those hips tight. She pulled away. Uh-oh.

"Don't you think you should take off your sweater, William?" she cooed. "You'll be more comfortable."

"Anything you say, Honey," I answered, as I tossed my sweater assertively onto one of the plush satin sofas. It's a little move I stole from Richard Gere.

"Let's relax. Come into my boudoir." She took my hand and let me there. The room was done all in shades of pink, and the heavy rose velvet draperies were drawn. She lit some candles. I noticed a fire-place.

"Would you like to light the fire, William?" she asked in that silky voice. "I do think that's a man's job."

Eagerly, I set to work at that fireplace. When I turned back to her, she had slipped out of her clothes and was laying butt naked on the pink satin spread. That girl was perfection and she wanted me.

I'm proud to say that Big Willie rose to the occasion. The two of us rolled on that bed and on the rug and in front of that blazing fire.

"It takes a strong man to be with a powerful wo-man, William," she whispered in my ear. "Are you that strong?"

I believe I proved I was, but I didn't recognize that Honey had other issues. From the sound of her she was a satisfied woman when I lay back on her bed. Frankly, I was worn out. She seized on my moment of weakness.

"William?" she moaned, as she straddled my naked body. Her hands stroked my arms.

"Honey, I think Big Willie needs a few minutes to rest," I admitted.

"Oh, no, baby. You take all the rest you need," she said. "Just give Honey your hands."

I lifted my hands up to her as if in prayer. If I told my mamma this story—which I won't—this is where she would remind me that maybe if I had been pray-in', instead of fornicatin', this would never have happened. But no, I lifted my hands as if in prayer and I felt something cold and hard.

Honey had handcuffed me, and she left me there

on her bed while she went to meet with clients Friday
morning.

CHAPTER
SEVEN

JOAN

Toni has been my friend since second grade and I can never stay angry with her. So don't expect me to beat her down because of the scene she made on the tour bus. Toni, Lynn, Maya and I had put that behind us and the four of us were having lunch at Lucky Strike on Grand Street in Soho. We were thoroughly enjoying the food when I got William's call on my cell.

"It's about time we heard from you," I said. "Where are you?"

"I'm tied up right now," he said. "I ran into a lady friend of mine from high school, and we've been catching up."

"Oh, William, that's so nice. I'm so happy for you." I soon let him get back to her. I couldn't wait to tell the girlfriends that Monica might have a rival.

"Is he coming tonight?" Toni asked. "I think we should check her out."

"Like he paid attention to our verdict on Monica?" Lynn said sarcastically.

"Easy," said Maya. "It was you that got him together with Monica in the first place."

"It was?" I said. I had no idea. Then Lynn explained how they met while Lynn was tending bar, before she got a real job. William used to stop by after work. One night, he was complaining about his love life and Lynn dared him to pick up a woman. And he did, and it turned out to be Monica.

"Maybe this new chick will bump Monica," Maya added.

"Amen to that," I said.

I looked around the restaurant. Lucky Strike was typical Soho with rough wood floors and seating enough for a crowd.

I was so happy that we were finally relaxing together. "Maybe it wasn't a good idea to start you guys off on a tour," I admitted. "Maybe I should have let you all rest up first."

"Or go shopping," said Toni.

"Well there's plenty of time for that this afternoon," I told them. "And the shopping down here in Soho is great."

"Too bad I've made other plans," said Toni coolly. "Sorry I can't stay for dessert, Joan." She put some cash on the table and stood up.

"What?" I exclaimed. "Wait! Where are you going? This is supposed to be our getaway weekend. Together!"

"I've had a lot of stress in the last 24 hours, Joan. I need a massage desperately. I need to be pampered. And Todd gave me a gift package for eight hours at Bountiful Spa. I need to get started right away."

"But don't you want to come shopping with us?"

"Joan, maybe you and Lynn and Maya have time to hang around eating and drinking and shopping all day, but I have a business to build," she said. "After my massage I intend to check out some real estate properties here. And I still haven't reached Derek Johnson. He'll be hurt—"

"—if you leave New York without seeing him." Maya finished Toni's sentence for her and made a hand gesture which seemed to indicate that Toni had dropped something. Toni looked down quickly while reaching for her earrings, then looked back up and sneered at Maya. "I'm out of here," she said, and with that, she was out the door, off on her trip to Bountiful.

"Wouldn't you like to be the masseuse who gets to meet Toni?" said Maya, with a roll of her eyes.

I moved to change the subject to our agenda for the rest of the weekend. If they didn't like my plan, I was willing to revise it. Doesn't that prove that I'm not a control freak?

"Bradley is going to meet us tonight at Chrysalis," I announced. "It's the hottest new club down here in Soho."

"I know. Malcolm already put us all on the guest list," said Lynn. "We're definitely getting in."

"Great," I said half-heartedly. I already felt like I was losing control of the weekend. And I admit—I didn't like it.

I'd been missing my girlfriends while I was working in New York for the last two weeks. Bradley was great but let's face it: there are certain things only your girlfriends can give you. And one of them was their opinion of my new guy.

"So tell us about this Bradley," Maya prodded. "I didn't notice his name in any of your reports."

I smiled and sipped my drink. "That's because he's strictly pleasure. There's no business involved." I told them about how I met Bradley in the rain and how he rescued me from my piggy client.

"But what do you know about him?" Maya asked.

"What does she need to know?" Lynn challenged her. "Bradley's hot. That's all she needs to know."

"Easy for you to say, Lynn. You've got yourself somebody whose whole life is a feature in *Black Enterprise*. You know Joan's track record with men as well as I do. She's gotta be careful."

"Relax, both of you. I know a lot about Bradley. You met his chauffeur. He lives uptown in Harlem. He's got a platinum American Express Card, a good heart and a sense of humor. And tonight," I gave a suggestive look, "tonight you'll see him dance."

"So have you had sex with him yet?"

Leave it to Maya to ask the direct question.

"No, Maya! You know my three month rule."

"Girl, I thought you gave that up. Anyway, I don't think rules apply during away games."

"Maybe not. But I only just learned that little exception from Ellis." I fumed a little inside. "Maybe I will apply it this weekend. Heck, maybe tonight."

"I'll drink to that," said Lynn, raising her glass. We clinked glasses in a toast.

"And to absent friends," I added. "To Toni and William, wherever they are."

At that moment, I noticed over Lynn's shoulder that there was a television playing at the bar. The sound was off, but captions were running underneath. It was showing some cable news station, and the clip was of an angry woman yelling at a bus driver. The caption read, "TOURISTS WE DON'T NEED."

"Oh, my God," I gasped. My eyes were huge.

"What's wrong?" Maya asked, looking alarmed. "You look like you've seen a ghost."

"I wish it was. Look," I pointed at the TV. "It's Toni!"

TONI

Before starting on my busy professional activities, I had expected to get a little pampering at Bountiful Spa. I desperately needed a calming Swedish massage. I was expecting to enjoy the full Mango Papaya Sugar Glow. That's the one where they rub you down with sugar, sweet almond, grape seed and more, then moisturize you with a mango-papaya lotion that makes your skin feel like Cleopatra's. Pre-death, I mean. But I never got past the front desk.

Bountiful Spa had the Soho feel with stripped brick walls and big antique mirrors and operators who were almost as beautiful as the clients. Ahem, almost. This much I could see from the reception area. There was a young Swedish woman seated behind the desk. I gave her my name and expected her to check the big appointment book in front of her. Instead, she looked at the small color TV that was next to it, then turned back to me.

"That woman, on the TV," she said, "she looks just like you."

"Ohhh, I don't think so," I lied, trying to mask my shock at what I was seeing.

"Oh, sure she does," she argued. Whatever happened to the adage that the customer is always right? "You've even got on the same outfit!"

Damn! I knew I should have changed clothes. I

stared at the screen. One of my fellow passengers from the tour bus must have videotaped the entire encounter this morning and brought it to a local TV station, where it was now being aired. It was not my finest hour. I wanted to get away from it as soon as possible.

"Guys, come see!" she bellowed. "The nightmare tourist is here!"

The operators, who clearly did not share my own dedicated work ethic, dropped what they were doing and crowded around me. They started arguing about whether it was really me on the screen. Meanwhile, I could hear the newsman's commentary, which was making me sound worse than Michael Jackson dangling that little baby out a window in Berlin. Soon they cut to the two cops who actually said that they wished people like me would stay home.

"Alright...yes, people, it's me," I admitted, hoping to end the matter.

"Well, then it's settled then," said the receptionist. "Who would lie about a thing like that?"

"Maybe you all have time to stand around discussing an invasion of my privacy, but I have an appointment for a Mango Papaya Sugar Glow," I jabbed the appointment book with my finger, "and I would like to get started. I have a very busy schedule," I explained in my most professional manner.

She looked at me as if she was surprised that I was still there. Really, I was finding New Yorkers incredibly rude. First the tour guide and now this receptionist. And I had always taken pride in my handling of the little people. Too late, I remembered my new compliment strategy. But that tape had already done the damage.

"I'm very sorry, Ms. Childs. We can't honor your appointment. Your operator was suddenly taken ill. Just before you arrived."

I didn't believe her for a minute, of course. Especially when she said that no one else could give me my massage either. No one else could even fit me in for a little touch up manicure! I understood how the Freedom Riders must have felt! Was I going to have stage a sit-in here just to get the spa treatment I so desperately needed? Unfortunately, I could see that there were several black clients there already, so it was not a race thing. This was utterly personal.

"Somebody is going to hear about this," I declared as I left. Defeat is a rare experience for me, and I don't like it.

I decided to call William, who has, on occasion, represented me in legal actions. He picked up after a few rings, sounding a bit breathless.

"William, it's me, Toni."

"Toni! I just saw you on CNN. Do you know they have people on there saying you should be deported from New York and returned to Los Angeles immediately? If I were you I'd stay off the streets."

"William, stop laughing," I snapped. "I never signed a release for that videotape. These stations have no right to use it. I want to sue them all."

"Sorry, Toni, you've got no case. This is news. Big news. They don't need your permission. Just be glad you look good. Has Todd seen it?"

"Oh, God, no. Fortunately, he's out of the country at a conference. They haven't heard the end of this, William. I'm embarrassed and humiliated. And Bountiful Spa refused to service me!"

"I don't blame them. You're a menace. Do you think this video is going to turn up on *Cops?*"

That was ridiculous. Right? No matter—'focus on the future' is one of my mottos. I decided to find the bright side.

"Maybe this is for the best, William. It gives me more time to check out properties. And I still haven't reached Derek Johnson. He doesn't even know I'm in town."

"Don't worry about that, Toni. Everyone in New York knows you're in town now."

In a sudden need for reinforcements, I hurried back to Lucky Strike to find the girls. At least I could always count on them.

LYNN

Joan and Maya and I were in hysterics watching Toni's video on the bar TV.

"Would you like me to turn the sound up?" the bartender asked us. He could see we were enjoying it.

"No, thanks. We can write our own lines," Joan said.

"We've heard it all before," Maya added dryly.

Poor Toni. At that moment, she walked back in.

"Is that thing *everywhere?*" she whined.

"What happened to your massage?" Joan asked.

"They threw me out. I've been banned. They treated me like a criminal! Or worse—like a regular person! Like one of you!"

The bartender edged over. "Is there...some kind of help...I can offer you?" he said gently.

She turned back to us. "And this one thinks I'm crazy."

Joan assured the bartender that Toni was not nuts. "She's just passionate," she added. "It comes across as crazy on the screen."

"I don't think that's helping," Toni said. Her big brown eyes were filling with tears. I was afraid we were going to see some genuine emotion from our drama queen.

"I know just what you need: some shopping therapy," said Joan, rubbing Toni's arm.

Toni perked up and the tears disappeared. "Yes, that might help," she nodded gratefully.

For the next two hours we made our way through damn near every shop in Soho. From Anthropologie to Harriet Love we took it all in. Joan and Toni did most of the buying. Toni really went wild at Hermes, scooping up a $1,500 bag. I have to admit I thought that was a bit excessive. That's when I told them I was taking off.

"Where are you going?" Joan asked. I could see she was going to freak out any time one of us veered away from her plans.

"I've got a four o'clock interview at a film school. Maybe you've heard of it? New York University?"

"You do realize that's in five minutes? How are you going to get there?"

Joan thinks if she doesn't tell you something, you don't know it. But I have to admit that I had no idea how I was getting to NYU. I'm a free spirit.

"I figured I'd just start on the sidewalk and the universe would provide my direction," I told her.

"Is the universe giving you cab fare, missy? 'Cuz if not, you're going to be late," said Maya.

"Here, take this," said Joan. She handed me some folded bills. "Pay me back later." Outside she hailed a cab and put me inside. I told the driver to take me to NYU.

"How's Washington Square," he asked.

"Is that where it is?"

"Pretty much," he replied, and we set off. See how the universe provides?

When we got to the Square, I paid the driver and looked around. I felt like I was home. The air was heavy with the smell of pot and the sounds of guitars and steel drums. The women on the streets of Soho were all artist-chic, but here, a few blocks uptown, the vibe was completely different. Most of them were dressed more like me, kind of retro hippie. I could have lingered there all afternoon, but I had my interview to go to.

It was in a building just off the Square. I took an elevator to the 24th floor and was directed to a conference room. It turned out that this was a marathon interview day. There were applicants ahead of me and others waiting behind me. Inside, three deans from the film school were waiting. Three conservatively dressed, solid citizens. The man in the middle looked like Sidney Poitier in *To Sir with Love*. Clean-cut, wholesome. He seemed to be the boss.

"Hello, Ms. Searcy," he said. "Have a seat."

I did.

"For starters, why don't you tell us why you want to come to the NYU Film School?"

I started to tell them about meeting my birth mother Sandy and how that tied into my decision to follow her lead and become a documentary filmmaker.

The man in the middle kept staring at me. "Have we met before, Ms. Searcy?" he asked.

"No, I don't think so. Unless you spend a lot of time in L.A. I've worked as a bartender there. Maybe I served you?"

"When did you leave L.A.?" he asked.

I was on a roll. I was going to ace this interview. I could feel it.

"Actually, I only left L.A. last night," I told him. "My friends and I came in on the red-eye this morning."

One of the two women who flanked him started whispering to him. He glanced at me and gave a nod of agreement.

"It seems that we were on your flight, Ms. Searcy. In first class with you. But, then, you probably didn't notice us. Nonetheless, I don't want to waste your time—or ours. I'm afraid we won't be recommending your application for admittance. Good day."

I guess Malcolm and I were not as discreet as I thought.

I forced a smile. "Well, I only hope that I gave you guys more education than you want to give me," I said, my dignity unscathed. I extended my hand, and he looked at it like it hadn't been washed since the flight.

"Good day," he said again.

With that I said goodbye to higher education. Not that I hadn't said goodbye to it several other times, but this time, there was no degree in my hand. Which, I might add, I had certainly washed since the flight.

MAYA

I could only shop with Joan and Toni for so long before I got bored. I swear, Coach must make a bottomless pocketbook for chicks like them. Besides, I'm more a mall rat when it comes to shopping. Their stores didn't have what I was looking for. My mind was also on my cousin Jacquie's party the next day. Our suite at the Soho Grand had a refrigerator, and I had stashed the ambrosia cake there. The woman on the plane had given me directions for taking the subway out to Fort Greene. So I was all set for tomorrow afternoon.

"Are you sure you girls don't want to come with me?" I asked again. "I do think it would be fun for us all."

"Are you kidding, Maya? No offense, but I have to leave time to catch up with Derek Johnson."

She didn't fall for the hand gesture this time.

"I wonder if William wants to come," I said, thinking out loud.

"Why don't you ask him?" said Joan. "Give him a call."

"I know he's answering his cell because I just talked to him," Toni added.

So, with their encouragement, I went ahead and dialed him. He answered, but there was something strange about his voice.

"William, are you all right?" I asked.

"Of course I am. Why do you ask?"

"You just sound a little stressed, honey. I hope the New York air isn't bringing out your asthma."

"I'm just fine, Maya. Don't worry about me. If I need help I'll ask for it."

"Sor-ry... I was only calling because we miss you. How come you don't come out and play with us?"

"I'm tied up," he said. "But I've got a TV here, so I've been getting a good look at you guys' idea of touring New York. Toni is on every channel."

"Where exactly is 'here,' William? We called your hotel, but they said you weren't in your room."

"Slow down there, partner. I don't have to check in with ya. You're starting to sound like Monica. Fact is, I've been visiting a friend. A very old friend."

"Well are we going to see you at Chrysalis tonight?"

"If she lets me." It was kind of mumbled, but I swear that's what I heard him say.

"Will she let you come with me to Fort Greene tomorrow?" I asked.

"I can't say, Maya. Gotta go."

I could see or rather hear that I was not going to get much more information from William, so I let him go. I looked at Joan and Toni.

"Something's going on with that boy. Mark my words. Something is up."

"He's playing around behind Monica's back. And that should be encouraged," said Toni.

Joan shook her head. "No, I think Maya is worried about him. Are you?" she asked me.

"I honestly don't know," I admitted. "It was just that he sounded—different—not like the William I know."

WILLIAM

I have to admit that sometimes I don't even know myself. That crazy Honey always brought out the worst in me. It was true in high school and it was just as true as now, when she had me trapped in her luxury loft downtown. But how trapped was I really? I woke up in four point restraints, but she had removed them and I was still here, with a dog collar and a very long chain anchoring me to her living room.

I had my cell and could communicate with the outside world. I could call the cops if I wanted to. I could call my buddy Rhamses. I could call Monica. I could call my girlfriends. I could be rescued at any time, if I was willing to be embarrassed for the rest of my natural life. I would never hear the end of it. So my pride kept me there, attached to a ten-foot long dog chain. I guess that was one of the lessons that crazy Honey was determined to teach me. Pride goeth before a fall.

"I'm glad you understand that, William," she said, when she got back from her meeting. She had dressed for it in a smart red wool suit with black braid trim and a cute little red hat. She was just as fine in daylight as in the club. The years had improved her outside while apparently doing much less for her inside. My dream girl Honey was one whacked out lady.

"You ruined my life senior year, William. You and your crew," said Honey.

"Honey, I'd hardly call the Young Republicans a crew. They weren't even a...a posse. Just a bunch of nerds with a dream."

"Yes! And that dream was to deprive me of my rightful place as president of our class!"

"Honey, it was a fair election. Our classmates spoke and they wanted me."

"They were misled. Your crew bribed them with

Tasty-Kreme donuts. My sorority was offering them fat-free cake. It was a tactical error."

"Whatever, Honey. It was more than ten years ago. We've both moved on. Can't you just forget it?"

"I thought I had, William." All the time we were talking, Honey was taking off her business suit and her cute little hat. She had stripped down to a bra and a thong. She kept on her high heels. Big Willie showed his appreciation. She noticed and smiled.

Last night I had thought that smile was sexy. This afternoon I recognized it for what it was: the grin of a madwoman. But she was a very beautiful, very sexy madwoman. I could not break away just yet. Yes, some of this was a nightmare, but some of this was a high school nerd's dream come true. And I never for a moment believed that she would kill me. At least not on purpose.

She laid down on the pink upholstered sofa and patted the space next to her. "Come over here, William. I missed you when I was out with my boring clients. I just kept thinking of you. My little politician. My little vote-getter."

"Honey! Let it go!" I said without thinking.

She got angry. "Don't say that! That's what my mother used to say. I have a right to my pain. I have a right to own my pain!"

"Okay, okay. But I believe in moving forward, in forgetting yesterday."

"That's the problem. I did that for years. But I've been in therapy since my last divorce, and I've recovered a lot of memories. Especially about you and how you ruined my life."

"Do you mind my asking what you plan to do about it?"

GIRLFRIENDS

"I have an idea, but I'm not ready to tell you yet."

EIGHT

JOAN

The weekend was coming together almost just the way I'd hoped. So what if Toni's videotape had made her the Notorious A.M.C. all over Manhattan? So what if Lynn called to inform us that her membership in the Mile High Club apparently disqualified her from film school! At least we still had each other! Except for William being M.I.A., the whole crew was together. I just knew we were going to have a good time clubbing Friday night. Bradley was going to make sure of that.

After our shopping spree, Toni and Maya and I went our separate ways. We agreed to regroup at the hotel at six that night.

Lynn was already there, wrapped in one of the thick sand colored terry cloth robes that came with the suite. When I walked in, I found her staring at a bowl of water. I looked closer and saw that there was a goldfish swimming in it.

"New pet?" I asked.

Lynn looked up at me. "Isn't this great?" she asked. "I told the bellboy that I missed my dog, and he told me the hotel lets guests have these goldfish for company. I think the little guy has an old soul."

"The bellboy? Or the fish?" Toni said, wrinkling her nose up at the bowl.

In between prepping for our first big night together in New York, we caught up on the last couple of hours.

"I'm sorry your interview at NYU went badly," I told her when she told us the details of her brief and disastrous interview.

She shrugged. "If they're that uptight, I probably don't belong there," she said. "I can't wait to tell Sandy. She'll love it."

We all knew by this time that Lynn's birth mother was even more of a sexual revolutionary than Lynn. I guess that answers the nature-or-nurture question.

"Maybe you'll use it in your own documentary," I added. I really wanted to encourage her in the first real career path she'd explored since I'd met her. Almost thirteen years ago. But who's counting?

Maya was the last to arrive. When she did show up, she was wearing a slinky new tank top that read "I Love New York" in red sequins. She was loaded down with shopping bags.

"Maya, I thought you didn't like the stores here," I teased her. "I thought you said you were a mall rat."

Maya shook her head. "Forget the stores. Take it to the streets! After I left you I wandered over to Canal Street, from here all the way to Chinatown. Do you know you can buy just about anything on Canal Street?"

Did that explain the glow? Was it the shopping glow? Because that girl sure was giddy. She started pulling out some of her stuff from the shopping bags.

135

"DVDs, CDs, Hermes scarves, video games. You name it and you'll find it for $5 or less on Canal Street!" she declared proudly, holding up a nice-looking fake Prada bag she had purchased. "Okay, so I paid fifteen for this."

It was a darn good fake. I stopped working on my hair to admire it.

With the four of us wrapped in those bathrobes and running in and out of the bathrooms, it was like we were teenagers getting ready for the prom.

"This reminds me of the time that we all bunked at your house last year," said Lynn. "Remember, Joan?"

"How could I forget?" It seemed as if everyone was going through things at once: Lynn was staying at William's until her dog gave his house fleas and he had to have the place exterminated. So they came to spend a few days at my place. Toni was there so much it felt like she had moved in, too. Maya's marriage was breaking up, and she and Jabari had moved in with me. They're still there, in fact, but the others are back where they belong. Isn't there an old saying about houseguests and fish starting to stink after three days? If not, there ought to be.

My mind had wandered as Maya brought out her purchases, although I have to admit that she had scored some big wins. I made a mental note to do Canal Street myself, if not this weekend, the next time I was in town. If I had a relationship with Bradley and shopping on Canal Street to look forward to, these business trips for Goldberg, Swedelson might not be so taxing after all.

"I've got something for you all," Maya was saying. That sure got my attention. Everyone loves a present, and I'm no exception.

"Sorry I didn't have time to wrap these," she added. "Consider them souvenirs of New York."

She tossed a small wallet to each of us. Mine was buttery soft cocoa brown leather.

"Maya, this is a Coach wallet," I said. "You shouldn't do this." After all, she works for me. I know what the girl makes, especially now that I know she pads her timesheet.

"Ferragamo! Cool!" said Lynn. She never has any problem accepting gifts. In fact, she encourages it.

"And for you, Toni, Louis Vuitton!" said Maya as she tossed the last wallet to Toni, Our Lady of Vuitton. "Something to remember your airport crisis by."

Toni stroked the wallet curiously then started examining it closely. There's a reason that sister is so successful in real estate. She has an eye for detail.

"Did this fall off a truck?" she asked. "Did one of your cousins come up with this stuff?"

Maya raised an eyebrow at her. I feared for a second that she might grab it back, but she was in too good a mood. I can't believe that shopping alone could do that for anyone.

"Sweetheart, this is what they're selling on Canal Street. I got all three of these and an Hermes for me for less than $25."

I could see us discussing Vuitton vs. Hermes all night, so I stepped in and reminded them that we had to meet Bradley at Grand Central Station at eight o'clock.

"He's taking us to dinner at Michael Jordan's," I explained.

"Oh, good," said Toni. "I'll leave a message for Derek in case he wants to meet me there."

"Still no contact?" Maya couldn't resist saying. "I thought he was dying to see you."

Nothing fazes Toni. If that was a dig, it went over her head. "The boy is crazy about me, I'll admit," she said serenely. "But the Yankees have a game tomorrow night, so he might be training or whatever it is they do to get ready."

"Cosmopolitans, anyone?" I said as I stepped behind the fully stocked bar. I started to mix up a pitcher for us while Toni turned her attention to her cell phone. Once again she got Derek's voicemail and once again she left a message.

"How many messages have you left for him since we got here?" Lynn asked.

Toni shrugged as I handed her a drink. The bar even had the right glasses, those nice oversized martini shapes that seem to add to the flavor of a cocktail.

"Lynn, the reason you are not as successful as I am is because you don't understand that you have to call, and call, and call again. Persistence is the key to being a successful diva like myself."

"Oh, excuse me," she said. "I forgot I was talking to a television star."

Toni's eyes flashed and for a second I feared we were going to have a catfight. I should know my best friend better than that.

"Thanks for reminding me," is all she said.

"You're welcome," said Lynn, looking surprised at the absence of backlash.

"No, really. I've thought over that tape and I've learned from it. I'm going to request a copy and see if I can use it for a TV commercial to promote Toni Childs Realty."

Lynn, Maya and I stared her blankly.

"Don't you see?" Toni said. "I can run it with a voice over. Imagine the voice of James Earl Jones saying something like, 'When Toni Childs wants results, nothing stands in her way! Let her find you the home of your dreams.'"

We were a little stunned at that one. Finally Maya found the words that expressed what I guess we were all struggling to say.

"I'll hand it to you, girl. If you were a man you'd have a pair of brass ones."

TONI

The four of us, Maya, Lynn, Joan and I, were looking rather devastating as we prepared to leave the suite. That goes double for me, of course. I could almost picture the four of us walking in slow motion toward a camera, like stars of our own show. But who are we kidding? I would be the star. Those three would only be my co-stars. Anyway, the night air had turned cool, which meant I had a chance to wear my new lynx coat.

"Bradley said we could take the subway up to Grand Central Station," said Joan as we headed for the elevator.

I looked at her like she was crazy. "Oh, no, Joan," I explained. "Toni Childs does not do public transportation."

"Come on, Toni. Didn't you ever hear the expression 'When in Rome'?"

"Didn't you ever read the headline, 'Tourist Robbed'?" I retorted. "I'm not getting on the subway in this coat."

Lynn shook her head. We all knew how she felt about fur. I wonder what she'd say, though, if someone gave her a coat as fine as mine.

Don't get me wrong. I'm not the scene-stealing diva some people think I am. Not on purpose anyway. I really am a down-to-earth person. But it's hard being a successful businesswoman, and I have to reward myself. That's why I bought myself the lynx. I didn't have many chances to wear it in L.A., but I was looking forward to giving it a workout in New York. After all, it hadn't traveled so far in its very own Vuitton garment bag for nothing. Maybe my girlfriends were disappointed that the weather had turned cold, but once again I saw a disappointment as an opportunity.

So the doorman at the Soho Grand called us a taxi. It was one of those little yellow minivans, so we could all pile in the back with lots of room. We were at Grand Central Station in minutes. The outside looked like something you'd expect in Paris, with huge arched windows, and columns, and on top of it all an enormous sculpture of three Greek gods, Mercury, Hercules and Minerva.

"This is the building that Jackie O. saved," said Joan. "Wait until you see the inside."

The interior lived up to her promise. It was a vast marble space with glamorous marble stairs at either end.

"In the daytime this is wall to wall people," said Joan, our self-appointed tour guide. "People are getting subway trains and Metro North trains from here that will take them to upstate New York and Connecticut. And there's a huge office building, the MetLife building, attached over there." She pointed to modern escalators that marked the entrance to the other building.

Maybe the concourse was crowded during the day, but it was almost deserted now. All the action was up in the balconies, which were crowded with my kind of people. We followed Joan up one of the marble staircase to Michael Jordan's Steakhouse. On the way inside, we passed a display of autographed bones. I wondered what they were about, but I was about to find out.

Bradley was already there, waiting for us at a table. Every other table was taken. The restaurant was filled to capacity.

"What are you ladies drinking?" he asked.

"I think we better stick to Cosmopolitans," said Joan who had switched from tour guide to mommy. But I have to give her credit for her new taste in men. And we'd soon discover that Bradley also had excellent taste in restaurants.

From our table we had a skybox view of the station's vast marble floor.

"Look up, ladies," he said.

We followed his eyes and for the first time we noticed the sky-blue ceiling, painted as a breathtaking mural of the night sky's constellations.

"Awesome," said Lynn.

Awesome, yes, but frankly I was more impressed with our fellow diners down on earth level. My eyes searched the tables for a familiar face.

"Are you looking for someone, Toni?" Bradley asked.

"She's expecting Derek Johnson to show up," Maya said.

"She left him a message," Lynn added.

"Oh, you know Derek?" Bradley asked.

"Not well," I had to admit. "Last time we were together he made it clear that he wanted me to contact him when I got to town. But you know how it is. Gatekeepers! They're so protective. Right, Joan?" Oops. I ignored her glare. "I'm sure that he has no idea how many messages I've left for him. When he finds out I was here and didn't see him, there's going to be hell to pay."

"Derek's a good friend of mine," Bradley said. "I'm sure you'll hear from him. But he's got a game tomorrow night, and before a game he's totally focused on preparation."

"I can appreciate that," I said. "I completely understand practice and preparation. That's why I'm so successful."

"What is it you do exactly, Toni?" he asked.

"You mean Joan didn't tell you?" I gave him the Toni Childs dazzle. I know that flirting with him was putting yet another bug up Joan's ass, but it served her right for not telling Bradley how fabulous I am. She left it to me to fill him in, even though I hate to brag.

Someone else who could brag is Michael Jordan. His restaurant served the five of us the bomb face-in-the-plate food. Bradley insisted that we start with broiled beef marrowbones. He said it was Michael Jordan's trademark dish. Then everyone but Lynn had one of their well-marbled ribeye steaks. She had some random array of leaves and potatoes. Her loss. Bradley knew his way around a wine list, too, and ordered us a fine Chianti.

"William would love this place," said Joan. "I'm sorry he's not here."

"Does he know we're here?" Maya asked.

"I called him this afternoon, but he said he thought he'd still be tied up."

"That poor guy," Maya said. "He's been 'tied up' all weekend." She made quote marks with her fingers.

"That can't be healthy," said Lynn.

"No, it can't," said Joan. "Sometimes I worry about William. He's so easily manipulated."

That gave the four of us a chance to rehash all our grudges against Monica for Bradley's benefit.

And then it was time to head downtown.

"Would you believe they wanted me to take the subway up here, Bradley?" I asked my new best friend. "In *this* coat!"

"People can be so unreasonable, can't they?" he concurred admirably. Instead of taking us through the station, he led us up the modern escalators, through the ultra-modern lobby of the MetLife building, and outside to a nearly deserted street. Instantly, a limousine pulled up. This was my introduction to Bradley's limousine.

"Hello, Khalil," I said. "It's nice to see you again." I don't know if I was feeling democratic or just buzzed, but I was definitely feeling the New York love. I should have known it wouldn't last.

LYNN

With Khalil at the wheel of Bradley Houston's limo, we sailed downtown. There was hardly any traffic on the avenues that chilly night, and it took us less than fifteen minutes to get to the Bowery. That's another example of the difference between New York and L.A.

At home, everything is a half-hour away; in New York, it's less than fifteen minutes.

I was excited about getting into Chrysalis, which was New York's latest club-of-the-moment. It was located in a former bank building, inside a big old granite box that looked like the U.S. Mint. At least we'd be safe inside—haha.

"Are you sure we're going to be able to get in?" Maya asked, not for the first time.

"Of course," I assured her. "Malcolm left our names at the door." I had only known Malcolm Diggs for 24 hours, but I had already seen enough to expect that everything would go smoothly. I didn't exactly expect Chrysalis to roll out a red carpet, and I assumed that we might even have to pay to get in, but I never expected to be barred from the city's hottest club on humanitarian grounds.

Would you be surprised to learn that Toni was at the center of this drama?

"What do you mean I can't get in?" She was standing in stunned disbelief that anyone could reject her in all her fabulousness.

"Does this have anything to do with that tape?" she demanded. "I've been a victim of cable news!"

"No, ma'am, we're a celebrity-friendly club," said the doorman. "We just can't let you in dressed like that."

That left Toni speechless. On the one hand, the doorman had just confirmed that she was a genuine New York City celebrity. On the other hand, he'd told her she was still unwelcome inside his club. To be barred because of her behavior was not exactly a new experience for our little diva. To be dissed because of her wardrobe—well, that must have been painful. I could see it in her eyes.

She stared at him in disbelief. "Are you kidding? This is a genuine lynx coat. And underneath it, a Badgley-Mishka ensemble. And under that—"

"Toni! Let the man explain," Joan said quickly.

Leave it to Joan to step in just when the scene was getting interesting. I, for one, would love to know what Toni was wearing under that dress. I'd bet it was a $100 silk thong from La Perla. Personally, I abandoned panties years ago, and not just for economic reasons either. The day I tossed my undies for good was the day I discovered true freedom. But that's a story for another time.

"This is a fur-free club, miss. I'm sorry."

Who knew? New York is an anything-goes town, but not for those wear fur.

As usual at a Toni event, a small crowd was gathering. A handful of clubbers who had been waiting started a chant, quietly at first, then rising as others joined in. "Fur shame, fur shame!" they repeated, like it was a staged rally. At least I'd dined on vegetables. I didn't trust what this mob would do if they learned that the rest of our group had just downed several pounds of red meat.

I turned to Bradley. It was the first time I'd seen him unsettled. He'd been so convivial, so worldly uptown at Michael Jordan's. Now I groped for a word to describe him and the only one I could think of was "young." Isn't that odd?

"Can you do anything, Bradley?" Joan asked him. "Can we leave Toni's coat in the limo?"

He shrugged. "I feel terrible about this. I let Khalil

go for the night. He's turned off his phone. We're stuck."

"Well, sorry Toni," I said. "Should we get you a cab?"

"What for?" Joan asked.

"To send her back to the hotel," I explained. "So the rest of us can go inside."

"Lynn!" she said in that prissy schoolteacher voice she gets sometimes. "Don't you think this is a time for us to support Toni and show a little solidarity?"

Like Toni would do that for me, I thought, but did not say out loud. Why make things worse than they already were. And furthermore, I'm anti-fur anyway. I had to bite my tongue to keep from joining in the "fur shame" chant. Meanwhile, at least Toni was wrapped up in a warm coat. The rest of us were standing around in the cold in lightweight L.A.-appropriate jackets. I wanted inside.

I turned to my only possible ally. "How about you, Maya?" I asked. "Don't you want to get inside? Malcolm did us a favor getting our names on the list. He's going to be disappointed if he finds out that we didn't take advantage of it."

But at that moment our black knight arrived again. Malcolm Diggs really has a wonderful quality: always in the right place at the right time. Maybe that's why he's so successful in the business world.

"Malcolm!" I said. I was so happy to see him, and not just because he could get us out of this mess.

He kissed me and I felt the warmth and the sensation that I was in a movie—not *Death to Smoochy*, mind you—and the focus was just on the two of us with the rest of the cast fading out. But just for a minute because he pulled away to address what was our most obvious problem.

"Toni Childs!" he said, smiling brightly. "Are you causing more trouble? You're going to get yourself tossed out of this town if you keep acting up."

"It's not my fault," she said in a voice that was almost babyish. "Nobody warned me."

"I should have thought of it, and I apologize," he said. He offered us a solution. He could leave Toni's precious coat with his own car and driver, or he could take us all on to a fur-friendly club. To my great relief Toni agreed to part with her coat. I really wanted to see the inside of Chrysalis.

MAYA

I have to admit that as I waited on the chilly sidewalk outside of Chrysalis, I wondered if it could really be worth all this aggravation. For once I actually felt some sympathy for Toni as those nasty people dissed her and her coat. She earned that coat, she had a right to wear it, and that's all I'm going to say on the matter. As far as I was concerned, I wasn't sure I wanted to be inside a club that encouraged people to be rude like that.

But once Malcolm led the five of us inside, I changed my mind. The music mixed hip-hop, reggae and R&B. The girls and I started dancing immediately, first as a group, then picked off one-by-one to dance with strangers. I could see that the guy I wound up with wanted more of my attention than just a dance, so I avoided his eyes. Dancing was all I had come for. I wasn't looking for anything heavier than that.

But this dude was not easily discouraged. He loitered around my group after I had thanked him and moved away. Then when we went to the lounge area and a human voice could be heard, he appeared again and spoke up.

"So wassup, L.A. Lady?" he said.

That took me by surprise. "How do you know I'm from L.A.?" I wanted to know.

He grinned. Do all the men in New York look young for their age? Bradley Houston looked to be in his early 20s, and this one looked like somebody's kid brother. Handsome, but young.

"You don't remember me?"

"No, I don't," I said firmly. I don't have a lot of patience with games. I could tell he liked them, especially the one he was playing now.

"Come on. Where's your fancy cake now?"

A light was starting to dawn. He did look a little familiar.

"Were you on my flight last night?" I asked.

He nodded, looking almost proud. "I'm a flight attendant. I worked the red-eye."

"How come I didn't see you?" I was still skeptical. He looked a lot like Jesse L. Martin but not like anyone I knew up close.

"Sista girl," he said impatiently. "I work first class. Ask your friend Malcolm. He's my buddy." He reached out for Malcolm's arm.

"Hey, Malcolm. Tell Miss L.A. Lady who I am."

Malcolm laughed. "Quentin Wright, meet Maya Wilkes. Maya, Quentin is U.S. Airway's finest first class flight attendant. A man whose praises are sung on two coasts."

"Enough," said Quentin, giving Malcolm the hand. "That's too much love. You're embarrassing me now."

From outside the lounge area, Quentin heard some song he liked and started moving a little. "May I have this dance?" he asked, with a slight bow to me.

"I suppose," I said, feeling a little flattered, and he led me back onto the floor. After that, we danced together for the rest of the night.

I could say blame it on the steak dinner, those Cosmopolitans that Joan mixed up for us, or the Chianti. I could blame it on the boogie—those damn Jamaicans and their winey-winey music. But for the first time that weekend, I felt truly free, and for the first time in a long time, I even felt sexy. The more we moved together, and we moved real well together, the looser I got. I hadn't danced like that in years. Maybe not since Jabari was born. Darnell didn't like to dance, and he never liked to see me dance with anyone else either. Not even my girlfriends. Maybe especially not my girlfriends. He always felt a little threatened by them. Maybe he saw what was coming before I did. But what's done is done. I've put my marriage behind me and I'm a free woman now. So there was no reason in the world that I should not enjoy the company of Flight Attendant First Class Quentin Wright—I gave him a little salute in my mind when I thought that—who so clearly seemed to enjoy mine.

As the night went on and the crowd surged between us, my girlfriends and I drifted apart in the club. I danced on and on.

When the reggae came back around and the beat

slowed, Quentin leaned in close and kissed me on my neck.

"Back up, junior," I ordered. I thought he was pushing it. "You don't know me like that," I warned him.

"You're right. My bad," he said, backing away. "But I'll have you know I'm going on thirty years old, so you can drop the 'junior' bit."

I was giving him an up-and-down once over when guess who bumped into us right there on the dance floor!

"William!" I practically screamed. I guess I'd been more worried about that boy than I wanted to admit to the girls. He might be a big shot lawyer, but he could also be a babe in the woods. Look at the way he'd gotten himself tangled up with Monica. No telling what could happen to him in a city like New York, or a club like Chrysalis. But one look at the woman he was with and I knew I didn't have to worry.

"Maya, I want you to meet my friend Honey Hayes," he said, presenting her. She was close to six feet tall, built like a brick mansion and just as well decorated. Her jewels and the strobe light were both blinding if you looked straight into them.

"Why William, I've been worried about you. Why didn't you tell me you were in such sparkly—I mean capable—hands."

Honey laughed. It almost sounded a bit wicked. "Oh, yes. I do have this boy under control," she replied.

WILLIAM

Yes indeed, that Honey Hayes was a head case. But I was intrigued. She pressed all my buttons. Those good boy, "behave yourself" buttons my mama installed for her use only. But mama installed those buttons for good things. She wanted to make me the successful, representing citizen I am today. Now Honey was taking the years of home training that those buttons represented and she was twisting them around into something evil.

Something evil and very, very sexy. It wasn't right, but it sure felt good.

By the time Honey and I made it to Chrysalis that Friday night, her big old dog chain was no longer necessary. I was totally enthralled with that woman. You could call me a prisoner of love.

Mama used to listen to old records from the 1950s. I remember one of them was actually called "Prisoner of Love" and there was another that was called "Chains." Did Mama know something that I didn't? Well, Papa did die a happy man. Could he have been a prisoner of love? Did Mama have him wrapped up in chains? Better not go there. Better concentrate on serving my own time because yours truly, the Mackmeister, was an inmate in paradise. I was Honey's humble servant. I see now, looking back, that the woman had me brainwashed. I was suffering from a clear-cut case of Stockholm Syndrome.

But at that moment, ahhh, at that moment, I was coming off 24 hours of the best sex I'd ever had. And I say that even after being one of the lucky men to have known the Lynn Spin.

Yes, Honey was a madwoman. But she was gorgeous, she was sexy, and she was convinced that she had issues to work out on me. As a kid I was always the last one off the roller coaster. Why should this ride be different?

CHAPTER
NINE

JOAN

Anyone who saw my girlfriends and me at Chrysalis on Friday night can tell you that we made L.A. look *good*. Malcolm got us inside the VIP room, and once we were there, he insisted on ordering a bottle of Veuve Cliquot, and then another. Between the champagne and the music, we didn't just party, I tell ya—we par-*tayed*! If the East Coast-West Coast rivalry was ever anything more than media hype to sell records, I think that Toni, Lynn, Maya and I established the winner once and for all. West Coast women rule! And three beautiful East Coast men, Malcolm, Bradley and Quentin, were validating my assertion.

By the time Chrysalis was closing around 4 A.M., the seven of us had bonded for, like, life. I'd only known Bradley a few days, and I'd only known Malcolm for twenty-four hours. Quentin I'd just met. Yet we all clicked that night. It wasn't just pairing off, either. If that had happened, poor Toni would be left on her own. No, it was more than that.

"Everybody," I shouted, "did we do the damn thing...or what?!"

"Gosh, Joan," said Bradley. "I've never seen you this loose!"

I was giddy from the champagne and totally pumped from the dancing. But all good things must come to an end, and we could no longer ignore that the club was shutting down. The bright house lights went on, the music was faded down, and the place was suddenly filled with the dull murmur of the people who were inching toward the exits.

"I think they want us to leave," I moaned. "But I don't want to go! I don't want this night to end."

"I have an idea, Joan," said Bradley. "Have you ladies seen the Statue of Liberty?"

I was sober in a minute. I was thinking about my disastrous attempt to take my girlfriends on the official tour this morning. "Toni doesn't do well with tours, Bradley," I said cautiously.

"Thanks, Joan, but I can speak for myself," Toni said, then to Bradley, "Sorry, but looking at that big, utterly unfashionable woman just doesn't do it for me."

"Ladies, have I steered you wrong yet?" Bradley turned to Malcolm. "How about it Malcolm? Are you up for the Staten Island Ferry?"

Malcolm grinned and then I knew that we were heading for the ferry. Malcolm had emerged as the alpha male of our little pack. Wherever we went depended on where he wanted to lead us.

We found Malcolm's car and driver waiting patiently outside, still guarding Toni's lynx coat from the anti-fur fascists. There was something cool and old school about Malcolm's driver whose name, I learned, was Wallace. He was older than us and seemed almost amused by our antics. I sensed he had a whole life of his own that he would be happy to get back to.

How silly were we? All the way to the Battery we sang along with the oldies station Wallace had been listening to in the car. We did a Sly and the Family Stone medley. Even Wallace harmonized along with us! Bradley had a beautiful baritone voice. And Malcolm was an alto. Quentin was keeping time beating on the back of a seat.

"You guys!" I giggled. (Yes—giggled.)

"You girls!" Bradley said after the four of us covered "Dancing in the Streets."

"Look out, Vandellas!" said Lynn.

In the space of a few hours we had moved from one of New York's finest restaurants to the VIP room of an exclusive new nightclub to the farthest end of Manhattan Island. We were about to take a 25-cent ride on a big, battered old ferryboat, twice the size of the ones that I've taken up in San Francisco. The shabby old ferry terminal was probably the same size as Grand Central Station but lacked the beauty and the grandeur. It sort of looked like it could have been the crate that Grand Central had been shipped in.

Lynn looked around at all the people waiting for the ferry. Some of them were partying like we were. But most of them looked like they were laborers. Some were in business attire, but many of them were men and women in uniforms, going home from work. "This is another thing I love about New York," said Lynn. "It's a 24-hour town."

Looking around the ferry terminal, you might not even know what time of day it was. There were lines of people, as well as cars, waiting for the next boat across. For many of them, 4:30 A.M. meant their work day was just ending. For others, the job was just beginning. It was kind of like being backstage at the show that is New York. These were the folks who kept the city running 24-7.

"These ferries run all night," Bradley said. "The only thing that changes is the frequency. This time of night, they run every hour."

Would you be surprised to learn that we waited less than ten minutes for the next boat? I told you we were on a roll!

Wallace drove Malcolm's limo up onto the old boat. We walked aboard on our own. I kind of dug the people watching us and wondering who we were. Maybe they recognized Malcolm from his magazine cover.

"Do you think they saw Toni on the news?" Bradley asked me. Some time that night Bradley and I had started holding hands and neither of us was ready to let go yet.

I shook my head. "And I'm hoping nobody makes the connection until this ferry ships out. Once we're on the water, they can't toss us overboard, can they?"

"I think that's up to Toni," he laughed. "They could just put her in a lifeboat."

We did manage to launch without another Toni episode. We gathered together on the prow of the boat as it slowly crawled across the Hudson River, on its way to Staten Island. Out there on the water, the only light was from the full round moon and the thousands of stars. The main sound was the rhythm of the water slapping against the side of the boat. It was a far cry from the raucous sounds of Chrysalis.

Together my friends and I stood against the ferry's rail and we watched as the New York skyline grew smaller and smaller, like a model city in a mall display. And then the Statue of Liberty came into view. Her torch was lit up. It was very grand. It seemed a moment to commemorate. I leaned over and kissed Bradley.

And he kissed me back.

TONI

For better or worse, I am used to being the center of attention. Whether because of my beauty, charm, talent or the sheer force of my personality, I am unaccustomed to being ignored. But at that moment, as I looked around me at the New York skyline behind me and the Statue of Liberty looming into view ahead, I felt very much overlooked. On my right there was my best friend giving the world a public display of her affection for Bradley Houston.

On my left there was Maya nuzzling girlishly with Quentin the sky waiter. They were giving me a high school flashback. Only the Lord knew where Lynn and Malcolm had disappeared to. I suddenly felt like the chaperone on the senior class trip.

Forced into this unaccustomed role, I started to think like a chaperone too. I asked myself what my girlfriends were doing with these two men. What did any of us really know about Bradley or Quentin? By now I had read so many magazine and newspaper articles about Malcolm Diggs that he was an open book to me. I had all the information that mattered: his credit rating (platinum), marital status (divorced for more than four years), and future earning capacity (limitless). But what about these other two? These two youngbloods were attractive representatives of the race, but other than that, I asked myself, what did any of us know about them? Were they fronting or were they the real deal?

Let's face facts. Thinking about other people does not come naturally to me. It put an unaccustomed strain on my brain. I found it tiring. I soon switched my attention back to myself. I was lonely. I missed my boyfriend. I wished I could share this moment with Todd, but my cell didn't have international service. So I settled for the next best thing. I pulled out my phone and punched up my own home number. Before he left on his trip, Todd had recorded a special message just for me. I guess he worries about me. He knows that I don't do alone well. He feared I might face a moment like this. Now I broke down and accessed his mercy message for me. I closed my eyes as I listened to his soothing voice:

"Antoinette Marie Childs, you are the most beautiful woman I have ever met," his recording said. "You are beautiful on the inside and the outside, even if you don't always show it. And dearest Toni, remember every moment of the day that I love you. Whatever time it is, wherever you are, know that I am thinking of you and I miss you with all my heart."

God has blessed me with many things, but the blessing I am most grateful for is Todd. His judgment is flawless.

I started to tear up. My friends were too wrapped up in their make-out sessions to notice, of course. I'm sure that our fellow travelers just thought I was feeling patriotic. I stared at the huge Statue of Liberty. She was a beautiful woman standing alone too. Just not as well dressed.

LYNN

Malcolm and I had slipped away and climbed up to the roof of the ferry's cabin. We were leaning against a pile of ropes and admiring our spectacular view. I looked down at my girlfriends at the ship rail when I saw Tony start walking away from the prow. She was dabbing at her eyes with a tissue.

"I could swear Toni is crying," I said. The ferry was just passing the Statue of Liberty.

"Is Toni that patriotic?" Malcolm asked.

"Toni? Patriotic? I strongly doubt it," I assured him. "Red, white and blue aren't her thing. Green is more her color."

Malcolm nodded gravely. "Ah, yes, I got a sense of that."

"You're cute when you're thoughtful," I said. "What are you thinking about?"

"I'm thinking about you, Lynn."

"That sounds promising," I said. "Because I've been thinking about you since this morning. This is the first time I've had you to myself since we were playing in mid-air."

He grinned at the memory.

"You know, Malcolm, when we were riding into the city from the airport this morning, and you were sitting in the front with the driver, and I was in the back with Toni and her luggage, I thought I was going to explode."

"Explode, Lynn? Was it something I said?"

I shook my head. "No, Malcolm. But I'd been having this fantasy that you and I were going to enter New York together. I imagined us crossing the water over one of those beautiful bridges, maybe to the tune of "Moon River."

"Moon River?" he repeated.

"Yes, you know. The theme song from *Breakfast at Tiffany's*? I never see a picture of the Manhattan sky-line without thinking about it." Joan isn't the only one with an Audrey Hepburn fantasy.

Malcolm very obligingly started to sing "Moon River," softly. He knew all the words! That man was gifted, at least as gifted as Andy Williams.

"So the sight of water makes you explode?" he teased.

"No, Malcolm. It was the sight of you. I thought I might explode with desire."

I tried to explain to him. "I've been thinking about what comes next with you. That quickie we shared in first class was just an hors d'oeuvre for me," I said.

"And a delicious one, too," he said slowly.

I could see that this conversation was making him nervous. He thought I was going to start talking about our relationship. For all his success, I could see that Malcolm was just like most men. Sex with a stranger was one thing. A relationship was much more scary, and talking about it could be downright terrifying. Men can be such little girls about sex sometimes. I tried to make my point a little better.

"I like to think the sexual chemistry we had this morning was something special," I went on. "And all day long, I've been wanting to do it again."

"Is that right?" he chuckled. "All day? No lie?"

"Well, most of the day, if you want to get technical. You were on my mind when I was at NYU."

"And I hope I'll be on your mind a lot in the future." He moved closer to me as the Verrazano Bridge came into view. It was all lit up like a Christmas display. At that moment, the bridge looked the way I felt if sexual attraction were expressed in watts.

Just that afternoon, after being tossed out of NYU, I had slipped away to check out the Museum of Sex. It had just opened up not far from our hotel. I was not impressed. There's something wrong about putting museum and sex together. Museums are about the old and the past. Sex for me is about the present, the now. The *right* now even.

"Lynn, I don't know you very well, but I do have feelings for you," Malcolm said.

"Well, okay," I laughed. I moved my hand to his crotch and was gently stroking it.

He didn't laugh. He looked very serious. "I hope you won't be offended by my question."

"I have a very thick skin. It comes from meditating every day." I smiled and stroked.

"Lynn, have you ever thought that you might be a sex addict?"

My hand froze mid-stroke. I hadn't seen *that* coming.

"A sex addict?" I repeated as I rolled that around in my head. "Wow, I don't think so. For me, sex is not about being horny. It's about the freedom to express myself. It's about feeling good, whenever I want or need to. Despite society's norms. And after the feeling fades and I want to feel it again, I can. As often as I want or need to."

"I think that's the definition of an addict, Lynn."

"Are you telling me this because you want to cut me loose?"

He shook his head and took hold of my hands, both of them. He stared into my eyes. "I'm telling you this because I want you. But I want you to want me as a man, not as some kind of love drug or…or rebellion against society. Do you think you can ever feel that?"

Now he was the one making me a little nervous. I can be such a little girl when it comes to relationships sometimes.

MAYA

I was standing with Quentin on the deck of the ferry. If I looked up I could see Lynn and Malcolm on the roof of the cabin. To my left were Joan and Bradley, making out like two bunnies. Toni had been on my other side a minute ago, but after making a call on her cell phone, she was walking away from the prow, dabbing at her eyes like she was crying. Since it was around 2 A.M. in L.A., I'm assuming that whoever she called just gave her a piece of their mind.

Quentin noticed. "Are you worried about your girl? Do you wanna go talk to her?"

I shrugged. "Toni can take care of herself." Let's face it, folks. If the roles were switched, you know where Toni would be, and it would not be by my side asking me what was on my mind.

"You know, it hasn't been long since I first laid eyes on you, but I'd swear, less that 24 hours in New York and I see a difference in you."

"How can that be?" I said. "I'm exactly the same person who got on your flight in Los Angeles."

He shook his head. "Nope. I saw you before I got on that plane. I noticed a fine-looking sista struggling to balance a very large box. I would've helped you myself, but Malcolm beat me to it. When he took the box away from you, I got a look at your frame and I saw you were more than a pretty face."

I felt my face warming as I thanked him. I was raised strict, with more punishment than praise. I have never gotten used to compliments, which was a good preparation for my marriage to Darnell. He was a good man, but he didn't believe in compliments. He thought it spoiled women and children. I never thought that other men might be different until I met Stan, and of course, the rest of that is history.

"I'm not sure I like compliments," I said. "They make me edgy. I always wonder if they're sincere."

"This one's sincere, Maya. I'm not kidding. Did you go to a spa today? You've got this glow."

I shrugged it off, but there was something. I had felt it myself since this afternoon.

"You know, maybe there is something," I said. "I was out walking alone this afternoon. I changed into my new top, the one that says 'I Love New York.' It's kinda tight, and I felt kinda sexy in it. I was just walking around, minding my own business, just trying to shop, trying to get a look around."

"That's it? Just walking around New York gave you this glow?"

"No, it's more than that, Quentin. It's that everywhere I went in New York, I saw men. I mean, I really saw them. I walked by construction workers who were digging up the sidewalk. I passed firefighters outside of firehouses polishing their trucks. I passed policemen on horses. I saw dudes in suits standing outside high rise office buildings. Everywhere I went, I saw men. I saw real men."

"That often happens here on planet Earth," he said

gently. Quentin didn't know me well enough to be more polite when I started talking about something he didn't understand.

"But it's not just that I saw them. They saw me. *Saw* me. They say you don't miss what you don't have, but I'll tell you, I think I was parched for appreciation. I felt like a flower that hasn't been watered in a long time. Walking around the street today, I felt like an attractive woman. Almost every brotha I passed had something to say to me. The latino brothas, too. I've been called mommy plenty, but the 'mami' *they* were saying was something totally different. Sometimes the men didn't even say anything, just whistled, or looked me up and down. And that was enough."

"Men don't look at you like that all the time?"

"Well, you gotta remember—nobody walks in L.A. So the answer is: No, not really. And if they are looking at me like that, I must just not have noticed."

Quentin shook his head. "I don't understand it, Maya. A woman like you. I'd be giving you praise every hour. I'd never let you run out of glow."

WILLIAM

I had made the mistake of introducing Honey Hayes to my girlfriends when we ran into them at the club. I quickly got her away from them. She was one of those women who is very docile, very supportive in public. I'm sure they didn't have a clue to what was going on between Honey and me. Maybe I didn't exactly understand it myself.

But here we were, back at her apartment. I had

followed her willingly, and once inside I had allowed her to put the chain on me. What was I thinking? Was I thinking at all? Was all the sex making me stupid? If I ever got away from Honey, would I ever be able to practice law again? Did I care?

"What's this about a girlfriend?" Honey asked.

My heart jumped a little double dutch at that question. With Honey I never knew how far I was from the danger zone. She could go over the edge at any minute. I tried to change the subject.

I was stretched out on top of her king size bed. A few feet away fragrant logs were blazing in the fireplace. Honey had slipped out of her dress and everything she had underneath it. She had wrapped herself in a shocking pink satin robe, but she had not tied the sash, so it kind of framed her breasts and the honeypot.

"Some of my friends get Brazilian waxes, but this is the first time I've seen one shaped like a heart before," I remarked politely.

She shrugged, and the robe flashed even more of her luscious curves. "It was my bikini waxer's idea." Her eyes flashed wickedly. " I could get your initials next time, if you'd like."

She had prepared us a tray with Cristal for her and a pitcher of apple martinis just for me. She handed me a glass, apple slice and all. "Now, William, what's this about a girlfriend?"

I sipped my martini. Say what you will about Honey, at least she lets me choose my own poison. Monica would freak if she saw me enjoying what she considers an inappropriate drink. I didn't want to think about Monica's reaction if she got a look at Honey herself.

"Girlfriend?" I repeated, trying to be cool. One of the first rules of the courtroom is that you never ask a witness a question that you don't already know the answer to. "Who told you anything about a girlfriend?"

"Those girls you introduced me to at the club, William. Don't play dumb," she said as she slid herself next to me on the bed. "They let it slip that you're taken. And that the taker plays hardball."

"They don't know anything about you and me, Honey. They don't know what we've shared this past day or so."

She sipped her flute of champagne. "Well, they didn't exactly discourage me. I could tell they don't like your girlfriend much. How come you didn't mention that you have one?"

Fear can make a man do strange things. "Yes, Honey, I did get involved not too long ago. But that was before..."

I let it hang there for dramatic emphasis. The Mackmeister knows how to set a seduction scene.

"Before what?"

"Before you and me. Before you...showed me things."

She started laughing. "Oh, William, I'm not after you. Your friends have it wrong. Your girlfriend has nothing to worry about!"

"But you've held me here as your sex slave, Honey. What do you want from me then?"

"I'm not sure," she said. She looked a little confused, a little vulnerable. "I just dreamed so much of this day, of getting my revenge on you for ruining my life. Now I don't know."

I could see why her former husbands lost patience

with Honey. "Woman, look around you," I commanded. "Look at how you live! You call this a ruined life?"

She looked up at me. Her big brown eyes were soulful. "William, I've never been able to enjoy any of it. I have an emptiness inside me."

"That's not something I can help you with."

"But it's your *fault*, William. All my previous psychiatrists danced around it, but my latest doctor finally got me to recover the memory. It all goes back to that election you stole."

"For the last time, Honey, I did not steal the election. Our fellow seniors elected me class president, fair and square."

"Are you sure, William? Suppose I told you that I have information that proves otherwise.

"If you're going to start complaining about the donuts my supporters distributed—"

"No. It's something more sinister. And as an attorney you ought to care," she pouted.

Where the hell were my girlfriends? My mind wandered. I'd called the hotel several times and gotten no response. It was time that those four young ladies were home in bed. Not that I thought they might in danger. No, if anyone was in danger it was me. I was still in the custody of hot Honey Hayes, but I felt like the loneliest man in the world.

And then, as Honey started to get into all her reasons why I ought to care about our long ago high school election, I forgot about Monica and my girlfriends, and started paying attention.

CHAPTER
TEN

JOAN

The girls and I actually managed to get in a few hours of beauty sleep back at our hotel suite. I think I was the first one up, and I ordered a room service breakfast for everyone. I had the waiters set it up out on the terrace, and I was sipping my morning latte out there when the others started to stir.

Toni wandered out first. She was already fully dressed in a smart pinstriped pantsuit. Her long black hair was tied up and hidden under a navy beret.

"Is that cappuccino I smell?" she said. "I need caffeine desperately." She sat down at the table and poured herself a cup.

"You're starting early," I said. I was still wrapped up in my bathrobe. "We don't have to be at the theater until two."

She looked at me as if I were crazy. "What theater? I'm going to work."

I didn't try to hide my disappointment. "Toni! I thought we could all go to a Broadway show together this afternoon. Bradley's getting us tickets to *Hairspray*."

"Joan, that show is sold out. But even if I believed that Bradley was going to come up with the tickets, I couldn't go to a matinee. I'm a businesswoman. I have appointments."

"And what kind of appointments would that be?" I said. "You've already been blacklisted at all the good salons and spas in this town."

"Thank you *so* much for reminding me of that."

"Sweetie, I wanted us all to relax this weekend," I said. "I don't want to see you working so hard you don't get to have some fun, too. So where are these appointments?"

Toni sighed impatiently. "You know that I have to look at properties today. I'm always reading in the trades about New York real estate going for millions. I want to see what makes a house in the middle of a city worth $12 million, or what makes a loft with nothing in it worth even more."

"And that makes this whole trip deductible," I said. "You're blowing off my *Hairspray* for a tax deduction."

"I admit it. I do need to conduct some business here to maximize the tax advantages. I'm not just all about playing around like the rest of you."

I hadn't notice Lynn walk in, yawning. She ignored the room service breakfast I had laid out and went to the phone.

"Hello, room service? Can you send up a case of Pedialyte to the penthouse? Thanks." With that she turned back to Toni and me.

"Well, don't look so surprised," she said. "Pedialyte is the best thing for a hangover. It puts back all the vital elements. I usually swallow at least a half-liter after a night like we had."

Toni sniffed. "I'll bet you swallowed a lot more than that last night."

"Toni!" I jumped in.

But Lynn was floating on cloud nine where none of Toni's barbs could touch her. She just smiled blissfully. "It's all good in the 'hood, Toni."

"How are you feeling, Lynn?" I asked, trying to avoid a catfight so early in the morning. And a cat is what Lynn made me think of as she sat there, looking very satisfied.

"I'll be able to tell you after I get that Pedialyte. And I'm going to sweat out the toxins later."

"Does the Soho Grand have a gym?" Toni asked.

"Better. I'm going hiking with Malcolm later."

"Hiking?" My voice went up a few octaves. I know I sounded whiny, but I couldn't help myself.

"Sure, Joan. I thought you wanted me to get into healthy sports and that's what I'm doing. Malcolm and I are going to be playing in the great outdoors."

"But what about *Hairspray*?"

Lynn shrugged. "I don't do Broadway. You should know that by now."

"Ha," Toni chimed in. "Finally something she doesn't do."

"Bite me, Toni."

"I bet you'd like that, wouldn't you?"

"Ladies!" I said. "Don't make me play Mommy. As our elder, that's Toni's job." I couldn't resist. Toni sneered.

"Sorry, Joan," Lynn said. "I'm sure *Hairspray* will be fabulous. But do you really expect me to pass up a chance to spend the day with Malcolm?"

"It's going to rain," I said.

"Not until later," she laughed. "April showers, you know."

"Know what?" asked Maya who had just walked in.

"April showers," Lynn repeated. "They bring May flowers."

Maya had moved over to the table where she started checking out the chafing dishes that were keeping our breakfast warm.

"Mmm," she said. "Eggs benedict. Orange juice. Cappuccino. You done good, Joan."

"You can have mine," said Toni. "I'm on my way to my appointments."

"Heard from Derek Johnson yet?" Maya said. She was also sounding a little catty, and she didn't even look up as she loaded up two plates. But if she wanted to rile up Toni, she didn't get the reaction she expected.

"I've learned that the Yankees will be playing the Toronto Blue Jays tonight, so I'm just going up there to corner him," Toni said.

"What about Malcolm's party?" Lynn asked. "He's expecting all four of us tonight."

"A-ha! Now you know how it feels!" I said triumphantly. "This is what happens when people don't stick to a plan!"

"Joan, chill," Maya said firmly.

"That's right, Joan. Chill," Toni repeated. She was checking out her cap in the mirror near the door, and now she added a pair of dark glasses.

"Disguising yourself today, Ms. Childs?" Maya asked.

Before Toni could answer, the suite door chimed. It was room service with Lynn's case of Pedialyte. I was still signing for it and Lynn had already opened the case and started downing the first bottle before she even got back to the terrace.

I should point out that the four of us had separate bedrooms in the suite. Each of us even had her own bathroom. Each of the bedrooms opened onto the large living room, so that was where we spent most of our conversation time. The terrace had a great view of the city, but when we were out there, the way we were that Saturday morning, we couldn't see inside the living room because the sliding doors had tinted glass.

Finishing with the waiter in the hall, I walked back through the living room towards the terrace. Maya was just coming in, carrying two plates piled high. She had the guiltiest look on her face.

My first reaction: I was happy she had an appetite. She's my assistant, she's my friend, and I wanted her to enjoy this.

"Don't look so guilty, Maya," I joked. "Here, let me give you a hand." I reached for the other plate and then I saw giving a strange head jerk to the right. She was looking over my shoulder, in the direction of her bedroom. I turned around to see the meaning of the gesture.

And there stood Quentin in her bedroom doorway, naked except for a tiny pair of chrome green briefs.

TONI

Among the many blessings that the Lord has given me is an exquisite sense of timing. I know when to hold and when to fold. I know when to close a deal and when to walk away. So I am grateful to the Lord that I had not yet walked away for my important appointments that Saturday morning. I am grateful to the Lord that he allowed me to remain in that hotel suite long enough to see the look on Joan's face when she saw Quentin there in Maya's doorway.

And while I'm thanking the Lord for his wonders, I must not forget Maya's expression either. That girl could have gone through the floor with embarrassment. She's the mother of a nine-year-old child, but right at that particular moment, she looked like a 13-year-old girl caught kissing behind the barn. Thank you, Lord. Amen.

Have you ever been involved in a car crash? If so, you know how it can seem to go on and on, and then when it's over and you step out of the rubble, you learn the whole thing lasted less than a few seconds. Well, the scene at the Soho Grand was a little like that. Joan and Maya and Quentin and even myself, all just stood there, frozen in place as we mentally processed the undeniable evidence that our little Maya had spent the night with a man she had known less than eight hours.

I don't know how long we might have just stood there staring if Lynn hadn't finally realized that she was all alone out there on the terrace and wandered inside.

"Hey, what's up, everybody?" She came through the door and looked around. "What's going—" she saw Quentin, "—ooh."

Somebody had to take control of this awkward situation, and as you know, I, Toni Childs, am fearless. I stepped forward to shake his hand.

"Hello there. I'm Toni. We met last night."

He looked relieved. Maybe he thought for a minute that we were going to tackle him. Maybe for a minute Joan wanted to. But she too had pulled herself together.

"Why don't you put on a robe, Quentin, and join us out on the terrace?" I suggested.

"Would you like a Pedialyte?" Lynn offered.

He shook his head. "Thanks, ladies, but I've got to run. I've got some commitments this afternoon."

"So do I," said Maya, a little too quickly. It was as if she wanted to make it clear to him that she didn't need to hang with him, that she had her own thing going.

"Broadway play," Joan beamed.

"Oh, that should be nice," Quentin said. "If you'll excuse me?" He headed back into Maya's room and pushed the door slightly closed as if he felt a sudden urge for discretion.

Maya moved toward the room, adding, "No, not a Broadway play, Joan."

"Oh, no," Joan whined. "You're not coming to *Hairspray* either?"

Maya looked genuinely sorry. "I told you I had my cousin's party this afternoon, Joan. You're all invited, you know."

Quentin stuck his head back out the door. "Mind if I take a quick shower, Maya?"

I've heard Maya say before that black people don't blush, but she was proving herself a liar. Her cheeks were fuschia, poor thing. I cut in, "Ladies, any further business to discuss before Malcolm's party tonight?"

Then Quentin spoke to us again. "Oh, Malcolm's party. I hope my family business is over in time for that."

I have a suspicious nature. I was the first person who saw Monica for the golddigger she is. And I'm not saying that I thought Quentin was using us, but I just wanted to be sure. I wondered out loud whether Malcolm had actually invited Quentin to the party, or did Quentin think he got to go because he had spent the night on the Staten Island Ferry with us?

"Oh, my man Malcolm and I go way back. I probably knew about this party before you knew about Malcolm," he said smoothly. "And I never trouble myself about who else he invites into his own home."

Well. My, my. I had just been one-upped by a sky waiter. And I was only trying to help my friends. Dammit...edge, Toni, edge.

"Well, I'm glad that's settled," I said. "Now I'm on my way to look at properties," I said.

Joan looked worried. "Toni, are you sure you should be going out alone? Remember what happened yesterday. Folks here don't like the way you came across on the news."

"Toni Childs does not live in fear," I told her. "Besides, I don't think anyone will recognize me if I keep my cap and sunglasses on. I'll see you at Malcolm's tonight."

Looking back on it now, I see that for once Joan was right. I really should have stayed behind. In the light of late events, I can honestly say that I would have been much better off at *Hairspray*.

LYNN

I was halfway through my second bottle of Pedialyte when I gave in to the urge to perform my homage to

Connie Francis. "This is dedicated to those two crazy kids, Maya and Quentin," I said as I started singing "Who's Slutty Now?" I broke into a fit of giggles.

"Shh! Lynn! They'll hear you," Joan said. Joan and I were alone on the terrace again, finishing up the remains of breakfast. Toni was gone and Quentin and Maya were wrapping it up in her bedroom. I just hope she wrapped it up last night, I thought, and giggled some more.

"Oh, I don't think they're listening for me," I said. "They're probably getting in a quickie before Quentin takes off."

"Maya looked so embarrassed," Joan said, sounding concerned. "And she looked hurt and surprised when Quentin said he was leaving."

"Joan, I don't have time to analyze Maya's sex life. I've got to manage my own. Do you realize I've got a second date this morning with one of the richest men in the country?"

Joan beamed at me. "I know, Lynn, and I'm so proud of you," she said. Then she added sternly: "Just don't blow it!"

The suite's telephone rang. Joan answered it. It was Malcolm and Joan chatted with him while I got more and more restless. I wondered if I was going to have to knock her to the floor to get that phone out of her hand so I could talk to him myself, but she finally handed it over. Malcolm said he was waiting for me downstairs in the hotel lobby.

I hurried down in the elevator to meet him. He looked mighty fine for a man who had been leading us on a charge to Staten Island only a few hours earlier. He was wearing expensive casual J. Crew chinos and a Missoni sweater. He looked me up and down with approval, then took my arm and led me outside to the street. I was surprised that there was no car waiting for us.

"Taxi, sir?" the black-clad doorman asked him.

"No, thanks," Malcolm answered and led me across the street.

"Where are we going?" I asked.

"I have a little surprise this morning," he said. "I thought we'd take the subway up to the park."

"The subway?" I repeated. "I'm a California girl. I'm very uncomfortable with underground transportation."

"Now you sound like your friend," he said. "I hope you're not going to turn into a snob on me, Lynn."

I hesitated, wondering just how much I wanted to tell him at this point in our relationship. Let's face it. While I'm not ashamed of anything I've ever done, there's no point in feeding someone like Malcolm information that could only confuse him. So I didn't go into my work history, but I did explain that I don't own a car for environmental reasons, and that I get around L.A. on the bus.

"Good," he said. "Then you'll like the trip we're going to take."

To tell you the truth, it wasn't as bad or as scary as I had imagined. The movies and *Law & Order* make the New York City subway look creepy, but that Saturday morning the people in our subway car were no more sinister than last night's crowd on the ferry. In fact, a lot of them looked like they came from the same open call.

"Joan sounded a little odd on the phone when I called," he said. "Is anything wrong?"

Wrong? What could be wrong? Joan's little protégé

Maya was dragging home strange men. Joan herself was hosting a theater party and nobody wanted to come. Poor Joan was completely losing control, and that's something she just can't bear.

On the other hand, folks, Joan is my best friend, and I was not about to discuss her tiny failings with Malcolm. I'd had great sex with him, but otherwise I hardly knew the guy. It wouldn't be right.

"Bradley is getting tickets to *Hairspray* this afternoon, and she wanted us all to go. But I told her I was going hiking with you."

"Really?" he said, giving me the cutest smile.

"Really," I assured him.

"I don't think she believes me, though," I conceded. "I mean, hiking in New York? I'm sure she thinks it's a code word for some kind of kinky sex." To tell you the truth, I wondered about it myself, but I'm a lot more open than Joan is.

"Oh, there's nothing kinky about Inwood Park," he laughed.

As the train moved uptown, he told me the story of the subway. He had a wonderful way of describing things.

"You'd make a great teacher," I said.

"I thought about it," he admitted. "I always thought I wanted to teach history. You know, 'those who don't learn the lessons of history are condemned to repeat it' and that kind of thing. I majored in history at Howard."

"So what happened?" I asked.

"I got sidetracked. Or maybe I should say I got on the *money* track instead," he said.

MAYA

I don't know which fact had me more embarrassed. The fact that I had spent one wild and crazy night with a man I just picked up at a club, or the fact that right in front of my girlfriends, the man in question had taken off and left me as soon as he could. Quentin kissed me and said he'd call later, but don't they all say that? Oh well, I consoled myself. We'd always have Staten Island.

It was almost noon, and Joan and I were still lingering in the suite at the Soho Grand. Now I was about to leave myself. I had packed up the ambrosia cake was getting ready to take it over to Fort Greene, but I felt funny about leaving Joan all alone. It just didn't seem right.

"Are you sure you won't come to Brooklyn with me?" I asked her.

Joan shook her head. "Thanks, Maya, but I really am looking forward to *Hairspray* this afternoon. And I'll see you at Malcolm's party tonight. I think we're all going to have to come back to New York. One weekend here is just not enough."

I had to agree. I said goodbye to Joan and headed out on my own. I followed the subway directions I'd gotten from Triplet Mom on our plane and made my way to DeKalb Avenue in no time. By 12:30 I was climbing the stairs out of the subway station like a native New Yorker. Actually, since Fort Greene was in Brooklyn, I had moved up from temporary New Yorker to temporary Brooklynite.

The buildings in Fort Greene were mostly two and three stories high. No Manhattan skyscrapers to block out the sunshine. I passed the office for Spike Lee's

40 Acres and a Mule production company and a lot of beautifully restored brownstones. I was beginning to understand that New York changed dramatically every few blocks. As I walked along the street of retail stores, folks smiled at me, but I sensed that everyone I passed recognized me as an outsider. Fort Greene was more than a little like the Compton I knew when I was growing up: a small town where everybody knew your business. I felt like shouting, "Hey, it's cool. I'm Jacquie Dawkins' cousin!"

My arms were full of the cake box, and I had to struggle to read the paper in my hand which had Jacquie's address. From the way she described her neighborhood in her last letter, I sensed that I was getting close to her house. I also sensed that I was not alone. I felt that someone was following me.

I guess my senses had been on alert since I got off the subway. I was more than a little nervous about the journey, but I had made it just fine. I had only relaxed a little, though. I was still in a strange territory and knew enough about the 'hood—any 'hood—to proceed with caution.

The cake box made it difficult for me to turn around without being obvious, but I was getting more and more uncomfortable about this presence behind me. To test my suspicions, I crossed the street. My shadow crossed too. I crossed back. The shadow followed. That was too much. I stopped and whirled around, ready to get ghetto on whoever this was. "You don't know who you're messing with," I shouted.

"Whoa, Foxy Brown, easy," he said, backing away and laughing at the same time. "So it is you," he added.

"Quentin?" I called his name in disbelief. "What

are you doing here? I thought you had family business. Don't you lie to me, boy!"

"I wasn't lying," he said quickly. "My family business is here."

He was holding a big brown shopping bag and I could see that it was filled with small junky presents, the kind you hand out at kids' birthday parties.

"My family's very organized. I was delegated to pick up the prizes for the games later. What about you? I thought you were going to some Broadway show."

"No, I passed up *Hairspray* to come out and see my cousin Jacquie."

"Your cousin Jacquie…who?" he repeated. "I hope you aren't talking about *my* cousin—Jacquie Dawkins."

My mouth fell open. All I could do was nod.

"Are you…serious?" he groaned.

I finally found my voice again. "She's your cousin, too? We're *related*?"

"Damn. Looks that way," said Quentin softly. He'd stopped laughing. "It looks like you and me are two relatives who just had relations. Somehow I don't think Cousin Jacquie is going to be handing us any prizes for that."

WILLIAM

Honey had quite a story to tell, and I had spent most of Saturday's early morning hours listening to it. It was now nearly noon and I was still in the Soho palace that Honey called a simple loft when she finally wrapped up her drama. The really scary thing was that midway through her sad tale, I started to see that Honey might actually have a case.

"So you see, William, it was all about voter fraud," she sighed.

"How about that?" I said, shaking my head in disbelief. "It was all about the chads."

She looked puzzled. "The Chads?" she repeated. "There wasn't anyone named Chad in our class, William."

It turned out that Honey's vast experience in the years since graduation had been limited to husbands, self-maintenance and shopping, not necessarily in that order. It did not include voting in a civil election. It's possible the woman had not read a newspaper either. I had to explain to her that some important recent elections had been full of charges of voter fraud.

"But folks have been stealing elections since Reconstruction," she said. At least she'd paid attention in our American history class. I guess that we had something to thank our teachers for, even if they had screwed her on the senior class election.

"Yes," I agreed, "you just don't expect it in a high school."

"So you do believe me, William? You believe me when I say that the voting machines our school used were defective and ignored a few hundred votes?"

I nodded. I didn't understand how we could have all ignored the obvious at the time. Yes, I won the election by an overwhelming majority. Out of around 200 votes cast, approximately 150 had gone to me and only about 50 to Honey Hayes, the favorite. It was an historic upset and a humiliating defeat for her. But thinking back on it, I recalled that there were more than 400 students in our graduating class. In those school elections, usually almost everyone voted. But somehow a good 200 or so votes had disappeared from our final tally.

"And when I told my parents that the election was stolen from me, they decided I was the crazy one and packed me off to the French Riviera," she added.

"Well, Honey, Cannes is not exactly the gulag," I said.

"The goolah?" she repeated. She had obviously never come across the word before.

"It's a prison camp in Siberia," I explained. "They could have sent you to worse places than the south of France. Reform school. Compton. Fresno."

She stared into space. "I suppose so, William. But I suffered a great deal, and it didn't have to be."

She cuddled up next to me like a kitten.

Funny thing about life. It had long been a fantasy of mine to reconnect with Honey Hayes. In the moments when I imagined us together I even pictured a fancy bling-bling kind of setting like this. Only I had not imagined I would be discussing something like this with her. Not to mention that I hadn't visualized the heavy chain still circling my neck.

"There's one thing bothering me about this," I said cautiously.

"What's that?" she purred.

"Suppose we could track down those missing 200 votes."

"Yes, William?"

"We have no guarantee that they'd be for you. I mean there could still be enough to declare me the winner."

"Oh, William, come on. We're talking about high

school. Remember what you were like? We know who won."

There was no point in arguing with a woman with a bullwhip.

CHAPTER
ELEVEN

JOAN

If my girlfriends had stuck with my plan, the four of us would have all gone to the *Hairspray* Saturday matinee together. Instead, Bradley Houston had me all to himself for the afternoon.

Question: What was wrong with that picture?

Answer: Absolutely nothing.

So I suppose you could say that I had just learned a lesson about my need to control things. If I had been able to control Saturday, I would have been in the audience at the Neil Simon Theater with Toni, Lynn and Maya. But when I lost control, I ended up with Bradley at my side.

I think that's what psychologists call "positive reinforcement." So, okay, consider me reinforced.

This weekend had given me a chance to get to know Bradley better. He was such a good sport about hanging with my friends. He got along great with Malcolm. He had a very nice singing voice and, last night, when we sang all the way to the Staten Island ferry, he was the one who came through whenever someone faltered on the words to a golden oldie.

Now I was discovering that he was that rare heterosexual man who loved live theater. He even revealed that this was his third trip to *Hairspray*.

"Oh, Bradley, I didn't realize that you'd already seen the show. You didn't have to come just to make me happy."

He waved me aside. "I love this show," he said. "I've followed it since its inception."

Bradley called himself a Broadway baby, and he seemed to know everyone who worked at the theater. The folks at the box office all had a few words to say to him. As we walked across the carpet at the theater entrance on West 52nd Street, we passed the uniformed ushers, mostly elderly women. They all greeted Bradley like he was their grandson. He had a kiss and a few words for each of them. It was another side of Bradley: similar but different from the club ringmaster that I'd seen performing late last night.

"I'm a Broadway baby, Joan" he explained. "I grew up in this business."

"I guess if I'd grown up in New York instead of Fresno, I'd be a Broadway baby too," I said. I saw *Rent* five times, and I played the album endlessly. Everything I'd heard promised that *Hairspray* was going to be the next *Rent*.

My heart leaped a slightly as an usher led us to our orchestra seats down in front. It was a smallish theater which I liked because it made it feel more intimate. There was a buzz among the matinee audience.

I'm sure you know that *Hairspray* is based on the John Waters movie starring Divine and Ricki Lake. It was set in the 1960s, and Ricki Lake played Tracy, a chubby Baltimore teenager who helps integrate an

American Bandstand type TV dance show. Well, to picture *Hairspray* the musical, just imagine the movie intensified. Take it up not one notch, not two notches, but maybe ten notches. Then you can picture the show that Bradley and I saw on stage that afternoon. The songs were hilarious, the dancing was non-stop, and the costumes and 1960s hairstyles were amazing.

We laughed, we cried. And when Tracy's parents got together to sing their big love song, "Timeless to Me," Bradley and I held hands.

By the time the curtain came down on *Hairspray* and the entire company had taken their final curtain call and bowed their last bow, we left the theater on an adrenaline high. Once again, I thanked Bradley for getting the tickets.

"You've made this weekend unforgettable," I told him. We were standing under the bright lights of the theater's marquee. All around us theatergoers were buzzing about the show we had just seen. The sky had started to darken while we were inside.

Bradley laughed. "Unforgettable?" he repeated. "Joan, you're the one who's unforgettable."

We began to walk east on 52nd Street. It was just a few steps before we turned right onto Broadway and headed south for a Bradley-guided tour of Times Square. The sidewalks were thick with people like us who were coming from other shows that had finished their own matinees at the same time. A knot of them collected at every corner while they waited for a light to change.

"Damn tourists," Bradley whispered playfully in my ear. "Come on. We know better. No red lights can stop us." He took my hand as we darted in and out of the cars, which were barely moving in the bumper to bumper traffic.

"Careful," I warned him. "In L.A. we could be arrested for this."

"That's one more reason to hate L.A.," he responded.

As we moved down Broadway, the lights got brighter and the signs got wilder. Every building seemed to be lighted more vividly than the next. Blinking, flashing, moving signs for Suntori whiskey, Tommy Hilfiger cologne, Calvin Klein underwear and SeanJohn clothes. There were signs promoting movies and signs promoting TV shows.

We had reached 42nd Street. There was a huge Disney store on the corner. He looked up at it and said, "It always seems so strange to me when I see this. I mean, when I was a kid my parents wouldn't even let me walk on this street, even in the daytime."

"I guess things have changed a lot," I said, looking around at the fancy theaters, the busses stopping at every corner, the yellow taxis and the sleek white limousines. Besides those things, the crowds on the sidewalk caught and held my attention.

"You just don't see people like this in L.A.," I told Bradley. There were tourists, natives and vendors all playing their parts. There was an Asian man who had set up tables on the sidewalk to give massages. An older white man sat at the beginning of a whole row of artists waiting to sketch portraits of passerby for a nominal fee. A West Indian couple was manning a table loaded with fragrant incense and oils. Further on, three young rappers were gathering a crowd of their own.

The lights all around us were so bright that I lost

track of the time. Only when I looked up did I realize that the sky had really grown dark with clouds.

"Worried about rain?" Bradley asked me when he saw me looking up.

"It does look a little sketchy," I admitted. "And I've got to get ready for Malcolm's party tonight."

"Come on," he said, moving faster as he signaled for a cab. "Let's get you back to your hotel. I don't want you getting caught if it starts to pour."

As we settled into the back of the cab and Bradley told the driver to take us to back to the Soho Grand, a loud clap of thunder split the air, signaling the start of a spring shower. What more can I say? The man had perfect timing.

TONI

I might not have been caught in the rain if not for my generous nature and my commitment to putting every millionaire in the mansion he or she deserves. Maybe that could be a slogan for me: "For every millionaire there's a mansion. Let Toni Childs Realty find yours." If Todd were here, he would add, "No regular people need apply." And I'd agree with that. They would just be uncomfortable.

That Saturday afternoon the millionaire that I had in mind was Derek Johnson. I simply could not believe that he had not gotten any of the messages I had been leaving for him all weekend. His people were obviously "protecting" him. Fortunately, Derek is not my first celebrity. I learned long ago how to break through these entourages. But so far, nothing I tried with Derek's people was working. I still had not heard from him and time was running out. If that boy was ever going to get the attention he deserved from me, he was going to have to return my phone calls.

After I left the girls at the hotel, I hailed a cab and began checking out the real estate on my list. "You look familiar," the driver said. She didn't turn around, but her eyes followed me in the mirror. New York cabbies post their licenses on the plexiglass that separates them from you, so I could see that her name was Sylvia Rivera. "Are you a model?"

New York taxi drivers are so observant. I shook my head. I was not in the mood for chit-chat with a cab driver.

There were three clusters of real estate that interested me: the East 60s, where people like Spike Lee, Ivana Trump and Tommy Mottola have townhouses; Greenwich Village, where all the big movie stars like Gwyneth and Richard Gere are living these days; and Soho, where, I discovered, you can buy 7,000 square feet of raw space for $16 million.

"What exactly is raw space?" I asked the agent who was showing me one of these so-called living spaces. As far as I could see there was nothing there. The entire expanse of loft was stripped with wires hanging from the ceiling.

The agent, Courtney, was icy blonde and Botoxed to the max so there wasn't much expression in her face. "Raw space is raw space," she said cheerily. "It's waiting for you to make it come alive."

"Look, honey, I'm in the business," I said as I handed her my card. "Let's get real here."

She looked at my card and hung her head. "Oh, I see. I thought you were Naomi Campbell."

Todd has told me many times that I do look like

Naomi, except that I have a much better rack. There was no point in bringing that to Courtney's attention.

"So what is raw space?" I demanded.

"It's nothing," she declared, throwing her hands up. "Nothing, nothing, nothing. I'm asking $16 million for a place that doesn't even have plumbing!" She started to cry.

Even Toni Childs has some compassion. I wanted to do something for my fellow businesswoman. There was no furniture, so she couldn't even sit down. I led her to the windowsill.

"Why don't you sit here. I'll get you a glass of water."

That only made it worse. "There are no glasses," she whimpered. "There is no water. It's just *raw space*."

I don't care what people spend, my clients were not going to go for this.

"You know what, Courtney? I've seen enough of downtown. Why don't we move up to the East Side?"

She nodded like a small child. We drove uptown in her van and talked real estate. She was divorced from a rock star, and I guess selling real estate was a way for her to meet a rich husband. I could tell she was not cut out for this business.

"What about you, Toni?" she asked. "How have you managed to be so successful?"

"I stopped competing, stopped worrying about the next broker. I just handle my business." But I'm not sure that would be enough for someone who didn't have all my other gifts.

In this case, as usual, my instincts were flawless, and Courtney was much more at home showing me three townhouses in the East 60s. A five-story building on East 64th Street was up for a mere $40 million. It was 1,500 square feet with an indoor atrium and a three-story living room. But $40 million. That would buy three times that back home, even in Bel Air.

"People used to want views and a fireplace," Courtney was saying. "Now it's all about outdoor access." She led me to the next townhouse, which was only $27 million and had a solarium and rooftop gym.

Soon Courtney suggested that we stop for lattes at Starbucks before we moved on to Greenwich Village.

"Sorry, Courtney," I said. "I can do the lattes, but the Village is off. I have to get up to Yankee Stadium by six."

"Oh, do you like baseball?" she squealed. "I used to date a Yankee before I got married." That started her tearing up again. "Would you like me to give you a ride up to the Bronx?"

"That's very kind, Courtney, but I'm fine on my own."

That was my mistake. I should have accepted Courtney's offer. But all I could see was this skinny blonde on a crying jag. I didn't want her depression around when I hunted down Derek. Besides, I intended to get that boy thinking Bel Air and Beverly Hills. If I let her near Derek, she might start pitching her $16 million dollar raw space to him. No way.

I did let Courtney help me get a taxi and we air-kissed before I sped off towards the Bronx.

I never got there. As we headed up Madison Avenue, the driver, this time an African man with a shaved head and an unpronounceable name, kept looking at me in the mirror.

"I know you," he said. "Are you Naomi Campbell?"

Let's face facts here. I don't have a lot of patience, even on a good day. And looking after Courtney had exhausted the little patience I have. I did not have the energy to chat up a cabby. I told him as much, then fumbled for my sunglasses. Unfortunately, I had left them behind at Starbucks. It was impossible to avoid eye contact with him as he kept staring me in his mirror. I could see a light go on in his eyes as he finally realized where he had seen me before. Another cable news watcher had busted me.

"You're very, very rude," he kept repeating, until I had enough. We had crossed the Willis Avenue Bridge and were in the Bronx when I told him that if he didn't leave me alone I would report him to the Taxi Commission.

"That's it," he exploded. The brakes screeched as he halted the cab in the middle of the street. He leaped out and opened the passenger door. "You. Out. Now."

I was too startled to object. I stepped out onto the deserted street. That was my second mistake.

There I was, standing on a corner somewhere in the Bronx, in a deserted industrial neighborhood. Within seconds, the clouds opened up and poured down on me.

LYNN

By the time it started raining late Saturday afternoon, Malcolm and I had hiked our way through most of Inwood Park.

We had started from the subway, through typical inner city streets. About half the people we passed were speaking Spanish, and even the billboards were in that language. I could have been back in East L.A.

As we entered Inwood Park, we passed men playing soccer, children tossing frisbees and all the other elements of a big city park.

Beyond the playing field and the playground, though, the park suddenly changed and became a true forest.

"This is New York's last wilderness," Malcolm said as we made our way up a rocky, steep slope. At the top we could look out at the city and the George Washington Bridge that linked the city to New Jersey. Standing there, surrounded by trees and rocks that had been there before the Mohawks and Iroquois arrived, was like stepping back in time.

"Like it?" he asked as he watched me staring.

"We seem a million miles from Manhattan," I said.

Malcolm nodded in agreement. "But the truth is that we're still in Manhattan. And these woods were here before us, before the English and the Dutch. Even before the Indians. I expect it will all be here long after we're gone."

"You're getting philosophical," I teased him.

"I'm always philosophical. You just don't know me well enough yet or you'd know that."

But I wanted to know him. For the first time since Vosco Wilde broke my heart, I realized that I wanted more than casual sex with a man.

"I want to get to know you," I said. "I want to get to know you very well."

We made our way through the woods, going ever higher. Soon we reached the highest point in the park. On one side was a huge building that looked like a castle out of Robin Hood.

"That's the Cloisters," Malcolm explained. "Someday I'll take you there to look at the tapestries."

I was about to ask him why we couldn't just do it now, but he clearly had another plan in mind. We headed in the opposite direction, down to a marina that had a large deck and tables where people were finishing lunch or enjoying cocktails in the spring sunshine.

"Do you sail?" he asked me.

"Not much, but I love the water," I said.

"Good." He led me down to the dock, and soon we were boarding a small cabin cruiser, the Sheba.

"I keep a sailboat up on the Cape," he said casually. "But some mornings I like to come up here and take the Sheba out on the Hudson. When I have the time, there's nothing like kicking back on the water."

He powered the boat away from the dock, and we were off. He stopped us when we were midway, with Manhattan on one side and the steep granite walls of the Jersey Palisades on the other. There, in the stillness, we opened up to each other in a new way.

"You know, I hate to be redundant, but for two people who've been as intimate as we have, we really don't know very much about each other," he said. He had reached into a cooler and got us both ice cold Heinekens.

"I usually prefer it that way," I said, as I sipped my beer thoughtfully.

"Don't be flip, Lynn."

"I mean it. I like to keep things light and casual. I guess you could say that, at least in that regard, I'm shallow."

"I don't think you're shallow at all, Lynn. I think you just don't let yourself feel."

"Maybe I don't, Malcolm," I said. "But I prefer it that way. I'm your poster girl for casual sex."

He shook his head. "I'm not looking for a casual relationship, Lynn. If that's what you're looking for, I'm not your man."

I took another pull on my beer. "Okay, Malcolm. You go first. Tell me your life story."

Malcolm had no problem opening up to me.

"My parents passed away quite young," he said. "I grew up fast."

"That must have been hard," I said.

He shrugged and looked off at the shimmering surface of the river as if he were watching pictures from his past. "My friends became my family. Their parents became my parents."

I couldn't help thinking how lucky I was to have three parents. The two who adopted me and raised me with so much love, and Sandy who had chosen to look for me and reconnect after all these years. And I had Sandy to thank for introducing me to Malcolm.

"You and your birth mother get along so well, Lynn" he said, later in the conversation.

"I had some bitterness at first," I admitted, "but I had to let it go. It was hindering my creativity and my aura."

"I feel the same way, Lynn. For me, the beauty of life experience is that through adversity strength is created."

We were each on our third beers by now.

"Do you mind?" he asked, as he pulled out his cell phone. "I want to check on the progress of my party prep."

I shook my head. No problem. I was almost sorry that we would be going to his celebration tonight. I could have stayed out there on the water with him forever. I didn't want the time to end.

As the sun faded, the air grew chilly aboard the Sheba. Malcolm insisted on fishing out a sweater for me. It was yellow cashmere and a little too big for me. "Keep it," he said. "It looks better on you anyway."

He looked up at the sky and frowned. "By my estimate, we have about ten minutes to get this baby docked before those clouds open up." He started up the motor and we headed back.

As usual, Malcolm called it exactly. We were snug inside the marina bar when a bolt of lightning shattered the sky, and we snuggled up by the fireplace as we watched the torrent outside.

MAYA

It seems poor cousin Jacquie had been fretting for days that a rainstorm was going to spoil her party. She was right that rain was coming, but she was wrong about the party. Nothing could have spoiled that afternoon for any of us.

Quentin and I had no trouble finding Jacquie's house. She'd sent us both before and after photos. Her little girls, Nina and Eve, answered the door. They were about eight and nine, and they both just squealed with delight when they saw Quentin and me.

"Cousin Maya!" they chorused. "You look just like your picture."

"Easy, girls, don't scare our relatives." Jacquie came from behind them, laughing. She had grown into an honest-to-goodness woman since she'd spent summers with me in Compton. She was now statuesque and regal, like a slim version of Queen Latifah.

As we stepped into her hallway, she took a peek outside and frowned. "Do you think it's going to rain?" she asked us.

"Mama, you ask everyone that question," said Nina.

"And you keep getting the same answer, Mama," Eve added.

Jacquie shook her head. "These girls are so bossy. I swear I don't know where they get it."

"I can't imagine, can you?" A tall, handsome man rolled his eyes light-heartedly as he stepped between the girls.

Jacquie quickly grabbed his arm and pulled him toward us. "Come on, Warren. I want to show my cousins my handsome husband." He gave me a big hug. He shook Quentin's hand as he took the cake box from him.

"This must be the famous ambrosia cake," he laughed. "I've been hearing about this for years."

"It's about the love, Warren honey," Jacquie said. She turned to me. "I remember those summers with you and your mom and all that love. It's what I'm striving for here today. I only hope the rain doesn't spoil it."

"Daddy, tell Mama that the rain doesn't matter," the girls chimed. "We already set up tables in the basement."

Good thing, too, because it did start to pour. Quentin and I moved through the house as Jacquie presented us to our relatives and everyone struggled to make the connections.

One elderly gran asked me if I was Leon Pickens' granddaughter. I told her I was.

"Then why are you calling yourself Maya Wilkes?" she demanded.

"I was married to a Wilkes, but we're divorcing."

"And what about you, Quentin?" she asked. "Are you divorced too?"

"No, ma'am. I've avoided that by not ever getting married." He winked at me. I shuddered.

Quentin seemed perfectly at ease. I was having a good time, but once in a while I would flash on the fact that Quentin was my cousin. I had spent the night with my cousin. I had made love with my cousin. It was bad enough when he was just a hook up. But I had hooked up with my cousin!

Jacquie had moved on to play hostess. I was eager to corner her to find out exactly how Quentin and I were related. Were we close enough go be breaking the law? And even if we weren't breaking the laws of the United States of America, where did we stand in the eyes of God?

There was no time to corner Jacquie on the Quentin issue, though. We were all too busy celebrating with the rest of Jacquie's guests. She and Warren had restored the house, which was at least a hundred years old. Someone mentioned that it was on the Fort Greene house tour.

Their kitchen was a dream, and in spite of the rain, Warren was happily barbecuing on the enclosed deck.

We feasted on home cooking. There were ribs and fried chicken and a peach cobbler good enough to make you smack somebody's mama. Even your own, if she never made one as good. And everybody loved my ambrosia cake.

Laughter and the pulse of music filled every room of that house. I never wanted it to end.

All my East Coast cousins were there. Some of them I'd never met, only heard about. There was Twinky, Dorinda, Karen and Denise. Pebbles and Zakiya and Isaac and D'Avila. Lowell and Rebecca and Kevin.

"I'm never going to remember all these names!" I said.

"How about if I remember the women and you remember the men," Quentin suggested.

I looked at him and could not help frowning. "I wasn't aware that we had become a team. When did that happen?"

"I believe it happened last night. For over an hour, if you recall." He shrugged. I couldn't believe how nonchalant he was about this. Maybe I was overreacting?

WILLIAM

By the time it started to rain Saturday afternoon, Honey and I were dressing for Malcolm Diggs' big party. She was quite a marvel of efficiency. She had sent a messenger for my clothes at the Mercer Hotel. She was not ready to release me, however, and I was still wearing her dog collar and chain.

She also apparently had a busy social life, for a madwoman. All afternoon she had been getting calls. I could mostly only hear her side of these conversations, depending on how close she was to me, but I could tell most of them were with her own girlfriends.

They were like, "Girl, you so crazy!" while I was

thinking to myself, damn, girl, you are crazy, which was a different thing entirely.

And yet a kind of peace had descended on me during my confinement with my beautiful madwoman. I felt some sympathy for Honey. She had a lot of pain inside that she needed to get out.

Unfortunately, Honey is not the only woman walking around who blames me for her pain. I know that my girlfriends still harbor some resentment toward me for ruining their Christmas plans. It was a turning point in our relationship. I found myself torn between my girlfriends and my girlfriend. I was supposed to play Santa for Maya's little boy, but Monica insisted that we host a big, expensive party for the Goldberg, Swedelson partners. I let her talk me into it, and I let my girlfriends down. That was a fine Christmas present I gave them and little Jabari. I still feel ashamed every time I think about it. Maybe the Lord was putting Honey back in my life to give me a chance to make up for it.

"Maybe I deserve this," I said to her at one point. She had just signed for the package of my dress clothes from my room at the Mercer. She was opening up it and laying it all out on the chaise lounge in her bedroom.

"Of course you deserve it, William. You stole my election."

"I thought that we had established that I was an innocent participant. I had no idea that the election was stolen. In fact, I don't know that we have established that it was stolen yet. We're only speculating."

"You're sounding just like a lawyer," she snapped. "I don't like lawyers."

"Easy, Honey. You might need a lawyer for what I have in mind."

"What's that, William."

Ever since I figured out that Honey was right about that long ago election, I had been mulling how to somehow make it right. I am embarrassed to tell you that I, a brilliant, rising young attorney, took 24 hours to come up with an answer.

"You could sue!" I said. "You could sue the school district!"

She looked thoughtful. "Are you saying that you would take my case?"

I backed off. "Not exactly. It would be unethical for me to tell you have a case then suggest that I could be your lawyer."

She frowned. The sight of beautiful, bonkers Honey frowning is oddly disturbing. I hastily amended my statement.

"I only mean I can't volunteer to be your lawyer, Honey. But you can ask me to represent you."

"Okay, I'm asking."

"Okay, I accept," I said. "At least now I know you'll have to let me go at some point to start putting together your case."

"Sure," she said. "But not just yet. We have a party to attend."

CHAPTER
TWELVE

JOAN

I was disappointed when our taxi pulled up to the curb outside the Soho Grand and Bradley told me that he would not be coming up to the suite with me. I was still playing that love song from *Hairspray* in my head. I was starting to think of it as our song. I guess I'm a hopeless romantic.

"Don't look so sad," he said. "I've got to get home and change for this party. If I'm going with you, I've got to look my best."

I could hardly argue with that. Besides, it gave me a chance to work on my own presentation. I intended to knock his socks off.

"I understand," I nodded. "Have you been to Malcolm's apartment before?"

"Oh, sure. I've played cards there a few times. But this birthday party keeps getting bigger every year. I think it's a hotter ticket by now than P. Diddy's birthday party."

Upstairs in the suite I was the first to arrive. I went to work, laying out my new earrings and a spaghetti-strap pale pink satin slip dress that did a lot for my bust. I checked my voicemail. There was a message from Toni saying she was on her way to Yankee Stadium and would meet us at Malcolm's. There was another message from Maya. She and Quentin were also planning to regroup with us at Malcolm's.

I had decided on a pair of strappy sandals to go with it all when Lynn barged in, glowing and wrapped in an oversized yellow cashmere sweater that made her look young and vulnerable.

"Where's Malcolm?" I asked.

"Oh, he wanted to check up on the party. I told him I'd come with you later."

"I guess I don't have to ask you if you had fun this afternoon," I said, as she started changing clothes. "I can see it all over you."

"Does it show that much?" she said, touching her face. "I don't think I've felt this way since—"

I cut her off when I noticed her outfit. She had switched to her t-shirt and peasant skirt from the flight.

"Is that what you're wearing? For tonight?"

"Don't scream, Joan," she said coolly. "Of course I'm wearing this. I only brought two outfits. I wore the other one last night, and I've been wearing this one all day."

"Lynn, " I said gently. "This party of Malcolm's is a local institution. This is big time. Do you really want to go in an outfit he's already seen?"

"Henry David Thoreau said to beware of any enterprise that requires new clothes," she said.

"Well Henry Thoreau wasn't invited to this party," I replied.

I have to admit that I do admire Lynn's resistance

to material things. She's our little flower child, and I love her for it. But there are limits to everything.

"Lynn," I said firmly. "We are going to a party at the home of a very rich man. A man who is crazy about you. Please let me give you something appropriate to wear. We already know that you and I wear the same size." We know that because when Lynn lived with me rent-free for a year, she helped herself to my clothes regularly. She wouldn't even have the job she has now if I had not insisted that she wear one of my suits to her first interview. Although I can't take all the credit for that. Maya and Toni held her down while I got the suit on her. Let me tell you, you'll never complain about putting pantyhose on your own self after you've tried to put them on someone else.

Lynn shrugged. "How about this dress?" she pointed to the pink silk slip laid out on my bed. "And I love the earrings."

Two steps forward and one step back. "No, Lynn," I said firmly. "This outfit is spoken for. But I have some other ideas. Let's start going through my suitcases and I'm sure we can come up with something."

Lynn might not have money, but she has great taste. She settled on some of the most expensive items in my wardrobe: a Charles Chang-Lima black lace jacket and black satin Chloe trousers. I even fixed her up with my sexiest Luca Luca sandals.

Our hotel suite had come with a CD player and a stack of the latest releases. Lynn put some music on while I mixed us a pitcher of Cosmopolitans. Soon we were giggling like sorority girls when we started on the next step. I went to work on Lynn's hair, pinning it up to show off her neck. I really got into it.

Since I never blow my hair out straight, playing with Lynn's was a novel experience.

"Maybe I missed my calling, Lynn," I mused with a bobby pin clenched between my lips.

"How's that?"

"Maybe I should have skipped law school and become a hair stylist. I love to work with hair!"

"You have a lot of talents, Joan," she said.

That made me glow. "Really, Lynn? Like what?" I should be ashamed of myself, but I have a secret: I crave flattery.

"I've learned a lot from you, Joan," she went on. "Like the way you make a plan and stick to it come hell or high water."

"Okay, I see where this is going…just because my plan for the weekend fell apart—"

"But you kept to your personal plan. You got us here, you showed us a great time, and you got to see *Hairspray*."

I beamed. "I did, didn't I?"

"Now, if we can just get you laid, my work will be done."

"Lynn!" I protested. Perhaps only half-heartedly, though.

TONI

I had strayed a long way from the chic streets of Manhattan's Upper East Side, and I was now stuck on God-Knows-Where Street in the South Bronx. With the luck I'd been having, it was probably at the corner of Smith & Wesson.

And I don't ever want to hear about Mother Africa

again! After my encounter with that Kunta Kinte cabbie, I am totally put off on the third world. Let them solve their own problems. My dilemma was much more serious. All I could think of was the movie *Fort Apache, the Bronx* as I stood in a doorway, soaked and shivering. My Rolex said it was seven o'clock. I didn't doubt for a minute that Derek's Yankee game had been rained out, so I had wasted my time trying to get to Yankee Stadium. And now Malcolm's party would be starting without me.

While the girls were on their way to the party, I was getting good and soaking wet. Of course, I'm sure that I could have called Malcolm myself and he would have sent a car for me. There are any number of calls I could have made to get me out of there but for the fact that, in my haste and distress, I had left my purse and cell phone in the taxi with Kunta Kinte. I didn't even have a quarter for a pay phone! I definitely intended to file a complaint with the Taxi and Limousine Commission. If I lived to see another day, that is.

The rain stopped, but the Lord was not through testing me. I felt like Job. I was about to move out of the doorway when two du-rag wearing, fake ice sportin', gansta rapper wannabes approached me. They had on extra-baggy jeans and quilted jackets, and they wore baseball caps pulled low over their du-rags so that it was hard to see their faces. Call me cynical, tell me that I'm profiling and playing into stereotypes, but I, personally, suspected that these two had robbery on their minds.

I played it cool. "Tough luck, boys," I said. "I left my purse in a cab. I'm broke." I held up my hands to show that they were empty.

That's when the taller one started staring at my Tiffany ring and my Rolex watch. This encounter was not going well at all.

"Don't get any ideas," I warned them. We were at a standoff. Neither side wanted to make the first move. Finally the short one broke the silence.

"You look familiar," she said.

You heard me. She. These weren't boys at all. These two juvenile delinquents were girls! Now I could see their problem. Dressing up like street thugs, how could they ever get ahead in this world?

"Oh, yeah! She was on TV, 'memba?" said the taller girl. "We saw you on the news. You think you a bad bitch, don'tchu?" she menaced.

I had become a prisoner of my fame. I knew now how women like Janet Jackson and Madonna must feel. If I survived this ordeal, I would certainly be better able to service my celebrity clients. Then it dawned on me—this was a great opportunity to use my compliment strategy!

"Hey, that is a *great*...," I scanned her quickly for something to compliment and spat out, "...tattoo." I pointed to the shorter one's forearm. "Who does your...ink?"

It worked immediately. I saw her posture change right away. "Oh, this one's new," she said, admiring her own arm. "I got it done at a spot in the Village not too long ago. You got ink?"

"Who, me? No. But if I ever decide to, girl, I need a Polaroid of that arm because that is just too...dope. What about you?" I asked the other girl. She was more than happy to pull up her pants leg and show me her right calf, the outside of which had a huge scorpion drawn on it. A representation of her zodiac sign, she explained. I fawned over that one, too.

They told me they loved my hat and my shoes, then showed me some other tattoos. It was a regular ghetto love fest. I even complimented their Air Force Ones, of which both girls assured me they had more than "two purr."

"Whew. You girls are just too fly for me," I said. Imagine that being true, but I was on a roll, so I added, offhandedly, "Say, does either of you have a car?"

"Huh?" the taller girl said. I could see the little one was the brains of this duo.

"Whatchu want a car for?" the little one asked. "Yo, you robbin' this place? What? You got peoples inside?" She looked conspiratorial, like she was ready to help carry the loot.

I shook my head. My friend Lynn has an advanced degree in anthropology, but I for one don't understand what's so interesting about primitive cultures. I had no desire to play Margaret Mead with these two miscreants, but they were my only hope of getting back to Manhattan.

"I'm Toni Childs. I specialize in results," I said, finally getting around to introductions.

"Huh?" said the little one.

"I'm Toni Childs," I repeated, leaving off my motto. There was no point in confusing them. "What are your names?"

"I'm Jocelyn," said the little one.

"Melody," said the other.

"Well, Jocelyn and Melody," I said. "I was dumped here against my will. But if you can find me a ride and get me back downtown, you can have my hat."

"How about the shoes?" the tall one asked.

My Jimmy Choos! These girls had good taste. I braced myself. Shoes could always be replaced, even at $500 a pair. "Sure," I said. "I've got more back at my hotel. Maybe you'd like to see them?"

Little Jocelyn looked at her friend. "We ain't got no whip, yo."

"So?" she shrugged. "We can boost one. Like you ain't never did that?"

"Ladies!" I intervened. "Can you come up with a ride without stealing a car? Think!"

This was obviously a struggle, but Big Melody finally said, "Aiight, I got uh idea. Let's be out."

So yours truly went dripping off into the dark night between two ride-or-die chicks in search of, well, a ride.

LYNN

By the time Joan and I arrived at North Moore Street in Soho, we were having a laugh attack. We just couldn't stop until we had arrived at the front of Malcolm's building.

"God, how long has it been since you and I laughed like this?" Joan asked.

"Too long," I answered.

"Funny, isn't it?" she sighed. "I see you all the time, but it's like we've been drifting apart for the last few years. I didn't realize until tonight how much I've neglected our friendship."

"We're always in a group, Joan. It's never just you and me anymore."

I know that I'll always take second place to Toni in Joan's friendship line-up. After all, Toni and Joan have known each other since second grade. I honestly didn't mind coming in second. But in the last few years I've been losing that spot to Joan's assistant, Maya. I've been slipping down Joan's speed dial. By now I'm below William and her boyfriend Ellis. I've sensed that Joan disapproves of my lifestyle. She was steadily moving forward on the partnership track while I was just staying in school.

It's not like I was just sitting around all these years. I had managed to collect a few impressive degrees. I just never clicked with a job. I'm not like Joan. Or William. Or Malcolm, for that matter.

Joan and I knew that our man Malcolm was rich and successful, but I don't think I understood quite how rich and successful he was until we arrived at his building on North Moore Street. There was an impressive-looking security guard standing in a spotlight on the sidewalk outside. The guard checked our names against a typed list and then buzzed us inside.

We stepped into an elevator and I almost collided with a wall formed by three tall, athletic-looking, black-tie-attired men who were already inside. I started to giggle when I recognized the one in the middle.

"Aren't you Derek Johnson?" I asked. "I almost didn't recognize you outside of those tight little pin-striped pants."

He smiled and introduced the other two men, who were his teammates.

"Shouldn't you be at Yankee Stadium?" Joan demanded. "Don't you guys have a game tonight?"

He shrugged. "Rained out," he said. They were on their way to Malcolm's, too. I wondered where Toni was. I was about to ask Derek why he didn't return Toni's calls when Malcolm answered his apartment door, looking sleek but casual in a Versace tux. (I might not need labels in my own life, but I can't help but pick up on a thing or two from Joan and Toni.)

One look at Malcolm's face and I silently thanked Joan and the Goddess for getting me out of my peasant clothes and into this outfit, even if it was only borrowed.

Malcolm led us into a three story living room that was already crowded with his stylish friends. All colors, all ages. None of the men was as elegant as Malcolm, though.

He was happy to give Joan and me a little tour of his triplex. I do believe I had entered the most beautiful apartment in New York City. The man should have been featured on *Cribs*.

Beyond the living room, which was the size of Joan's house, we followed Malcolm down a hall lined with photographs of relatives and friends. There he was with Derek Johnson. With Lennox Lewis. In front of a bunch of little kids, giving them some kind of prize for a spelling bee. There was a sweet one of a very young Malcolm standing with a couple who I assumed were his parents.

Next, Joan and I stood in the hallway that lead to the master bedroom suite. "One of these closets is a humidor," Malcolm explained, "for my Hoyo de Monterrey Double Coronas. The other closet is for wine." The bedroom was beyond plush, and inside the master bathroom was a sunken tub.

"Wow," I said. "This is like something out of *Architectural Digest*." (Another of the things-or-two I'd picked up.)

"You've got a good eye, Lynn. This apartment was featured in *AD* last summer."

Once among the partygoers, I kept bumping into people I recognized, but everyone was cool. Waiters kept coming through with trays of divine food and flutes of champagne.

Malcolm plucked a mini quiche from a passing tray and popped it into his mouth.

"Mini quiches are Toni's good luck food," I said. My eyes searched the crowd. "I wonder where she is."

Except for Toni's mysterious absence, the party vibe was great. A gathering of old friends and new ones to laugh and talk.

I headed for the buffet. There was a pile of sushi and a mountain of Oscetra, a golden imperial caviar. (Okay, maybe it's been more than a thing or two I've picked up on.)

"Would you like to try the vegetable tempura?" asked the server behind the table.

"Would I?" I repeated. "Just try and stop me."

There was a cheese souffle and pate and bananas flambe and lots of other fancy ay's.

I had hardly eaten since breakfast. All that time on the boat this afternoon had left me starving. I plunged in.

The universe was supporting me tonight, I could feel it. The way I had met Malcolm, the way he had presented himself to me this afternoon. There could be no other explanation: Malcolm was a gift to me from the great Goddess. She had let me find my purpose. When I went home to L.A. on Sunday night, I would not be returning to a job that sapped my spirit. I would be going toward my destiny.

MAYA

Quentin and I wound up having such a good time at Jacquie's that we didn't want to leave. We finally tore ourselves away and took the subway back to Manhattan.

"Do I look okay?" I asked him over the roar of the train. There simply wasn't time to go back to the hotel and change.

"You look beautiful, Maya," he said. Good answer, I thought, wondering if that black people don't blush thing was holding true.

"I didn't realize you were married, Maya," he added. "You don't seem old enough to have a nine year old son."

"I married young," I admitted. "We had a few good years. I know how you feel about marriage. You made it clear back at Jacquie's."

He chuckled. "I was exaggerating for effect, Maya. I'd love to get married someday myself. But women like you are too independent for me." I admired his honesty and his flattery and found myself regretting having found out the truth. I should have known a man that good had to be kinfolk.

When we reached Malcolm's apartment in Soho, I watched as Quentin mingled as smoothly in this crowd as he had mixed with our cousins in Brooklyn. He could really do the levels, from the 'hood to high brow.

We were both stuffed from all the food at Jacquie's, so we walked right past the buffet tables and downstairs to Malcolm's private disco where the music was mostly current R&B stuff. I found my mind dwelling on last night and today again. I sat stiffly next to him on a sofa, and he called me on it right away.

"Listen," he said. "I know what you're thinking. But what happened happened. We're both adults. It's not like I pulled a Jerry Lee Lewis. And besides—we didn't know. And even if we did, it's not like we're first cousins. At most we're second cousins. Maybe even once removed!"

I nodded.

"Can you just forget about it? And enjoy the party?"

I wanted to. A song I liked was playing.

"That used to be my song," I told Quentin as I nodded my head to it and he insisted on pulling me up by arms to get me to the dance floor.

"So what is it now?" he asked.

"I think I'm feeling kind of foolish," I replied.

"Oh, Ashanti?" he asked.

"Huh? Oh, yeah. That, too."

He laughed and gave me a little tickle. I giggled and relaxed and gave in to the music.

WILLIAM

Two gorgeous young women wheeled in a cake for Malcolm. Somebody said that the cake came from Cakeman Raven, the celebrity baker. It was a reproduction of one of Malcolm's most recent projects: a hundred story office building on North Michigan Avenue in Chicago.

In spite of unlimited caviar and champagne, in spite of the delicious cake, yours truly had kept his head clear. Clear thinking under fire is the first tool of a good lawyer. And Honey and her problems were forcing me into a greater clarity. By the time we arrived at Malcolm's party I was thinking so clearly it was as if my head was made of glass. Whether or not that was a good thing remained to be seen.

I had managed to carry my cell phone with me, and at Malcolm's I disappeared into a bathroom to make a private call to my girlfriend in L.A. There was no real advantage to telling her that Honey had brought me to the party, but I knew that Monica would be impressed to learn that I had just met Malcolm Diggs.

"That's my boy!" she raved. She does know how to encourage me.

We chatted, but I didn't want to linger. She had a way of getting information from me. The Mackmeister had to watch his step. I let her go and returned to Honey's side. She was a good mixer, and we sailed through the crowd getting face time with much of Malcolm's mixed bag of guests. There was a chilly blonde real estate agent named Courtney who seemed to be stalking Derek Johnson. Seeing him, I wondered where Toni was. I thought she was getting together with him when she came to New York. She was the only one of my girlfriends I didn't see. From where I stood, I saw little Maya with the same guy I saw her with at Chrysalis, and I saw Joan laughing it up with Lynn. Then Joan sort of lit up as a good looking young man in a tuxedo joined them. I waved at her, and she just could not wait to show him off to me. I'm surprised she didn't knock anyone over as she rushed him to my side of the room to introduce us.

CHAPTER
THIRTEEN

JOAN

The party at Malcolm's triplex was still going strong when Bradley took my arm and suggested that we move on. As we moved through the rooms to say our good-byes, I could see that all my girlfriends were doing fine on their own. Malcolm was keeping Lynn by his side as he played the perfect 21st century host. Maya and Quentin were dancing like two kids in the private disco. Even William had finally turned up with his mysterious new friend, Honey Hayes.

"Do you think William is serious about that woman?" I whispered to Lynn as I was saying goodbye. "He never seems to leave her side."

Lynn shook her head. "There's something going on with those two, Joan. I can smell it. Those two are getting kinky."

Just then Derek Johnson passed by us and shook hands with Malcolm. A blonde woman was hanging on his arm. She was slightly intoxicated, and he looked uncomfortable and embarrassed.

"Maybe I'll catch up with you guys later," he said to Lynn in passing.

I looked at her. "Don't tell me you're planning on mixing it up with Derek, too, Lynn!"

She shook her head. Lynn really did look beautiful with her hair pulled up, and my ensemble that she was wearing flattered her figure. I realized that I was going to have to let her keep it because it had never looked as good on me. "I'm sticking with Malcolm," she said firmly. "But Derek is one of his best friends. I think we're doing something later, if he can ever peel that blonde off his arm."

"Who is she?" I asked.

"Courtney something. She was married to a rock star, divorced, and now she sells high end real estate."

The words real estate made me think of our own little sales dynamo. "Have you seen Toni tonight?" I asked.

"No," Lynn answered. "If she was here, she'd be on Derek Johnson like butter on toast."

"Should we be worried about her?" I asked.

Lynn laughed. "Relax, Joan. We're here to party. Toni is over 21 and she can take care of herself."

"Maybe I should give her a call," I said slowly.

"Oh come on, Joan. Stop playing mommy. Besides, maybe she wants a little privacy. Maybe she's up to something she doesn't want the world to know about." Lynn smiled lewdly. Sex is never very far from her thoughts.

Bradley tugged at my arm. "Ready?" he said.

Lynn looked him up and down. I was very glad that she was so happy with Malcolm because otherwise the way she looked at Bradley would have made me very nervous.

"You and Bradley go have a good time," she encouraged. "I'll see you in the morning."

So Bradley and I were soon out the door and into an elevator. Downstairs on the street, his chauffeur Khalil was waiting in the line of limousines. It was nearly one in the morning, and the streets uptown were almost deserted. We sailed up the West Side Highway to 125th Street in less than twenty minutes.

"This is it? This is Harlem?" I asked. "I feel like I've crossed some great divide."

Bradley smiled. "Yes, this is Harlem. I can't believe that all these years you've been coming to New York and you never got yourself up here."

I resented that a little. "What are you saying? That I thought I was too good to come here? Because that's not true."

"Okay, okay. Easy, girl."

"I've been coming to New York on business trips, Bradley. My time is limited. I've never had much time for side trips."

"You had plenty of time for shopping," he teased. "I'm just surprised that a sista like you has never been to Harlem before. But I'm honored that you've come up here with me."

"That's better," I said. We were moving further uptown, finally stopping at 139th Street.

"This is it, the famous Striver's Row," he said as he helped me out of the limo. I looked around at the street in the moonlight. It was lined with old-fashioned brownstones, like something in an Edith Wharton movie. I'm sure that those buildings hadn't changed in a hundred years. I was so absorbed in the scene that I barely registered when I heard Bradley tell Khalil that he would not need him for the rest of the night. But when that did click, I knew for sure that Bradley and I had the same thing in mind.

It was time to waive my three-month rule, I told myself, as I followed Bradley up the steps to one of the brownstones. A small brass plate on the door read "Houston."

The street outside was like something frozen in the past, but the inside of Bradley's brownstone was strictly 21st century. It was also surprisingly peaceful and still after all the party noise at Malcolm's. Most of the first floor was an enormous living room that looked designed for entertaining. There was a bar in the corner stocked with all the best brands.

"Drink, Joan?" he asked.

"Actually, I could go for a coffee," I suggested.

"Then step this way," he said, and I followed him into the next room, which was a huge, state of the art kitchen. He began fumbling with a cappuccino machine.

Everywhere, the walls were covered with paintings by artists like Romaire Bearden and Sam Gilliam. That surprised me since up until then Bradley had never mentioned an interest in art. I had a lot to learn about this guy, and I was eager to learn it.

"Are you a collector, Bradley?" I asked him.

"Hmm?" He looked puzzled, then he caught on. "Oh, the paintings. They came with the house."

I could see that he was having trouble with the cappuccino machine. "First time using that?" I joked. "Let me help. I have one like it at home."

I fixed us two cups and Bradley suggested that we take them upstairs.

"My playpen is on the third floor," was the way he put it, actually. I followed him up the narrow stairs. We skipped the second floor, but I noticed that the walls of the landing were lined with family photo-graphs, and I insisted on stopping to look.

"That's so sweet," I said, pointing at one shot of Bradley in a cap and gown standing between a handsome middle-aged couple who I assumed were his parents. "You've hardly aged a bit. What's your secret?" I asked.

He didn't answer, just kept tugging at my arm to move on to the next floor. That boy was eager, and, to tell the truth, so was I.

TONI

"Harlem's just over that way." Jocelyn pointed to a steel bridge in the distance.

"Yeah, thass the Willis Avenue Bridge," Melody added.

Jocelyn continued, "We could walk across that bridge and be in Spanish Harlem in a few minutes."

This was Jocelyn's plan for getting me out of the South Bronx? What was wrong with that picture? Try everything. Toni Childs does not do Harlem, Spanish or otherwise, on foot and in between two thugged out juvenile hall escapees.

"I'm not walking into Harlem at 2 A.M.," I said patiently. "Can't you just get me a cab?"

They shook their heads. "You see some cabs around here, you go right ahead and flag them shits down," Jocelyn said.

I had to acknowledge that in the time we had been walking, we hadn't passed a single human being, much less any kind of vehicle.

My clothes were soaking wet, I'm sure my beautiful

Jimmy Choos were ruined, and my hair desperately needed attention. I was still hoping that I could get myself to Malcolm's party, but there was no way I could show up looking like this.

Suddenly a truck came barreling down the street. The noise it made seemed loud only because there was no other sound around. I had an inspiration. I leaped into the path of the truck. Brakes screeched. Strong hands pulled me backwards and down toward the curb. I closed my eyes and hit the ground hard.

"Yo, you alright?!" Jocelyn asked me. We could hear Melody exchanging loud curses with the truck driver. She was daring him to get out and fight her. He finally sped away, and she stormed back to us.

"Punk ass," she said angrily. "He almost killed you."

"Whachu thoughtchu was doin'?" Jocelyn asked. "You just walked in front of a truck. You coulda got killed."

I was furious at these two dumbelinas. This was the last straw in a very difficult night. I'd never made contact with Derek, I was missing Malcolm's party, and I didn't know if I was ever going to get out of this horrible place.

"You dolts!" I screamed. "You ruined my plan! He was supposed to stop! I was supposed to pretend I was hurt and he'd have to take me to a hospital. I'd be out of this hellhole! That was my plan, and you ruined it!"

They looked stunned and hurt. "We was gon' getchu out," said Melody.

"Then call me a car service," I said. "Surely there must be a phone somewhere."

"No pay phones in this neighborhood," said Jocelyn.

"Yeah, and in case you ain't notice, Jocelyn and me ain't got no cell phones neither," Melody added.

I began to rethink the bridge. After all, it wasn't like I would be crossing into Harlem all alone. These two were not letting me out of their sight until they got the stuff I had promised them.

"All right, ladies," I said, standing up to my full, glorious height and collecting myself as best I could. I took a deep breath and said, "Let's see that bridge."

LYNN

"I think it's time to go," Malcolm said to me.

It was nearly three in the morning and I had just said goodnight to Maya and Quentin. They were among the last guests to leave Malcolm's party.

His words took me by surprise. Malcolm had kept me by his side throughout most of the evening. Now that it was winding down, he was kicking me out?

"But I don't want to leave you now," I said.

He grinned. "I'm talking about the two of us. Let's both of us get out of here. Leave the cleaning people alone to do their thing."

Even now there were still a few stragglers scattered throughout the triplex. I noticed that Courtney-the-real-estate-lady had passed out on a sofa in the living room. She was snoring softly.

Malcolm saw me looking at her. "Don't worry, Lynn. My people will take care of all that. Let me take care of you."

"I like the sound of that," I said. Again, I silently thanked the Goddess and my girl for talking me out of my original outfit and lending me this one. Thoreau did warn me to beware of any enterprise that required new clothes, but my relationship with Malcolm was a worthwhile enterprise for sure. He was unlike any man I had ever known. And to make it even stranger, I was behaving differently, too. I'd hardly flirted with any of the men at Malcolm's party. I mean, I have eyes. I have a pulse. It's hard to ignore sexy men like Derek Johnson or Bradley or Quentin or hell, even a good half of the wait staff. I just wasn't acting on any of them tonight. I was actually sort of saving myself for Mr. Malcolm Diggs.

The rain had stopped long ago, and the full moon was lighting up the streets. We were just a few blocks from the Soho Grand. I suggested that we walk back to my hotel. Malcolm thought that was a good idea.

"And I can give you back your sweater," I added.

"My sweater?" he repeated.

"That beautiful yellow cashmere you lent me on your boat this morning." I reminded him that when the weather turned chilly out there on his boat he had found the sweater and wrapped me up in it.

"That's one of the things I like about you, Lynn," he said.

"What's that?" I asked.

"You don't want anything from me," he said. "A guy in my position hears from people all day long and most of the time they're trying to get something from me."

"I met a lot of your friends tonight, Malcolm. It didn't look like they were looking for anything but a good time," I said.

He shook his head. "You'd be surprised, Lynn. Everybody's after something. Derek is looking for a job after he leaves baseball. Courtney sold me my triplex, now she wants me to trade up or buy a loft from her. Whether they're investors or clients, they're all looking for something."

"Gosh. You're...a cynic." I said.

"I don't deny that at all," he said. "It's not something I've been trying to hide from you. It's hard to have a lot and not have your eyes opened to the real nature of most of the world."

I shook my head. I was still trying to wrap my brain around this piece of news. I'd been falling for a cynic? I thought I could usually pick up on that kind of negative vibe from a person's aura.

I looked at him cock-eyed. "You don't look like a cynic," I said. "You had me completely fooled." I pulled away when I said that.

He bristled. "Listen, it's not like I'm a...a Republican or something. Why are you making such a big deal of this? It's just the way I see the world."

We had reached the Soho Grand. It was make or break time. If I invited Malcolm into the hotel it meant that I accepted him despite any negative energy he brought. Or I could send him back to his lavish triplex to enjoy his negativity alone.

"I'm not sure, Malcolm," I admitted. "It's just that you're my first cynic."

"You're the one who told me you like to push the envelope. You want to try new things. You could try getting me to be less jaded, for one."

He was right, and I was suddenly lusty for him again. I grabbed him by the arm, and we headed inside, into the lobby of the Soho Grand.

MAYA

Well, as Mama always says, nobody's perfect. Not me, for sure. The shock and shame I felt when I discovered that Quentin was my relative had taken a back seat to my earlier feelings about being with him. And although I know that the Lord is everywhere, I still felt like anything I did during this get-away weekend in New York was not going to count on the permanent record of my life, which God of course keeps in L.A.

After Quentin and I left Malcolm's, we moved on to the bar of the Soho Grand. Most of the hotel's street level lobby was this fancy bar with lots of padded sofas and armchairs you could curl up in. It seemed to go on and on like a set in a movie. The people lounging around the lobby were all dressed up and glamorous.

Quentin and I headed for a corner and I settled into a sofa. There were a few chairs opposite me, but he sat right down beside me. He put his arm around me. We could have been curled up at home watching TV instead of in the lobby of a fancy hotel watching a crowd of trendies. I knew then that he had not changed his mind about me either.

"Dancing with you was one thing, Quentin," I said slowly.

"No pressure, Maya. That's my motto," he said. He turned his attention to the room. At that moment, we could see a tall man in a tuxedo stroll in and look around the lobby as if he was searching for someone.

I tugged at Quentin's sleeve. "Isn't that Derek Johnson?" I said.

"Derek! Derek!" Quentin shouted. "Over here!"

Derek looked relieved. I suppose even famous ballplayers are shy about walking into a crowd without any familiar faces in it. He started to stroll our way.

Quentin turned to me and put his hand under my chin, lifting my face to his. "Relax, Maya. You call the shots tonight, and I'll just follow your lead."

Derek took a seat in one of the plush armchairs in front of us. Soon, a waiter came by to take our drink orders. Heinekens for the guys and a Cosmopolitan for myself.

Derek stared at me. "You're a friend of Toni Childs, aren't you?" he asked.

This was not the time to analyze my relationship with Toni. I acknowledged that Toni and Joan and Lynn and I were spending the weekend together at the hotel.

"Then do you know where she is? She's been calling me all weekend," he said.

"I know, and I'm surprised that a gentleman like yourself wouldn't return her calls."

"I was in batting practice," he shrugged. "The Yankees had a major game tonight. I didn't know we were going to be rained out. I'm an athlete. My whole focus has to be on my game."

"Well, have you heard from Toni tonight?" I asked. I was surprised that she never turned up at the party.

"No. I tried to call, but she wasn't answering her cell. She had mentioned Malcolm's party so I came downtown expecting to run into her there."

I suppose that Quentin was feeling neglected because I was talking to Derek. A lot of men get to feeling insecure around professional athletes. In my estimation, however, most of them are just like Derek.

They're so focused on their jobs that they don't have much left for a woman, if you get my meaning. There's no fire in the oven, no flame in their game.

I think Derek was very happy to recognize more of our group turning up in the lobby. I saw William and his tall new friend stroll in.

Quentin saw them, too, and signaled for them to come over and join us.

WILLIAM

As I followed Honey Hayes across the vast lobby of the Soho Grand, I felt a wave of fear. When Honey had seen fit to let me off my chain, we had encountered my girlfriends at Chrysalis and, earlier tonight, at Malcolm's party on North Moore Street. Each time I had been able to brush off their questions about Honey. I told Joan that she was an old high school classmate. True. I told Toni that I'd run into Honey at a poker game. True. And I told Lynn that Honey was a lifestyle consultant. Also true, more or less.

But now Maya Wilkes was waiting for us. Maya with her street smarts and her skepticism. I did not trust myself to put anything over on that sister. I was expecting us to face an endless parade of prying questions designed to expose what was really going on in our relationship.

I gave Maya's friend Quentin the high sign and indicated that we would be right over. But first I insisted that Honey and I stop at the bar and fortify ourselves. I was not in the mood to wait for table service.

"Trust me, Honey, you don't want to face this without chemical assistance," I said.

"That's another difference between you and me," she said coolly. "When I go into battle, I insist on being totally clear-headed."

Clear-headed? This madwoman was lecturing me about being clear-headed? I ignored the comment and brought us to the table, where Maya was chatting it up with Derek Johnson and Quentin.

"Where are your other partners in crime?" I asked her, trying to take early control of the dialogue.

Maya shrugged. "They don't answer to me, William. But, oh...there Lynn is right behind you."

I turned around to see Lynn on the arm of Malcolm Diggs. The two of them were glowing, and frankly, if I had not been with one of the most beautiful women in New York, I might have been a little jealous.

To my surprise and relief, Maya never had a chance to cross-examine me about Honey because all attention was suddenly focused on a noisy encounter in the doorway. This is New York, of course, so one gets used to the occasional unfortunate street people trying to wander into places where they aren't exactly wanted. In this case, it was a motley crew of three, two of whom had obviously mistaken the Soho Grand for the set of a Nelly video shoot.

But one of the voices became louder and more difficult to ignore.

"I know that voice," I said.

"We know that voice," said Maya.

Together we stood and hurried to the front of the lobby. The others followed, concerned that we were going to need help. My worst fears were confirmed. There stood Toni. Her suit was completely disheveled,

she was barefoot, and she was flanked by two dangerous looking young brothas wearing low caps and du-
rags. My first thought was that I would never be able
to pick either one of these guys out of a lineup.

"Toni!" Maya shouted. "What on *Earth*?"

Toni stopped and threw herself into Maya's arms.
"Oh, Maya. Thank the Lord you're here. I've missed
you so!"

Maya looked as stunned as I did at the greeting.

"Do you know this woman?" the doorman asked
politely. After all, the hotel is used to rock stars and
whatnot. They know how to handle eccentric, demanding personalities. But Toni was clearly testing their
limits.

"Of course I know her. She's staying with me at
this hotel," Maya said defensively.

"That's what I've been telling them!" said Toni.

"I'm very sorry," he said. "But she had no I.D., and
under the circumstances...," he nodded pointedly at
her two companions.

Toni saw us staring at them too. "Oh, meet Jocelyn
and Melody," she said. "They saved my life tonight."

Her two companions looked uncomfortable and
then, after nudging each other, they removed their
caps. Then their du-rags too. That's when I realized
that they were actually woman. I mean, females. Not
women like Honey or my girlfriends. Not women like
Monica. Or my mother. Or even my lesbian sister
and her lover. No, these two were another sex entirely. But I'm yammering again.

CHAPTER
FOURTEEN

JOAN

Sunshine poured through the windows of Bradley Houston's bedroom and woke me up early Sunday morning. I lay there content in Bradley's bed as he slept soundly in my arms.

If I ever have the time to take up needlepoint, I plan to make myself a pillow. On it I intend to stitch my life's motto: How Could I Have Missed It?

Maybe I'll even stitch on the other side: "Beats Me."

Because I have no idea how I could have missed the truth about Bradley. I can even look back now and see that at least Maya was giving me subtle little hints. She just didn't want to rain on my parade and tell me flat-out.

I see that in hindsight, but at that moment, alone with Bradley, all I could think about was: daaaaamn, that was good.

He was so much fun! We had such a good time together! I had honestly begun to think of Bradley Houston as The One. My soul mate.

My mind was on that instead of picking up on the clues around his house.

Maybe it was the full moon. Maybe it was all the champagne that I had been drinking this week. Whatever it was, when Bradley opened up my lace tuxedo jacket—which I'd wound up wearing instead of the pink dress—and started to kiss my breasts, all I could think of was getting him out of his own clothes as soon as possible. As I unbuttoned his shirt, sure, I noticed how hard his abs were. I remember thinking that even Ellis, who works out in a gym five days a week, does not have a stomach that hard. It was a stomach you could bounce quarters off.

Fool! I say to myself now. No man on earth over the age of 25 has a stomach that hard. But my attention soon moved to other areas of Bradley's fine frame, and we rolled around on that king-sized bed like two alley cats in maximum heat.

I was thinking about all that as Bradley slept, and I leaned over and kissed him, which of course woke him up, which I supposed was my plan all along.

He sat up in the bed. "Sleep well?" he asked.

"Like a log," I said. "But I'm wide awake now." Hint, hint. I have learned that hot sex and subtle don't mix.

He started kissing me again, and I was soon responding.

"Feel good, baby?" he whispered, his hand slowly working me while his lips explored my neck.

"Oh, yeah," I answered. My voice was hoarse with desire.

It had been too long. I didn't want to think about how long Ellis had been gone because that would make me think of Ellis, and I didn't want any other man in that bed with Bradley and me at that moment. Bradley was doing things to me that took all my attention. I could not silence myself if I had wanted to. He had me facing his wall, on my knees. He was taking me from behind, and I was damn near climbing that wall.

I started moaning loudly and banging the wall with my hands, so I didn't have a prayer of hearing the front door open three floors down.

Nor did I hear the people who had entered making their way to the second floor.

But when one of them started shouting, "Bradley? Bradley? What's all that noise? Son, are you alright?" That I heard.

Bradley leaped off me like a flea off a skillet. I turned to look over my shoulder, and I saw a middle-aged woman draped in sable standing in the doorway getting a full moon in broad daylight. I grabbed a sheet to cover myself as quickly as I could.

"What is this, Bradley? We told you no strangers in this house!"

"Relax, Mom, she's...umm...a lawyer," he mumbled. Was it my imagination or had his voice just gone up a few octaves. He no longer sounded like Bradley the baller I'd spent my weekend with. He sounded like Bradley the 22-year-old college graduate. Yes, he was, like, ten years younger than me, which I would have seen if I had not been blinded by lust.

"A lawyer?" the man behind her repeated. He was an older, bigger, grayer version of Bradley. "Son? Is she trying to serve you with papers? I'll call my own lawyer."

"Would you two chill?" He turned to me, rolled his eyes and said, "Joan, this is the parental unit.

They've been in Italy at a film festival." Toward them, he added, "They're supposed to still be there."

"We got tired of watching the movies. When you father's film didn't get the prize, we decided to come home. Good thing, too!"

Now I recognized his parents. His father was an independent producer. He worked in theater and film. I'd even seen him at some galas in Los Angeles. With parents in the business, it was a wonder that Bradley and I had not crossed paths before. But, of course, he'd been in high school until four years ago!

"How do you do," the mother said. She turned back to Bradley. "You settle up here, young man. We'll talk to you downstairs."

I was furious. What had I done? Had I learned nothing? How could I be so blind?

"Come on, Joan, what's the big deal?" Bradley pleaded. "My parents will get over it."

"Who cares about them? You played me for a fool!" I screamed. "You lied!"

"All men lie," he said. "Besides, I never actually lied. Maybe I *withheld* something—"

"Like the truth!" I snapped back.

"Look, you drew some conclusions that were wrong, and I didn't correct you. That's just good manners."

"Don't' give me that!" I shouted. "Don't make this any worse than it is by acting innocent!"

I was mad at Bradley, but I was even madder at myself. How could I not have seen this? How could I have missed it?

It took me all of ten minutes to pull myself together and storm out of that house and onto 139th Street.

So there I was on Striver's Row early Sunday

morning in the middle of Harlem, where I had never been before. I silently thanked God that I had at least worn a pantsuit and not that pink slip dress I originally picked out. In that get-up I definitely would have been taken for a hooker. Now I just looked like a slut.

TONI

I never thought I would be so happy to see the disapproving scowl of Maya Wilkes, but I was last night when she came to my rescue in the lobby of the Soho Grand. I believe that if she had not admitted knowing me I would have been tossed out along with Jocelyn and Melody. I might have ended up in a homeless shelter, or at Bellevue, trying to convince them that I was Toni Childs the real estate broker and them telling me I was just a ragged crazy lady.

Clothes do make the woman, I guess. My beautiful Jimmy Choos wore out halfway across the Willis Avenue Bridge, and we tossed them into the Harlem River. I just wanted to collapse at that point, but mean Melody forced me to continue on the march towards Harlem.

A lot of good it did us, though, because even though there were taxis up there, none of them would stop for two thugged out girls that looked like guys and a ragged, barefoot black woman. Instead, Jocelyn and Melody got me to the train station at 125th Street and showed me how to jump the turnstile. I was now guilty of a crime, too. But at least it got us back to my hotel and my friends. I almost cried when I came face to face with Derek Johnson, but I was already all cried out.

There was no way we could linger in the lobby, so all of us, even Derek, crowded into the elevator and headed back to our suite where my friends passed the Courvoisier while I took a shower and freshened up. At the same time, I told Melody and Jocelyn to go through my closet and pick out what they wanted.

When I had pulled myself together and was wrapped up in a nice thick robe, I found them sitting on my bed in front of a little pile of clothes.

"Is that all you're taking, Jocelyn?" I said. "I can see you and I wear the same size."

She shrugged. "I don't think we gon' get out of this hotel with no box of clothes. They'd bust us at the front door."

"All I want is Derek's autograph," Melody added. "I can sell that."

I went outside to the living room where the others were still socializing. I got Derek to consent to the autograph for Melody, but he insisted on giving it to her in person. She was like a kid talking to him.

When he left, I made Maya and Lynn come back to my bedroom with me.

"Look at these two," I said, pointing at Melody and Jocelyn. "Can't we do something?"

Well we did. It was like the time we ganged up on Lynn and forced her into one of Joan's business suits. Only this time we had willing participants. By the time we got the cornrows out and the clothes and make-up on, they looked like bona fide ladies.

"Here," I said. "I'm packing it all up for you." I retrieved two of my carry-on pieces of Vuitton luggage and started packing up my precious hair supplies and make-up as well as the clothes and shoes for Jocelyn.

I made Malcolm call the front desk and get them a

car back to the Bronx, and I told him to confirm that, yes, Ms. Jocelyn and Ms. Melody would be accompanied by two pieces of Vuitton luggage.

"You know they're going to sell those bags the second they get back to the Bronx, don't you?" said Maya.

I shrugged. "What they do with it is their business. At least I'm square with the Lord."

So I slept soundly and alone that night, and when I woke Sunday morning, it was I, Toni Childs, who began to round up my friends to attend services at a church uptown.

I grew up in the church, but I stopped going regularly when I got to college. I never stopped praying, though. When I wake up, I thank God for giving me another day. I thank Him for my family and Todd and even my girlfriends. And of course, I have to thank Him for making me so fabulous.

LYNN

I woke up spooning with Malcolm in my bed at the Soho Grand. "Don't you have a home of your own?" I teased him. "Why do you have to stay in a hotel?"

"I like the room service here," he said, his hands stroking my thigh.

"And I like the service in this room," I answered. We were in the middle of a romantic kiss and I was thinking that this was the perfect way to start my last morning in New York when we heard Toni banging at our door.

"Is she in trouble *again*?" Malcolm asked.

I rolled my eyes. I did not want to leave that nice

warm bed to answer her, so I just shouted, "What is it?"

"Sunday morning, time for church!" she yelled back.

"Oh, Jes—"

Malcolm put his large hand over my mouth. "Try not to blaspheme on Sunday. It's probably twice as sinful."

"Don't tell me you're going to make me go to church with her!" I wailed.

"I don't know about you, Lynn, but I'm going with Toni. I think we all have a lot to be thankful for."

He leaned over and kissed me on the forehead. "I know I do," he added.

MAYA

The banging on doors woke Quentin with a jump. "What the hell was that?" he responded from the side chair in my room, which was where he had slept this time. He had said I was calling the shots, and that was my call.

"That was Toni. I think she wants us all to join her for church." I sat up and started mentally putting together an outfit for service.

"Church? It's Sunday morning!"

I laughed. "Maybe it's different in New York, but back in L.A., Sunday is the Sabbath. That means church."

"Sure, Maya, sure. But that doesn't mean that we have to go there."

"I think we have some issues, you and me, and maybe a little guidance from the Lord is just the thing. It won't kill us to go to church with Toni."

He smiled as he reconsidered. "You know what I like about you, Maya Wilkes?" he said.

I cringed. "If you tell me I remind you of your mama or something, you're definitely going to church—in a hearse!" I warned.

"No, Maya. It's that you're smart. And you have a lot of common sense," he paused. "It must run in the family," he added and ducked right away as I screamed and hit him with a pillow.

WILLIAM

I was waking up in Honey Hayes' loft for the last time, and she had let me off the chain. I sensed now that she trusted me completely. Or at least she believed that I was going to help her wreak revenge on our high school for doing her wrong.

I was surprised that Honey was already up that morning.

"I'm taking a taxi uptown, William," she said. "Can I drop you off at your hotel?"

"Is that New York talk for 'get the hell out of my apartment and do it fast?'" I asked.

"William! How could you think such a thing!" said Honey. "I just have other plans."

"What kind of plans can a woman like you have at this time of the morning. It's Sunday for God's sa—"

I stopped abruptly and said, "Why, Honey! You're a church girl, aren't you?" If only I had known that sooner, maybe I wouldn't have come over on the first night. Or I would at least have known what to expect. You know what they say about church girls and sex.

239

She nodded. "I'm singing in the choir this morning. I have to be uptown soon."

"Aren't you going to invite me along?" I prodded, since she apparently wasn't going to volunteer.

"Do you really want to come, William?"

"Of course!" I said grandly. I'd score points with God and Honey at the same time, and besides, what else was I going to do on a Sunday morning? My girlfriends were fed up with me. The good poker games didn't start until after 6. And at least I'd have a good accounting to Monica for my Sunday morning whereabouts. The rest of that story I'd work out later.

CHAPTER
FIFTEEN

JOAN

The weekend that I had planned so well was supposed to take all of us out of our comfort zone. That Sunday morning, as I stood on 139th Street in the middle of Striver's Row at the foot of the steps of the Houston family's brownstone, I had to admit that I was way out of my comfort zone.

I didn't know where my girlfriends were or when I was ever going to see them again. I didn't know where my hotel was or how to get back to it.

And Bradley was running after me, his fine form naked except for the towel he was trying to keep wrapped around his privates as he tried to catch up with me. I had the advantage since I had shoes on. And clothes.

"Would you let me explain, Joan?" he called. "Just let me talk to my parents. We can work everything out."

I kept walking. The street was quiet and still except for the two of us. He stopped chasing me after a few feet. He was barefoot and undoubtedly cold in the chill of the early spring morning. "Joan, I can't follow you like this," he shouted. "Everyone on this block knows my parents!"

I turned around. "Then your neighbors know more about you than I do," I said angrily. "Go home, Bradley. You've already poisoned our relationship. Work on the one with your mom and dad."

I walked to the corner of Adam Clayton Powell Boulevard and 139th, still not sure where I was or where I was going. It had been dark when Khalil chauffeured Bradley and me up here last night, and I had barely noticed the street signs. Now I could see that the Boulevard was almost a freeway, maybe three lanes wide in each direction with an island running down the middle. Unlike the quiet of sleepy Striver's Row, the Boulevard was alive with traffic and people. Busses were stopping at every corner. Harlem was waking up.

"Wake up, too," I told myself. What had I done? Would I never learn? Why was I always attracted to men who lied to me?

I supposed that I could have taken the legendary A train from Harlem downtown to the Soho Grand, but I had no idea where it was. As I walked along, dressed up in my lace jacket and pants silk pants, I was convinced that anyone who looked at me could tell where I'd been: out all night and slinking home like an alley cat.

I looked around for a taxi to take me downtown, but there wasn't a yellow cab in sight. I was in no mood to go back to Bradley's and ask for help. I think I could have handled Bradley, but I could not face his mama. Mrs. Houston and I had started out on the wrong foot, or the wrong end you might say. It was too soon to try to change her mind about me. I wanted to redeem myself, convince her that I was not a bad person, but somehow this morning seemed too soon.

I pulled out my cell phone and punched up the hotel's number. I wanted to make contact with my girlfriends and give them the 4-1-1 on this latest development. Let them laugh, I thought, consoling myself that at least I found out that Bradley was 10 years younger than me after we did it. Because let me tell you, it would take more than a little ribbing to make me regret those few hours of mattress magic. It had ended badly this morning, but I could not deny that the boy was gifted. Of course, some of his gift might have to do with him being 22 years old.

"Damn," I swore to myself as I frowned at the cell phone. There was no answer in our suite. I didn't just want to share my latest drama. I was hungry for details about everyone else's night, too. Had Toni ever turned up last night? I tried her cell, but it went straight to voicemail. Had Lynn spent the night at Malcolm's? Was Maya with that cute flight attendant? I tried Maya's cell, too, but there was no answer. I had no idea where any of my girlfriends were. There was no point in trying to reach William, either. Sure, he'd been nice enough when I crossed paths with him and his new friend Honey Hayes at Malcolm's party last night, but I did not think he was going to going to share anything about what he had been up to this weekend on his own.

All the time I was punching up these numbers and getting no response, I was walking along Adam Clayton Powell Boulevard, keeping my eyes open for a cab, but there were none to be had. Once in a while, a plain sedan would pause at the curb and the driver would honk to offer me a ride. I always shook my head to say no. I'm still squeamish about getting into one of New York's gypsy cabs. Besides, after my encounter with Bradley's parents, I didn't trust my own judgment. I could get into a cab with the bone collector and not know it until it was too late.

As I moved through the swelling Sunday morning pedestrians, I noticed that the best dressed men, women and children were all turning off the Boulevard and onto 138th Street. I could see that many of them were carrying Bibles. I followed them as they moved down the street to a big gray gothic church that sat in the middle of the block.

I recognized it at once. It was the famous Abyssinian Baptist Church I'd heard about for years. Through Afro-American History class in college, I was familiar with the careers of Adam Clayton Powell, Sr., once pastor at Abyssinian, and his son, who was a powerful Congressman in the 1950s. I also knew that Fidel Castro gave a speech at Abyssinian in 1995. I even knew the name of the current pastor, the activist Dr. Calvin O. Butts, who had crusaded against negative billboard advertising.

Bradley had teased me about never coming to Harlem, and he once accused me of knowing nothing about our history. That rankled, but it wasn't the only reason that I followed those folks up the steps into the church. I felt something calling me, drawing me inside. Besides, it was a Sunday morning in Harlem, and I could think of nowhere better to be.

TONI

I think it was Malcolm Diggs who suggested that if the five of us were going to church we ought to get ourselves up to Abyssinian Baptist in Harlem. The hotel doorman started hailing a cab, but one was already there. I took one look at the driver and exploded. My plans to praise the Lord came to a screeching halt.

"It's you!" I screamed. "You…you abandoner! And purse snatcher! What now? Did you come back for my Rolex?"

"Calm down," Lynn said through gritted teeth, holding me back by my arm. "Are you sure this is the driver?"

"Of course it is," I roared. "I'll never forget being abandoned by Kunta Kinte!"

I ran to the driver's side before he had a chance to raise his window. "Wasn't it enough that you dumped me in the middle of nowhere?" I demanded. "Did you come back to finish the job? Huh? Here to kill me are ya?" I spread my arms open. "Well come on. Bring it, Shaka Zulu!"

As usual, my friends were acting like they were embarrassed by my behavior. Everyone but Malcolm stayed on the curb while I called that little cabby out. And I do mean little. When he stepped out of his taxi he only came up to my chest. I couldn't believe he was that small. Last night, he'd seemed like a giant. My blood was really going now that I believed I could take him.

"Let's go! Here, I'll even help you out," I said, reaching to take off my shoes.

He was just chattering on and on, jumping up and

down, banging on the side of his taxi. I couldn't understand a word that little man was saying. He was making no sense at all. The only words that came through loud and clear were the ones from last night, "You are very, very rude! You are a rude lady!"

"Big deal!" I shouted back. "Tell me something I don't know!"

We might have gone on like that for a while, neither of us giving an inch, but Malcolm stepped between us. He had seen the little cabby's name on the license and could actually get his tongue around all those letters. I can't repeat it for the life of me, but it did seem to involve several clicking sounds, too. That alone made some points with the little pygmy, and he stopped shouting back at me and turned his attention to Malcolm.

"This woman," he said. "She is very, very rude!"

Malcolm smiled patiently. "Yes," he said, making that funny name sound again, "but my friend is upset and confused. She thinks she left her purse in your taxi last night."

"Thinks? Left?" I shouted. I would have added a lot more but at that moment both Maya and Lynn had flanked me and each put a hand over my mouth.

"Hush, Toni," Maya whispered. "You can lay him out or you can get your stuff back. Which is it?"

Shaka Kinte had slipped into his own language which I guess Malcolm understood because he was nodding sympathetically as Kunta Zulu went on and on, waving his arms about and sometimes hitting the fender for emphasis. He finally stopped to draw a breath. Malcolm addressed him in his own language then turned back to us and smiled.

"I think you owe this gentleman an apology, Toni.

246

It seems he's already left your purse for you at the front desk. That's what he was trying to tell you."

"That's ridiculous," I snapped. "I just came by the front desk. And don't tell me he didn't expect a reward."

Even Maya agreed with me on that.

That really made Malcolm laugh. I'd seen the man smile before, but I hadn't seen him break into a big old country boy laugh. He was breaking up so hard that he could hardly get his words out.

"That's what he's trying to tell you, Toni. He doesn't want a reward. He just doesn't want to see you again. The poor man just wants to get our of here. He thinks you have a bad mojo."

"Bad mojo! Me?"

"Maybe that explains how you got stuck in the South Bronx last night," said Lynn nodding. "Bad mojo."

"Why don't you go back inside and get your purse, Toni," said Malcolm.

I went back to the front desk and sure enough the clerk recognized me. "Oh, Ms. Childs. I must have just missed you leaving this morning. We've been calling your room."

"Well that won't do any good, will it, since I'm standing right here," I replied. "I understand that you're holding my property?"

"Yes, Ms. Childs. And I don't even need to ask you for a photo I.D.," he said smoothly. He handed the bag over, and I rifled through it. Everything was still there, including my cell phone and my credit cards. Even my cash. Not a dollar was missing.

Now I had even more reason to thank the Lord.

I turned my head up and whispered a thank you, then smoothed out my suit and headed back outside.

It was well after 11 o'clock when we and the rest of the crowd waiting outside were finally allowed to enter the Abyssinian Baptist Church sanctuary for 11 o'clock service. Morning sunlight poured through the stained glass window at the front of the sanctuary. Behind the pulpit, robed members of the choir were taking their seats.

An usher directed us to follow him down the center aisle. By the time the Reverend strode to the pulpit and greeted us all, there was hardly a vacant seat to be found. Folks had filled the second level above us and were still slipping in as the sound of the organ began to fill the air.

I looked up and saw a familiar face strolling tentatively down the aisle, searching for a seat.

"Psst, Joan!" I whispered, thrilled to see her. "Over here!"

She turned around and her eyes widened with relief when she saw me. "Oh, Toni," she squealed quietly, just as pleased as I was. There was no more room in our pew, but I pointed to an empty seat in front of me. She could squeeze in there, beside a woman in a sable coat and a smart little hat.

A few minutes later, I felt a tapping on my shoulder and turned around to see William squeezing into the pew behind us.

"Good morning, Sister Toni," he said.

"Good morning, Brother William," I responded in kind. "Where's Honey?" I asked.

William pointed to the choir loft down front. "Third row, second from the right," he said. Indeed, there she was.

"Isn't the Lord good this morning?" Rev. Butts began his sermon. "I ask you, isn't the Lord good?"

"Amen," I answered, joining in the roar from the congregation. "Amen."

LYNN

"Amen," I repeated along with the rest of them in the pew. I wasn't sure if it was the right thing to do, but I tentatively raised my fist when I said it. Until this moment, I had real doubts about coming up to Harlem just to go to church. All the way uptown I had been wondering if I really belonged here. To be honest, if Malcolm had suggested that he and I take off for another romantic ride on his boat, I would have happily blown off the whole church idea completely. Sitting around praising the Lord is just not my idea of a good time. Not while there was a beautiful sunny spring day outside and we had only a few more hours in New York City.

I was surprised to see Joan slipping into the pew in front of us. She is no more of a church girl than I am.

Unlike Toni and Maya, I never was a church girl and never will be. Sure, when I was growing up, Mom and Dad took my sisters and me to church on Sunday, but I guess that Christian stuff never stuck with me. All my psychology, sociology and anthropology studies have left me very skeptical of organized religion. Today I consider myself a pagan. Usually, when I want spiritual guidance from the universe, I invoke the great Goddess. Or consult the Tarot deck. And when I need advice, I turn to my psychic.

The show—I mean, the service—started with the choir. They sang "Precious Lord, Take My Hand," and I have to admit it was very moving, though it wasn't a song I was familiar with. I was raised "white" by my adoptive parents, so most of these old time gospel standards were new to me. I didn't know the words, but to my surprise, Malcolm started singing along in that rich voice of his. I just followed his lead throughout the service. He seemed to know what he was doing.

"Have you done this before?" I whispered.

He just smiled and patted my knee.

I cringed when the ushers moved through the aisles, passing the collection plates. As usual, I had no cash. I handed the plate over to Malcolm, sheepishly, and my eyes popped when I saw him drop a $100 bill in the basket. His was not the only big bill in there, either. "You're very generous," I said.

"I have a lot to be thankful for," he answered. The way he said it gave me a warm glowy feeling. I wanted to kiss him right there, but that was one thing I knew wouldn't be appropriate. So, instead I laughed and squeezed the back of his neck. That's when William, who was in the pew behind me, tapped me on my back and whispered, "Hush!"

"Well excuse me," I said huffily. How was I supposed to know that all of my friends are closet church folks?

The preacher man had come back to the pulpit and was about to begin his sermon. He went on for over thirty minutes about the need for love in our lives. More than once I was tempted to make sarcastic comments in Malcolm's ear, but I could see that his attention was completely on the preacher's words.

Like I said, organized religion is not my thing, so my own concentration kept wandering around the huge sanctuary. I took in the stained glass windows, which were as beautiful as the ones I'd seen in cathedrals in France. I took in the organ and piano on either side of the stage area, as well as the tall plants that nearly obscured the others on stage behind the reverend. I looked at the choir and at the folks in the pews around me. They weren't all bourgeois types, either, I have to admit. There were regular working-class looking folks among us and a well-known rapper, who had arrived with an entourage of bulging body-guards in black suits. They kept their dark glasses on throughout the service. Does he really think he needs protection here, I wondered.

I hardly listened to the preacher's sermon, but every once in while a sentence of it would force itself into my consciousness and drag my attention back to the man at the pulpit. He did have a way about him, especially when he got all fired up. "When you call on the Lord, the devil has to flee," he said.

And another time, he called out, "The beauty of life experiences is that through adversity, strength is created." I could sure relate to that. My life experience is all about overcoming adversity.

"Where is the love?" he questioned us. "I ask those of you, my brothers and sisters who are gathered here today, where is the love?"

Every time he stopped to catch a breath there would be shouts of "Amen," "Praise the Lord" and "Hallelujah." Malcolm and Maya were always among the first to give it up.

At one point the preacher invited us all to shake hands with our neighbors. Poor Joan looked very nervous as she offered her hand to the tall woman in the sable coat next to her. Then I saw that the tall woman was with an older man and Bradley Houston. Recognition dawned: these were Bradley's parents. Joan looked stunned as the woman gave her a warm smile and patted her back with her free hand. It made me wonder what kind of drama had gone on between them. But then I was also wondering where Joan had been all night.

MAYA

What a beautiful Sunday morning. Everyone was together. We joined our hands our voices and gave glory to God, Hallelujah. That sanctuary with the love that Dr. Butts was preaching about. The church was so crowded with love, in fact, that once in a while someone would get overwhelmed with it and just pass out in their pew. An usher would rush to their side to prop them up. Sometimes, if they were really gone, the usher might lead them out into a side room to recover. Most of them returned to their seats eventually.

I thought about my son and how I wanted to share this moment with him. I thought of Mama and how much she would love this preacher. She would have loved visiting with Cousin Jacquie Dawkins, too. I wondered what Mama would say about Quentin, and I wondered what I was going to tell her about him. I prayed for guidance as the preacher called on the Lord for our final blessing.

As I stepped out of the church and into the afternoon sunshine I was surprised to see that the service had lasted almost two hours. I think Quentin spoke for all of us when he said, "I'm starved."

"Do you know this neighborhood?" I asked. "Is there somewhere nearby where we can have brunch?"

At Quentin's direction, we cabbed it over to 125th for the gospel brunch at Bayou, a sleek, second floor restaurant overlooking Lenox Avenue. We were seated at a table larger than we needed as there were still a few empty chairs.

"Do we really need a table this big?" Joan asked. "Are you guys expecting company?"

"It's Sunday, Joan," said Malcolm. "You've always got to be ready for company. When I was growing up in my Aunt Verona's house, we never knew who'd turn up for Sunday dinner, but she always set a place for anyone who did."

"Yeah, Joan," Lynn chimed in. "Feel the love. Open yourself up to whatever the universe brings you."

Malcolm was staring off as if remembering those days at his aunt's. "The funny thing was, my aunt didn't have much, but we always had enough to feed our guests. I guess the Lord does provide."

"Like the loaves and the fishes," said Quentin. He turned to order a pitcher of mimosas for our table.

"Yes, small miracles happen all the time," I added.

"I experienced a miracle yesterday," said Toni. "It's a miracle that I'm alive."

"And you got your purse and your cell phone back," I told her. "I hope you thanked the Lord for that."

"I had my own miracle this morning, folks," Joan chimed in.

"Was the miracle that you finally got laid?" Lynn cracked.

"Lynn!" I said. "Not the time, baby, not the time."

"Oh, it's all right," Joan shrugged. She was a lot more relaxed than usual, which should have been a hint that Lynn was right.

Conversation stopped when the waitress brought us our pitcher of mimosas. She took our order—New Orleans style french toast for me—and departed. As soon as she was out of hearing distance, I nudged Joan.

"Okay, Joan," I said. "Give it up. Tell us where you were last night."

She started giving us the all the details. I don't think she held anything back, even the parts that she thought made her look silly. As far as I was concerned, they only made her human. I didn't bother to give her an I-knew-that, even though I had pegged Bradley for a youngster from the beginning. I really admired Joan's honesty. She was braver than me, child, 'cuz my little family ties episode was going with me to my grave. We were all still laughing about Joan's evening, Joan included, when William appeared with Honey Hayes...and the whole Houston family.

WILLIAM

"Amen to that, Brother Quentin," I echoed in the spirit of the Sunday service we had just attended. I had gone downstairs to the choir room afterward to help Honey and the rest of the choir hang and store their robes. By the time Honey and I left the church that afternoon, the crowd outside on the street had thinned considerably. The Reverend was still on the church steps, glad-handing the faithful.

I shook his hand and thanked him for the sermon he had just delivered.

"Are you a vistor?" he asked. Of course he knew the answer.

"Yes, Reverend," I acknowledged. "I'm a guest of Ms. Hayes."

"Ah, yes, Honey," he said, his eyes following her as she moved through the folks who were still on the sidewalk. She was wearing a shimmering fitted turquoise suit and a wide brimmed hat the same color, which flattered her dark complexion. Maybe it was my imagination, but the woman seemed warmer and more relaxed since we had begun to work out the burden she had been carrying all these years.

When I started my wild weekend with Honey, she had acted the role of dominatrix. She had later moved on to client, and now I was seeing her in another role: church lady. She was circulating among them like a preacher's wife. I wondered how many of them knew about the cage and the bullwhip in her fancy loft downtown. Did any of them know about her high school heartache? Honey, I decided, was just as complicated as the rest of us.

"I'm taking Honey to brunch, Reverend," I said. "Can I invite you to join us?"

But the Reverend had other commitments. He did suggest that we try the brunch at Bayou. That's how we happened to join in on my girlfriends. They insisted that we join them as well as the Houstons, who came in right behind us.

Bradley and his parents were surprised that most of our group had not been up to Harlem until that day. "All the times you've been coming to New York on business, and you never took the A train?" his mother teased me.

"The law firm works us hard, Mrs. Houston," I explained. "It doesn't leave us much time for play." I could feel Honey squeeze my knee playfully under the table.

"You all call me Geneva," she said. I recognized that Geneva Houston was not a woman that one argued with.

"And I'm Walter," her husband added. "And we're not going to let you leave town today without seeing the rest of our neighborhood."

Joan and their son Bradley had stepped off to a corner where they were engaged in a heated discussion. But the rest of us cast our votes without them, and we were all for a tour.

Outside as we began our walk, I said to Honey that I thought of 125th Street as the heart of Harlem.

"I don't think it's much different from 42nd Street," she sniffed.

She had a point. We looked around and saw a Starbucks and a Disney Store. But then I saw the marquee for the Apollo Theater and I knew we were in the right place.

The rest of the afternoon sped by as we walked along the wide boulevards and fabled side streets. The whole neighborhood was in the process of being reborn. You could tell it from all the construction signs outside the old buildings. Every rundown tenement was getting some kind of face-lift. The buildings that had already been rehabbed all seemed to have real estate placards posted.

"The speculators are moving in," Walter Houston

said dryly when he noticed me looking at one 10-story building that had a for sale sign posted.

"Would you recommend an investment here, sir?" I asked.

"You could do worse," he answered. He wasn't nearly that terse when it came to describing the wonders of his beloved neighborhood.

"My dad's third generation Harlem," Bradley said with pride.

Geneva Houston pointed out that we had missed the Schomburg Center back up north on Lenox. "They're closed on Sundays anyway," she added, "but they've got a treasure trove of documents you'll want to look at some day. And some wonderful photos of the Harlem Renaissance."

Honey and I were very interested in all this, and I know that the sight of all this real estate opened little Toni's nose. But my other friends seemed more interested in the men they were with. That went double for Joan, who seemed to be getting her own private tour from young Bradley. Whatever had gone on between those two earlier, it had all been worked out by now.

Geneva and Walter led us into a bakery. "They're famous for their coconut pie," Geneva explained, as she ordered one. "I want you all come back to the house and try some."

So we all followed Geneva back to Striver's Row. It was a long way from Los Angeles, and a longer way from Kansas City, but it felt a lot like I was coming home.

CHAPTER
SIXTEEN

JOAN

What can I say about the last few hours of our weekend in New York? Only that our time together—and apart—made me realize that the love I share with my friends is priceless. I love Toni and Lynn and Maya and William, and I love them as much for the differences between us as I do for the things we share.

And speaking of sharing, we shared a most beautiful tea at the Houston home on Striver's Row. The brownstone was a very different place in the daylight. Now I could see that it was not some cool bachelor pad at all. It was the cozy and comfortable home where Bradley had grown up and where he had lived with his parents all his life.

Ah, yes, the parents. This morning, I thought I would never be able to face Mr. and Mrs. Houston again, and I admit, my face was beet red when I realized I had sat myself down right next to his mother at the church. But it had probably been the best thing I could do. I think the sermon had calmed us all.

When Mrs. Houston insisted that we all come back

to her home for tea that afternoon, we fell into line. We walked out onto the enclosed deck behind her kitchen and found a beautiful spread laid out for us. Her tea was worthy of Martha Stewart or B. Smith.

"My son Bradley is very mature for his age," Geneva said when she and I were alone in her kitchen. I watched as she sliced a pound cake and laid the slices out on top of a paper doily-lined plate. I silently thanked the Lord that she had not been holding that knife when she discovered me with Bradley this morning. "He tells me that you two haven't known each other very long." I blushed again at the memory of this morning.

Bradley walked in, and I handed the plate of pound cake to him to take out to the deck where a long table was already piled high with goodies. The table itself was covered with a linen tablecloth, and there was a silver teapot and a complete china service. I recognized the Lenox pattern from a friend's recent wedding.

When Bradley came back to the kitchen, Geneva was fussing over the coconut pie. "I'm so sorry about this morning, Joan," she said, "but Bradley should have prepared us. When we walked in, I didn't know what to think."

"He should have prepared me," I said. "I thought he lived alone." I didn't add that I thought he was ten years older.

Bradley shook his head. "I don't know if I like the idea of you two becoming friends," he said. "I can see you ganging up on me."

"That's right," Geneva said, "watch out." She pointed at her son playfully with a pie serving utensil. Soon we joined the others out on the deck. Geneva began to pour the tea while we helped ourselves to the sweets at the table. There were benches all around the deck, and we made ourselves comfortable there. Soon William announced that he and Honey had to leave.

"I'd love to stay, but we have things to do," he said breezily.

"Places to go, people to see," said Honey who was starting to sound a lot like William's California girlfriend Monica.

Walter and Geneva wanted to hear all about our weekend in New York.

"When you live here all the time like us, you get used to things," Walter Houston said. "We don't do a lot of sightseeing in our own home town."

"It might be fun to take one of those tour busses some time, Walter," Geneva said.

"I wouldn't recommend it," said Toni. "Those tour guides can be very unpleasant."

I was relieved that the Houstons had been away while Toni's videotape was airing all over town. With luck they'd never see it.

"We took the Staten Island Ferry, Mother," said Bradley. "You two would like that."

"Yes, I believe we would," she laughed. "But if it were up to my son here, I would think all you had seen would be nightclubs."

"He did take us to some good ones," said Lynn.

"But you all have to come back to New York again," Geneva went on, "so we can show you our own favorite places. Did you see a Broadway show, for example?"

"Joan and I saw *Hairspray*," said Bradley.

"That's a start, I suppose. But you've got to let us

take you to some of the little theaters off-off-Broadway.

"That's something I'd go for," said Lynn. "I want to see the kind of work that pushes the envelope."

"Well if it's envelope-pushing you want, you should go down to the art galleries in Chelsea. You'll see some amazing sights there."

"I saw some amazing sights up in Inwood Park," Lynn said, putting her arm around Malcolm's shoulder.

"Oh, I love that park. And the Cloisters is right next to it. Did you go in there and look at the tapestries. And those wonderful gardens?"

Lynn shook her head and hit Malcolm's arm playfully. "No, I missed all that. Malcolm made me go boating with him on the Hudson River instead."

"Oh, my," Bradley's father laughed. "Don't tell my wife that you'd rather be outside sailing than inside looking at art with a capital A."

Geneva frowned at him, but I could see she was playing. I guess they had been going through this act for many years. The sight of Mr. and Mrs. Bradley together made me feel a little wistful. I don't know too many happy couples, especially not couples their age. Lynn and Toni are blessed. Their parents are still living together and loving it, at least most of the time. I wondered if any of us would ever know that kind of longtime loving. At least Toni had a boyfriend. She and Todd were on their way.

"I'd love to stay here forever," I said, "but my girlfriends and I have to catch a plane from JFK at 5:45 tonight. We've got to get back to our hotel and get our bags."

"Then I insist you let our chauffeur take you," said

Geneva. "Khalil can wait and then he'll take you to the airport."

"Oh, really—" I was about to say that it wasn't necessary, but Lynn and Toni cut me off.

"That's so generous of you," Lynn said.

"Have you ever considered property in Los Angeles?" said Toni. She handed Geneva her card. "I hope that you don't mind if I call you with some potential investment properties for you."

"Why thank you, Toni," she said, and turned to her son.

"Bradley, dear, I think you'd better go with them too. These ladies are going to need help with their bags. And I'm sure you want to say goodbye to Joan in private."

TONI

Spending Sunday afternoon with an old married couple like Walter and Geneva Houston made me miss my boyfriend even more. I looked at the Tiffany bubbles ring he had given me, glittering in the afternoon sunlight, and it was a big blinking sign that reminded me how lucky I was. This little farm girl had come a long way from Fresno, but after three days in Manhattan, I was ready to leave the big city behind. I wanted to go home to Los Angeles where I was appreciated.

"Will it take you long to pack, Toni?" Joan asked me as the Houston's sleek black limousine pulled up to the front of their townhouse. Mr. and Mrs. Houston were standing in the doorway at the top of the steps to their townhouse, watching us prepare to leave.

Quentin and Bradley were coming along with us for the ride, but Malcolm said his good-byes to us at the curb. He explained that he had his own business to get to. He apologized for leaving us and wished us all a safe trip home. I suspected that this wasn't the last time we would be seeing this gentleman. I think he was a little sorry that he couldn't come along.

"You remember to call me when you get to L.A.," I said. I could see Lynn cutting her eye at me, so I quickly added: "Or Lynn can let me know when you come to town. I want to show you some houses appropriate for a man of your achievements. A man at your level should have a base in Bel Air or Beverly Hills."

"Thank you, Toni," he grinned. "I'll take that as a compliment." He turned and took Lynn in his arms for one last embrace. And that was some embrace. That guy didn't do anything halfway.

"That Malcolm Diggs really has his act together," I whispered to Joan and Maya. "I still don't know what he sees in Lynn. Maybe it's true that opposites attract."

"That would certainly explain your pairing, wouldn't it?" said Maya. "Tree and grass. Good and evil."

Distracted by Malcolm and Lynn, I guess that I had not answered Joan's question about my luggage fast enough. I turned around to give one last wave to Mr. and Mrs. Houston.

"Hello?" Joan said impatiently as we stepped into the limo and settled ourselves in the back. "What about your bags, Toni? Will it take you long to pack? I heard all about your carry-ons incident at the airport Thursday night. I hope we're not going to have to go through that again. I'm begging you, please, no repeat performance. You won't have Malcolm to rescue you, and I want to get home!"

"Girl, you're out of touch," I replied. "This weekend has changed Toni Childs. The carry-ons are gone. I'm traveling back a little lighter than when I came."

"Yeah, you didn't hear," Maya chipped in, "Toni gave back to the community. The South Bronx just came up a notch, and its got the genuine Vuitton and the Manolo Blahniks to prove it."

Joan's eyes widened. "Oh, Toni, I'm so proud of you. That's so generous! How'd that happen?"

"Generous, nothing," I whined. "While you were sneaking off with manchild in the promised land, I was fighting for my life on the streets of Fort Apache!"

Joan looked horrified. "Were you in danger? I had no idea!"

I filled her in on my misguided trip to Yankee Stadium.

"So you own Jocelyn and Melody your life," Joan said.

"Well, they helped, of course. But in the end it was my own brilliance and resourcefulness that got me back to Manhattan," I said.

Joan shook her head. "No taxi cabs or tour busses for you from now on," she said.

"Yes," I agreed. "I seem to function best in limos."

It was smooth sailing after that. We got to the Soho Grand in ten minutes and raced to our suite. We pulled our luggage together, loaded up the limo and headed across the Manhattan Bridge to JFK.

"Look down at the water," Lynn said as we made our way across the bridge. She pointed at a boat and said, "Malcolm's is a lot like that one." She looked wistful, but I had no doubt she'd be over it by the time the next cute boy said hello. Maybe even on the flight, knowing her.

Checking in at the airport was a breeze, now that I was travelling light. I sailed through JFK Airport as if I were a hippie like Lynn.

We were all relaxed during our flight. The plane was half-empty, and even though we were all in commercial class, there was so much room we all got to spread out like a slumber party. Nothing could bother me now. There was only one crying baby this time, not triplets, and he went off to sleep quickly. I didn't even take the time to put the arrogant sky wai—flight attendants—in their place. It was a new, mellow Toni Childs who was returning to L.A.

And when we landed at LAX Sunday night, my baby was there to welcome me home.

For just a minute, when I saw him waiting by the baggage carousel, I froze. He was holding a bouquet of yellow roses for me. Until that minute, I had completely forgotten to pick up a little something for him. And then I remembered Maya's shopping trip to Canal Street. She brought me back a wallet that I had planned to pass on to my assistant Shelby. I fumbled through my bag until I found it. That's another good thing about a Vuitton wallet. It's unisex.

"And for you, honey," I said, handing Todd the wallet. "I'm sorry I didn't have time to wrap it."

He smiled. "Oh, Toni, you shouldn't have."

"She didn't," mumbled Maya, who was standing next to me and saw the whole thing. Before I could kick her—not that Todd heard, just that I would have found it amusing to kick her—she said in a full voice,

"That's just the way she is, Todd. Just generous to a fault."

LYNN

There was so many empty seats in the plane's commercial class cabin that the four of us could spread out. Joan and I were separated by an aisle, but she heard me heave a great sigh as I settled back into my seat.

"Do you miss Malcolm already?" she asked.

"Yes," I admitted, but I was also missing the luxury of the first class cabin. I was all too aware of the difference. "You know, I flew to New York with Malcolm in first class, and I think it has spoiled me forever."

"I think everything about being around Malcolm could spoil a girl forever," said Joan.

"Yeah," I concurred, thinking back to his triplex apartment and his boat. And I have to admit, I was hoping that he might invest in the documentary that Sandy and I are putting together. "That man knows how to live."

"Do you think you'll see him again, Lynn?" Joan asked.

"I hope so," I said. "I most definitely hope so."

"You hope so?" Maya repeated. She and Toni were spread out in the seats in front of Joan and me, and they could hear every word. "Girl, we all hope so. That man could be the best thing that ever happened to us. I mean you."

The flight attendants came through to fuss around and make us buckle up. After that, it only took a few minutes for the plane to take off. As soon as we were in the air, the buckle light went off and Toni was on her feet and moving down the aisle toward the front of the plane.

"Excuse me, ladies," she said, "but I have to check out first class."

"Toni!" said Joan. "I don't think you can go in there."

"It's strictly business," Toni said without even turning around. "I have to know if any of my clients are up there. You know that I never stop looking after my clients."

"Yes," said Maya sarcastically. "You are so generous, aren't you?"

"Besides," Toni added, "they serve terrific cookies up there in first class."

"You're not starting up again, are you?" Joan demanded. "Please don't get us banned from U.S. Airways. We'll never forgive you!"

I think I spoke for us all when I warned Toni: "If you get busted for breaking into first class, you're on your own this time."

Toni wasn't paying any attention to us. She had reached the front of the cabin and was tugging at the heavy curtain that separated us from a private world of expensive luxury. Joan and Maya and I braced ourselves for the explosion. Minutes passed. Nothing happened. A pair of flight attendants came through with the beverage cart. I insisted that we all have mimosas, in memory of our brunch at Bayou.

"What about Toni? Should we order a mimosa for her?" Joan said.

"Sure," I said, "I think she's going to need one."

At that moment, Toni finally emerged from behind

the first class curtain. She was grinning like a kid full on pre-dinner cookies.

"I know that grin," said Joan nervously. "When Toni smiles like that she looks just like she did when we played together in elementary school. That grin means she got away with something."

Behind the flight attendants' backs, Toni was holding up her prize: a platter of the famous first class cookies.

She slipped slipped into her seat, and as soon as the flight attendants had moved out of hearing distance, she passed the cookies around.

"You are baaad," said Maya.

"Toni, you *stole* these cookies," Joan laughed nervously.

I corrected her. "Toni didn't steal these cookies. She *liberated* them."

"Relax. I didn't swipe anything. These cookies are a gift from a friend of yours in first class."

"You're looking very pleased with yourself," I said. "It can't just be the cookies."

Toni shook her head. "Nope."

"Is it somebody famous?" Joan asked.

"Not exactly," said Toni.

"Then who? Who's up there?"

"Girl, none other than William Dent. Just all up in first class looking like somebody died and made him the first black President. He insisted that I take these back to you."

"That rascal," said Joan. "He didn't say he was coming back on this flight. We could have all gone to the airport together."

I tried to break it to her gently. "Joan, honey, I think

that's the idea. William is trying to distance himself from us."

"But he sent us the cookies!"

"Lynn's right," Maya added. "You know he's been doing that for months. He and Monica are trying to change his image."

"But Monica isn't here. Monica isn't on the plane. Why doesn't he come back and say hello?"

"Why didn't he get his ass into a Santa suit at Christmas so he could play Santa for Jabari?" said Maya. She had still not completely forgiven William for that one.

"Yeah," I added. "William established where his loyalties were. And they're not with us."

Joan shrugged. She's very resistant to change of any kind. I blame it on her parents' separation when she was young. She's always struggling to control her environment. But guess what? It can't be done. I wish she would learn from me to just go with the flow.

"William's made his choice, Joan," I added. "Go with it."

Joan looked at the cookies. "Now I'm not sure I even want these," she said.

"That's the difference between us, Joan," I said. "The rest of us don't have your problem. For us, a cookie is just a cookie."

"And a damn good one at that," added Maya. "Anybody got some foil? I wanna wrap some of these up for Jabari."

MAYA

It's not that I was sorry that I had taken time out for

a weekend with my girlfriends in New York; I was just very happy to be home. And my heart almost exploded when I saw Mama and Jabari waiting for me at the luggage carousel.

"Mama!" my son shouted when he saw me. He came running at me like I'd been gone for months.

"Mama," I shouted and went running at my own mother, so I guess you can see where he gets it.

Mama was wild for the Prada bag I bought for her on Canal Street. And Jabari couldn't wait to try out his video games.

"But now, Maya, what's this I hear about you and Quentin Wright?" she asked.

I stared at her.

"How do you know about me and Quentin?" I asked.

Mama shook her head. "Apparently Jacquie was onto you guys from the minute you walked in the door together. Honey, it's been on the family drums. Your cousin Ronnie came out to San Bernadino yesterday just to give me the 4-1-1."

"I'm so glad that Ronnie has time to put his nose in my business," I said.

"Now, Maya, don't be harsh," she said. "Peaches tells me that Quentin is very handsome. I haven't seen that boy since he was learning to crawl. And anyway, it's not like you guys are related. You're both cousins to Jacquie, but on different sides of her family. You aren't cousins to each other, for crying out loud. You knew that, right?"

"Of course I did, Mama," I slapped her arm. I would have cried with relief, but at that moment Joan came up to us and gave my mom a big hug.

"Oh, Jeanette, it's so good to see you," she said.

"You too, Joan. And I want to hear all about this wild weekend," Mama added.

"I was just going to ask Maya if she wanted a ride, but I see she's in good hands." Joan grabbed her bags off the carousel. She had been in New York for two weeks, so she had a lot more than the rest of us. Well, except for Toni, of course.

"I hope you don't think you're getting a car service," said Mama firmly. "You're coming in my car."

"Oh, you don't have to do that, Jeanette," she said.

"I wouldn't argue with my mother, Joan," I said. "She's made up her mind."

"Now I know where your daughter gets it," Joan smiled.

"Enough of that, girls," said Mama. She started barking orders which is one of her talents. "Maya, you get some of Joan's bags. Jabari, you grab us a luggage cart and we'll pile it all on that."

We took time to say goodbye to Toni and Todd.

Toni started smirking. "Look behind you," she said.

We all turned around. There was Monica.

"Don't you think that's something?" said Toni.

"No, I don't," I said. "There's nothing unusual about coming out to LAX to meet somebody. Look around you. There are hundreds of folks here doing the same thing."

Toni shook her head. "That's my point exactly. It's folks. Monica is not folks. Monica is a diva gold digger. She doesn't put herself out for anyone. And she has had William jumping through hoops for months."

For once, Joan came in on Toni's side. "I agree with Toni," she said. "Monica doesn't put herself out for anyone. I wonder what she's up to."

"Maybe my cousin Ronnie heard about William and Honey Hayes," I said.

"What's that?" Joan asked.

"Oh nothing. But you know how gossip flies across the country. You'd be surprised how much people already know about our weekend." I was still more than a little steamed that Ronnie had gotten to Mama before I did. Who needed e-mail? If you want to get the word out, just tell my cousin Ronnie.

Since he knew we had seen him, William was forced to come over and say hello to my mama. He even had to introduce Monica to Mama, and Monica had to pretend she was happy to see us.

"Well, we've got to go," William said. "We've got a lot to catch up on."

"And you'll be taking Lynn too?" Mama said. I have to give her props for that because it was obvious to us all that Monica was not intending to do any such thing.

"I do live in your house, William," Lynn added sweetly. "At least until Toni finds me some digs I can afford."

"So now it's my fault you can't find a place of your own?" Toni said.

Mama intervened before another fight broke out. "I think you're all getting tired and cranky from your trip," she said, "You should all be getting home and getting some rest."

Mama's organizational skills rival Joan's, and she had out of that airport and into her car in just a few minutes.

There was more surprise in store for us when we pulled up outside Joan's bungalow. The lights were on inside.

"Did you have someone staying in your house while you're away, Joan?" Mama asked.

"Only Maya and Jabari. And they're both here in the car," said Joan.

"Maybe we should call 911," Mama said nervously.

"No," said Joan calmly. "I have a pretty good idea who it is."

She went inside and was back in a few minutes, smiling broadly. "You guys can come in. It's only Ellis."

I was about to express my feelings about Ellis and remind her that she was cutting him loose when the man who would be Denzel appeared behind her. Call me old-fashioned, but I was too tired to be doing all that heavy lifting by myself and was glad to turn the luggage chores over to him and Jabari while Mama and I followed Joan inside the house.

"That's the spirit, Joan," said Mama. "You make that man work." But she didn't know half the story.

"Joan, what's going on?" I asked. "I thought you were through with Ellis? Didn't you call his room and find another woman in his *bed*? And what about all those messages you left for him in Vancouver?"

Joan shrugged and pointed to her answering machine next to the phone in the kitchen.

"No system's perfect, Maya. Ellis had no idea I was calling his hotel because he wasn't even there when I called. He left Vancouver early and accidentally left the bag with his cell and his two-way at the hotel. He didn't realize it until he was on the plane. So he didn't have my cell number because it was programmed into his phone. He said it's all explained on those messages—which I never checked."

"And I suppose that was because you were having

273

such a good time with Bradley," I muttered, then kept it moving, adding, "Okay, but why didn't he leave a message for you at the office too?"

"He has that number programmed into his cell too, I guess."

I raised an eyebrow. "And you believe this story?"

She thought about it for a minute. I knew it wasn't like her to swallow such a tall tale, but she'd done a few things that weren't like her in the last few days. We all had.

"Well, he's got his story...and I'm going to have mine." She gave me a conspiratorial look.

What could I say?

At that moment Ellis came in with the last of the bags.

"You sit yourselves down, ladies," he said. "I want to hear all about this weekend."

"Oh yeah! I want to hear this, too," I smirked at her, wondering just what kind of tale I was about to hear now.

WILLIAM

"If it don't apply, let it fly." That's my new motto. I am a new man since my adventure with Honey Hayes in New York. I have moved to a new level of awareness. And I couldn't wait to get back to Manhattan.

But for the moment, I am deep in my relationship with Monica.

I was surprised to see her waiting for me at LAX. We immediately got off on the wrong foot when she saw that my girlfriends had also been on the plane.

"You didn't tell me you were with them," she said.

"You know how I hate it when you keep things from me."

If she only knew. I prayed to the Lord she never found out what I had been up to. So it was fine with me if she focused her attention on the girls. She never understands that Joan and Lynn and Toni and Maya are not her enemies.

She especially dislikes Lynn. Actually, I can hardly blame her on that one. You know how women are. She probably sensed that Lynn and I had shared more than a dip in the hot tub. And she was not happy that I was still allowing Lynn and her dog to live in my house.

I don't know what got into me. Maybe I was feeling a bit frisky myself after my weekend with Honey, but I actually insisted that we stop at the kennel so that Lynn could get back her precious Vosco. The big old hairball was all over Lynn and me and the upholstery of Monica's Mercedes.

"Now that's love," I joked to Monica. "That's the real thing."

Monica doesn't have much of a sense of humor, she doesn't like animals unless they're served cooked on a plate, and I've already mentioned that she doesn't like Lynn. So you might think there was a little tension in the Mercedes as we sped along to my house. You would be wrong. There was a lot of tension in that car. I was never so glad to see my little ranch house.

Vosco started barking as soon as we pulled up, and he ran out as soon as Lynn opened the door, pulling Lynn behind him.

"William, I'm glad we're alone," Monica said. "I want to prepare you for something."

Uh oh. With Monica that could be anything.

"You know I've been wanting to make some changes," she said.

"Yes, dear." Drastic changes in my work, my life and my friendships. Most of them had been thwarted so far.

"So don't be surprised when we go in."

But I was. The woman had completely redecorated my home. Every room, even, I soon discovered, the guestroom.

"What happened to my room?" Lynn was screaming.

"Your room? I thought this was William's house," Monica replied coolly.

"Now, Monica, Lynn is our guest. And what in heckfire have you done here?"

"Why, I've only hired the finest decorator in Los Angeles to give this place a complete overhaul. Now it's a proper setting for a prominent attorney and future partner in Goldberg, Swedelson."

"But where's all my stuff?" Lynn was asking. We stood in the doorway of the guestroom where she had been camping for the last year. Like the rest of the house, it had been completely done over, this room in brown leather and bronze. I have to admit—it was quite beautiful. I dreaded asking how much it cost. Monica has an unpleasant habit of charging first and asking me to pay up later. I could get a massive bill for all this.

"I intended to pack it all up and send it off to Goodwill, but there wasn't time. So it's all in some boxes in the basement," said Monica.

Poor Monica. As if in keeping with the idea of not having anything, Lynn commenced to strip down to her skin right in front of us. I don't think my girlfriend had ever seen the tattoos on Lynn's stomach before. They are quite extraordinary, especially when they're flexed during the Lynn Spin. But I'm yammering again. And perhaps oversharing. That's a natural reaction, I believe, for any man confronted with the spectacle of Lynn standing there completely naked. The damn thing is that she's so un-self-conscious about it. So free. It would take me a fortune in therapy to ever reach that point.

"I'm going to take a soak in the hot tub, William," she announced. "I hope you haven't remade that, too, Monica."

Monica shook her head with disgust. "No, darling. You'll find that just the way you left it."

"Good!" Lynn said. "Come on, Vosco, we need a soak!"

Monica shook her head as she watched Lynn disappear. "We've got that girl on your to-do list, William. You've got to do some housecleaning. I can't do everything."

"Sure, Monica. Sure. But don't you want to hear about my weekend in New York?" When Toni saw me in first class, she thought I was just taking it easy. Far from it. I'd spent the entire flight working on my cover story to account for my weekend. Preparing for a discussion with Monica could be harder than preparing a closing argument.

But Monica didn't seem all that focused on hearing about my adventure. She pulled me toward the living room where she showed me more of the changes, including a fancy new bar. She stepped behind it.

"I have a new drink for you, honey," she purred. "It's a French martini. Made with apple slices and

Chambord and vodka." She was shaking up the silver cocktail shaker like a maraca.

When Monica serves me a pink drink with apple slices, I know she's up to something, but it would take a while to figure out what. I settled back.

I missed my girlfriends already.